SUMMER'S SWEET SPOT

SYLVIE KURTZ

OLIVERHEBERBOOKS

Published by Oliver-Heber Books

Cover art by Dar Albert at Wicked Smart Designs

0 9 8 7 6 5 4 3 2 1

❀ Created with Vellum

For my mother, Nichole—I hope it's "one more chapter" you would have enjoyed.
For my daughter, Cassie—never doubt I love you.
And for all mothers and daughters everywhere, and their complicated relationships.

"Baking isn't just about mixing ingredients together; it's about the heart and the soul together." — Paul Hollywood

1

MAEVE

Finally, alone! I surveyed the bakery's white tables with their blue chairs, empty for the first time today, and sighed. With the bakery's lunchtime rush over, I had a chance to focus on the hand pies for my Strawberry Festival booth. The kitchen smelled of sugar and strawberries and flaky pie dough. I planned on making at least five hundred this year. Last year, I'd run out by Day 2 of the four-day festival.

This was income I could count on. Income I needed to keep Brightside Bakery afloat. Income that would help pay for all the mounting bills following my daughter's diagnosis. Income that would, one day soon, mean I could move out of my parents' home into my own place.

Kayla, my only full-time day help, hadn't shown up for her morning shift. When I'd called to check in on her, she'd offered only a flimsy excuse. I'd fire her, except I needed all the help I could get, reliable or not. Her absence also meant I'd had to split myself in two all morning, out back baking goods for the bakery cases and servicing the café out front. Working for someone else was so much easier than being the boss.

A truckload of grit seemed to rub against my eyelids. My aching muscles yearned for a nap. My bread baker Natalie's classical playlist— something she swore helped make her bread rise —still played over the speakers even though she'd left hours ago. That wasn't helping my sleepy state. I switched the station to soft rock that wouldn't annoy the customers, made a large mocha latte, and drank half of it in one gulp.

The jingle of bells signaled a new arrival. I groaned. I just wanted to be out back baking, not chit-chatting with customers. I swiveled my head to find my sister gliding in as if her feet weren't touching the floor. How did she do that? The spring-green yoga T-shirt that said Breathe and the matching knee-length yoga pants told me Zoe had come straight from teaching a class. Probably looking for a tea handout.

"Hey, Maeve," she said, setting her forearms on the oak counter.

"Tea?" I asked, already plucking a large to-go cup from the stack on the counter.

"If you're offering."

I snorted, not quite able to round up a laugh at the usual routine. "Like that's not what you came in for."

"The green with strawberries. And no, actually, that's not why."

"No?" Zoe didn't like conflict of any kind, which had me curious, but there was no way I'd let her know. I took my time scooping out her tea, pouring hot water from the spigot on the coffee machine, and setting a timer, waiting her out. I drained what was left of my mocha latte and refilled the mug with black coffee.

She parked a hip on one of the blue-topped stools at the counter our brother Aaron had crafted for me. "I wanted to talk about Mom's birthday cake."

There it was. Not something big; just a gnat of a bother I

wanted to swat away. "I have a wedding cake to make for Saturday, then I'll get to it."

"What kind are you making this year?"

"Still debating." One thing for sure, there wouldn't be a strawberry in sight. I was sick of slicing strawberries. I didn't have the brainpower right now to think of something Mom would actually enjoy as ornery as she'd been lately.

"Maeve! It's the big six-oh. It has to be special."

I grabbed a cloth and swiped non-existent crumbs off the counter. Both Aaron and Zoe had an easy relationship with Mom. Mine was... complicated. "You would say that."

"You're in a mood today."

"You get the best of Mom."

"She treats me like I'm six, always checking on me and bringing me food."

Mom did treat Zoe as if she was egg-fragile. "If you ate a decent meal, she'd leave you alone."

Zoe's eyebrows rose in a game-on way. "She helps you take care of Neve."

I snorted, but I really wanted to growl. "She forgets that Neve is my daughter and ignores my rules."

Zoe laughed in a you're-kidding way. "Rebel Maeve has rules?"

"It's not a joke, Zo." Why did every conversation with my family have to devolve into a fight?

My nine-year-old daughter's welfare was my number-one concern. She had a rough year between her new ADHD without hyperactivity diagnosis, a teacher who was less-than supportive and her best friend moving all the way to Colorado. We still had a long way to go to get her ready to handle school next September, especially because I wanted to try the drug-free option first. I wasn't sure how exactly I would pay for the therapy, nutrition counseling and ADHD coaching, only that I somehow had to. I couldn't fail her. "Would you give an addict drugs?"

Zoe dismissed my concern with a flap of her hand as flippant as Mom's disregard of my rules. "Maeve, come on, it's not the same."

"Sugar is a drug for Neve's brain." My whole body tensed, ready to slay dragons for my daughter. "The therapist said the high-protein diet works. Mac and cheese and cookies for lunch don't fit the bill."

Zoe shrugged a shoulder, trivializing my daughter's health. "We turned out okay."

"Says the girl who hasn't dated in almost a decade."

Zoe's face fell, and immediately, my heart took a dive. *Filter, Maeve, filter.* I'd wanted to dig but not to hurt. "Zo, I'm sorry."

I pulled a brownie from the case, put it on a napkin and pushed it toward her, a peace offering. "Your favorite. Caramel-pecan."

Without a word, she pulled the napkin closer with a stiff movement and broke off a bite. I breathed a sigh of relief when her face softened from prey to cautious.

"Pot, kettle," Zoe said with a flip of her blond braid. "From the girl who has a boyfriend who treats her no better than a dog."

Fair enough. I'd started this. "Are you calling me a dog now?"

"Your obsession with a relationship that will go nowhere isn't healthy."

"It's called love, Zo. Loyalty."

"Don't you think you deserve someone who treats you better?" She tipped her head, scrunching the dewy skin on her forehead. "We worry about you wasting your life waiting for Patrick."

Patrick had called two nights ago and mentioned he was coming home soon. That he had some news. I couldn't help hoping that, this time, he'd stick around, that we'd be a real family. "He's Neve's father. She needs to know him."

"Not this way. He comes. He takes her out. He leaves again. That's not the way to make a girl feel good about herself. Isn't that what you want for Neve?"

That was why I'd come back to Brighton when I found out I was pregnant. I'd wanted my baby to know that she was loved and wanted and surrounded by people who cared. I wanted her to have the safe, secure, carefree upbringing I'd had. Especially because Patrick wasn't ready to act like a father back then. Which didn't alter the fact. "He is her father."

Zoe hitched her chin in the direction of the engagement ring Patrick had given me three years ago. "If he hasn't followed through by now, he never will."

I looked down at the ring on my left hand, a cushion-cut emerald surrounded by chips of diamond. He was the only person who knew and loved the side of me that everyone else wanted tamped down. That was worth waiting for, wasn't it? Everyone else in my life wanted to whittle me into someone I wasn't.

"About the cake...." Zoe pressed a finger into the brownie crumbs on the napkin and licked them.

I breathed a sigh of relief that Zoe was letting this go. The tea timer went off with a small ping. I slammed a lid on her tea and plopped it in front of her. "I'll get it done. I always do."

Zoe aimed her chin toward my mug. "You might want to cut back on the coffee."

"We can't all be green-tea-drinking yogis." I deliberately took a big gulp of coffee, and my nerves jangled like an alarm.

"On that note...." Zoe wrapped the napkin around the brownie, tucked it in the side pocket of her yoga pants, then, tea in hand, headed toward the door where she paused. "We're counting on you to make Mom's cake special."

For all my faults, when I made a promise, I kept it. Zoe

should know that by now. I'd promised Patrick I would wait for him, no matter how long it took. I'd promised Neve I would take care of her, always. I'd promised myself to do whatever it took to make the best life possible for our family. "It'll be spectacular!"

With a we'll-see smile, she floated on her way.

When the bells stopped jingling, I let my head drop and groaned. Why, why, why did I always let my family get to me? *Because you care.* And yes, I'd make the darn birthday cake. And, yes, it would be spectacular. My bakes put a smile on people's faces. That was why I'd gotten into baking, wasn't it? To make people happy.

"You know you're lucky to have a family that cares, right?" came a voice from the kitchen.

More like a pack of busybodies always sticking their noses in my business. Living with all that constant judgment could wear a person down.

"Well, well, look who finally showed up for work." I took in Kayla's appearance, cheeks sunburn-red, sweat stains under her arms, straight black hair mussed as if she got caught in a rainstorm. What was going on with her? I glanced at the clock. "Only four hours late."

"I told you," Kayla said, tying on a blue Brightside Bakery apron around her slim frame. "I had something to take care of that couldn't wait."

"How long were you snooping?"

"Long enough."

I snorted like this wasn't something new. "I'm leaving in an hour to pick up Neve from school. Last day. You're closing."

"I know. That's why I came in at all. And don't I close every day?"

"I'm docking you the four hours."

"Yeah, yeah." Kayla stepped toward the coffee machine and filled a mug with coffee, then handed it to me. She nudged her chin toward the kitchen. "Go bake or something. You always get crabby when you have to deal with people."

Coffee in hand, I turned toward the kitchen only to feel a chill go down my spine. A shadow fell across the bakery's picture window and obliterated the sun.

2

MAEVE

"What is *that* about?" Kayla asked, craning her head over my shoulder. A white truck, plastered with neon-colored donuts, rolled to a stop right in front of the bakery.

"I don't know, but I'm going to find out." I didn't have a good feeling as I strode toward the door. Something about the food truck— maybe those giant neon donuts aiming for a spot right in front of my bakery —spelled trouble.

Pedestrians turned, watching the behemoth attempting to park. One wheel raked over the sidewalk before plunking back onto the street. The engine sounded as if it would die at any second. *Please, not in front of my bakery.* My patrons enjoyed basking in the window's sunlight. That monstrosity was a blight to any view and belonged nowhere near our quaint downtown.

"Keep an eye on the cookies," I told Kayla, and headed outside. "They need to come out in two minutes."

A puff of black smoke blasted out the truck's back, spewing an evil stench that clouded even the sweetness of the strawberry thumbprint cookies baking in the kitchen. I waved my hand in front of my nose to dissipate the burnt-oil scent. The passenger's side opened with a creak, revealing a twenty-something girl with timid movements, bleached-blond hair streaked with pink, and nose and brow piercings I'd once coveted but was now glad my parents hadn't allowed. She wore jeans with gaping holes at the knees and a pink T-shirt two sizes too big that read, "Eat More Hole Food."

A deep bass voice came from the driver's side. "Dani, wait up a minute!"

"Why?" She reached inside and pulled out a magazine I recognized— *603 Things to Love About New Hampshire.*

Tourists— from Connecticut, according to the truck's plate —who'd probably seen the blurb on the bakery in the magazine.

"I get that you're excited but don't just rush in like that." The voice held a gentle laugh, as if that would make everything okay.

A door slammed, shaking the truck. For a second, I thought the whole thing would fall apart like one of Neve's Transformer cars. A man rounded the front of the truck, broad shoulders breaching first, then a long, lean body coiled with potential energy just waiting to spark. The only hitch in the otherwise juicy image: the skip/limp that slowed his chase.

I pulled my gaze up to his face and sucked in a breath. No, it couldn't be. What would *he* be doing here in the middle of nowhere? And why would he be driving a truck sporting donuts?

"Hey, there," he said, gaze zeroing in on me, eyes gray like a summer sky about to storm. The slow-swelling smile reminded me of too many after-game press conferences meant to charm reporters and fans alike. A smile so sure of itself. A smile that said the wearer was aware of the little curl of pleasure it created in whoever basked in it. "Sorry about barging in like that."

He reached out a hand. Before I knew what I was doing, I accepted it. He sandwiched my hand with his other hand, making it feel warm and safe. "Apparently, your pies are swoon-worthy, and Dani had to drive all the way out here to try them."

I extricated my hand from his, fingers tingling as if he'd cut off circulation. I knew who he was. Of course, I did. Dad and I watched baseball together whenever we could. Once a year, we trekked down to the Green Monster for the Sox vs. Yankees game. I'd had a baseball crush on Luke Saunders since he'd joined the Portland Gulls as their shortstop. He'd helped the fledgling major league team make a good showing its first two years in the National League and helped get them to the World Series in their third year. I'd even seen him play live a time or two when the Gulls had faced the Sox. And, two years ago, Dad and I had watched the World Series game on TV when his career came to a spectacular end.

I was right. The truck had brought trouble. What I couldn't figure out was why.

The girl clutched the magazine to her chest, heels pumping up and down, face aglow. "You're her! You're Maeve Carpenter!"

I let my gaze study the girl. The enthusiasm rising off her like steam from a hot pie took me back a decade. "I am."

"I'm so excited to meet you." She reached for one of my hands and rattled it up and down. "You started your bakery from nothing and built it into something special. That's what I want to do, too."

Not quite from nothing. It had been a sandwich shop before. I'd worked hard for the past three years to earn the success I had. I nodded, the flattery finding a mark with a rush of heat to rival Luke Saunders' smile. Then I took my hand back from her sweaty palm, waiting for the real reason she was so excited.

"After culinary school," Luke said, leaning a hip against the truck, going for casual, but not quite hiding the wince. Who was this girl to him? Daughter? Couldn't be unless he was a teenage father, and even then, he'd have to have been precocious. Wife? Girlfriend? "We have a plan."

"Yeah, yeah." Dani shoved the magazine my way, along with a Sharpie. "Would you sign it for me?"

She'd opened the magazine to the Top Ten Bakeries page that showed a rather unflattering picture of me, standing in front of my bakery case. My hair sprouted Medusa-like curls around my face. My arms were crossed. So was my expression. Aaron and Zoe had teased me mercilessly about the too-good-for-the-neighborhood tilt of my chin. The reporter had arrived at the end of a long day, asked a few questions, taken the hasty photo before I was ready, then moved on to her next victim.

I scrawled a signature at the base of the photo— I'd never given an autograph before and wasn't sure what she expected —and handed back the magazine and marker, feeling like an imposter.

She hugged the magazine to her chest. "Thanks." Lips pressed tight together, she glanced at the bakery. "I can't wait to try your pies."

That, I could deal with. I crossed the sidewalk, opened the door, bell tinkling a happy tune, and swept a hand in invitation. I'd feed her pie, then send her on her way. Problem solved. "Come on in, then."

Dani headed straight for the bakery case, examining its contents with both hands pressed against the glass like a kid at Christmas. "I can't decide."

"Why don't you sit down, and I'll bring you a sampler."

Her eyes went wide. "Really?"

Her admiration was endearing. "For a fan."

She turned to Luke. "I finally get all the girls pawing at you. I want to hug her so bad."

His laughter sounded like summer, full of warmth and sun and sparkle.

"Is that Luke Saun—" Kayla started as I stepped behind the counter.

"No."

"Are you sure?"

"Positive." The last thing I wanted was to feed his ego. According to online gossip, he enjoyed all the female attention those dirty blond, gray-eyed good looks got him. Not to mention all that lean muscle that made them shiver in delight.

Kayla sent me a quizzical look. "Ooo-kay."

A timer's ding came from the kitchen. "Can you go switch out the cookies?"

"Yes, ma'am." She marched away, military style.

I chopped four slices of pie with the speed of a hibachi chef and placed them on a dinner plate. Usually I'd have more variety, but with unreliable help, I did the best I could. I brought the plate over to them, along with two forks and two coffees.

Dani picked up a fork and hovered it over each pie in turn.

I pointed at the lemon custard pie. "Start with lemon, then peach, deep-dish strawberry, chocolate strawberry."

"Good plan." She dug into the lemon custard pie.

I turned to go back to the kitchen, but Dani called after me, "Stay!" Her eyebrows with their rings at the corners rose. "Pretty please. I want to learn more about the pies."

Okay, so I was tickled. People rarely wanted to talk pie, other than to just order a slice. But this girl seemed to hold genuine curiosity and appreciation, judging from her purr-like noise as she ate.

"I've heard so much about your pies," Luke said, "it feels like I've tasted them all already."

That smile, again. It should be against the law.

"This crust," Dani said, picking at the flakes with her fork, "there's something different."

"Caramelized it."

"You can do that?!"

I chuckled. Her enthusiasm reminded me of mine at her age, all eager to learn and experiment. "You can."

She grabbed my hand and squeezed tight. "Show me, please, please, please!"

"Dani," Luke said, low so his voice wouldn't carry. "We talked about this. You're making a scene." He turned his gray summer-storm gaze toward me. "You're all she's been talking for the past three weeks."

"Why?"

"Because I want to learn from the best, and you're the most creative baker I've investigated. Your ideas are fresh, innovative. I like the rebel flair of some of your flavor combinations. And this—" She stabbed her fork toward the peach pie "—is insanely good. I can't quite figure out the taste of the filling around the peaches."

"Rosé," I said, then frowned. "Investigated?"

That sounded stalkerish and a little scary. I lived in a small town where most people didn't lock their doors. Did I have to worry about this girl invading our home and putting Neve or my parents in danger?

Dani dug into the strawberry cobbler pie.

"We've been following the baking contest circuit," Luke said, his full attention on me in a way that made me feel as if I were in a hot oven.

"Uh-huh." The things you didn't have time for when you worked too many hours. Luke hadn't touched any of my pies, which for some reason irked me.

"Dani wants to earn enough money to pay for culinary school," he said.

Can't you just fork out the tuition with the millions you made playing baseball? Of course, I couldn't ask that out loud. People were touchy about money. "How's it going?"

"So far, more losses than wins. Which is why I'm so excited to meet you." She talked around a mouthful of chocolate strawberry pie. "Oh, my, this is so, so good." She placed a hand over her heart and kept eating with the other. "I'll do anything you want— wash dishes, mop floors, bus tables —if you let me watch you bake. I just want to learn from the best."

As enticing as having free labor and someone to boost my flagging confidence was, I just didn't have the time to take on a rookie right now. Not with the festival only a few weeks away. "I'm sorry."

Her smile melted like ice cream on a hot July day, showing off a bruised self-esteem. This girl seemed to have heard "no" too many times. "I promise I won't get in the way."

"It's not that, Dani. I really do have too much to do before the Strawberry Festival opens."

"I can help. I promise." She crossed her heart, showing how young she was. "I'm a good baker. I know I have a lot to learn. But I want to learn."

Luke hobbled to standing, then leaned over and whispered in my ear, sending an electric tingle down my spine. "Can we talk for a second?"

"Want a refill on that coffee?"

He nodded and we headed toward the counter. He stopped in front, and I went around the back to fetch the coffee pot.

He leaned an elbow on the wooden counter and slid his mug forward. "Do you know who I am?"

His scent of fresh-cut grass, sunshine and rain distracted me for a moment. I shook the distraction away, then hummed the re-mixed version of "Fought the Law" called "Fought the Ball" that played on the YouTube video, showing Luke Saunders misjudging a hardline drive. It missed his glove and shattered his tibia into a hundred pieces. I couldn't watch the often-rebroadcast video without flinching and feeling his pain.

He tilted his head in a touché move. "My sister's been through a really hard time, and this is the first time in over a year she's shown an interest in anything. It would be a huge favor to me if you could give her a few tips."

I filled his mug with hot coffee. Dani was his sister. Now that made more sense than daughter or wife.

"She made me drive all the way here just to meet you. All she wants to do is learn from you. Surely, you remember what it's like being young and eager."

"Oh, wow, that's not gaining you any points, mister."

He had the decency to blush. "You know what I mean."

"I'm not sure I do."

"She looks up to you. You're a success now, and she's just starting out. Someone must have helped you up."

My grip on the coffee pot's handle tightened. Shirley Burgess and her husband Wilbert had given me a job when I most needed one. After Shirley died, Wilbert had sold me the shop at a below-market-value price. Something I would forever be grateful for.

But Dani shouldn't look up to me. Between the mortgage, the resupply bills and the bills for Neve's therapy and ADHD coaching, I was barely hanging on. And if I wasn't careful, the rest of my life would fall like a bad cake. "I really don't have time right now. Come back after the festival, and I'll be glad to show her a few tricks."

"Time's short. She needs to win *this* contest," he insisted.

"Why? What's so important about this contest?"

"It's a long story." His eye contact didn't waver, making me feel too exposed.

I shoved the coffeepot back onto the coffee machine. "It's not like I have any say about who wins. I'm not even a judge."

"But you have the skills to show her what she's doing wrong with her bakes. You have that flair with flavors, all those awards." He pointed at the "Best in New Hampshire" plaques on the wall. Two of which I'd earned while still working for Shirley and Wilbert.

"How would you know?" I aimed my chin toward his empty plate on the table. "You didn't taste a single bite of pie."

He rubbed a hand up and down the thigh of his bad leg. "Dani rhapsodizes for hours on end about the stuff she reads on your website. I feel like I've tasted them all."

"Remind me to take that down."

He tilted his head to one side, flashed his winning smile, and I resented that it had my middle sizzling like browned butter. "Come on, you seem like a decent person. Why won't you help her? Pay it forward?"

I wasn't going to let him get to me. For him, this was part of a game. He had nothing to lose. "I have a business to run. I'm short-staffed. And I have five hundred hand pies to bake in less than two weeks."

"She can help you. She really is a good baker." He hooked a thumb over his shoulder. "The donuts are hers, and we sell out every single time we make a batch."

"I don't have time to babysit."

The gray of his eyes darkened. "You're being unreasonable."

"Wow, unreasonable? Really? You're a perfect stranger—"

"To be fair, you know exactly who I am."

"Doesn't mean I know you." Baseball Luke was focused and driven and precise. Internet Luke flirted with anything in a skirt. He was used to winning on and off the field. I didn't have that luxury. I had to stay the course and work hard for everything I had. "You come waltzing in, throwing your name around, asking for a favor. Then you try to make me feel bad because I'm not bending over backwards to say yes. What if I brought my kid to your ballfield? Asked you to let her play on game day? As a favor. You'd give her a shot just because I'm Maeve Carpenter, award-winning baker?"

"It's not the same. It wouldn't be up to me. There's a whole team involved."

I tilted my head. "You're asking me to give professional advice for free when I don't have the time."

"I'll pay you. I'll sign autographs for your customers. Whatever you'd like. Just name it."

Before I could tell him just how I felt about him trying to buy time I didn't have, his phone rang. He glanced down. "Sorry, it's business. I have to take this."

"Be my guest." I pointed at the door. "Outside."

As her brother strode/limped toward the door, Dani meandered to the counter. "Did he offer to pay you? He can't afford to, you know."

I filled a mug with coffee, then shoved the coffee pot back in its place. "Why not?"

"It's complicated."

The sigh that followed held a whole history that piqued my curiosity.

"Bad investments?" I asked.

She shook her head but wouldn't look me in the eye. "Look, it's okay." She twirled a hank of pink-tipped hair in a way that said it was anything but okay. "I'm sorry I put you in this position. I just really wanted to see you work."

I got that. I'd wanted so badly to go to pastry school in Paris at her age. "Come back after the festival."

She nodded, but her whole expression dimmed. "I really liked your pies, especially the chocolate-strawberry one. There's something about your crusts I haven't tasted anywhere else. I'm glad I finally got to sample them."

Not going to do it, I told myself. *Not going to let her sad story make me do something I can't afford.* I retrieved what was left of the chocolate-strawberry pie from the bakery case and slipped it into a box, then handed it to her. "Come back in July."

Hugging the pie box to her middle, she gave me a sad smile and left.

Ten minutes later, the truck with the neon donuts hadn't moved.

Twenty minutes later, the scent of fry oil crawled into the bakery and the donut truck's side yawed open like a mouth ready to swallow.

3

GRACE

A sea of cans, pasta boxes and baking supplies littered the kitchen table and the granite counters all around me. This was, to use my daughter Maeve's favorite expression, ridiculous. I sank into a kitchen chair, picked up a can of diced tomatoes so I could rest an elbow on a scrap of table.

"How has my life come to this?" I asked the can of tomatoes. "Creating busy work just so I don't have time to think?"

It's the darned birthday, I thought. In just over two weeks, I would turn sixty. It seemed as if only a short while ago I'd walked down the aisle with Ansel, a bride filled with hopes and dreams. And now, here I was on the brink of old age, reorganizing an already perfectly ordered pantry so I wouldn't have to face the fact that I'd become, well, stuck.

"Do you think they'll remember?" I asked the can. Part of me wanted everyone to ignore the date, for my birthday to be just another day. But then if they did, I'd feel forgotten, unloved.

"I know," I told the can. "I'm making no sense."

My father's voice came back to me. *If you want something to feel sorry about, I can give you something to feel sorry about.*

Right. Ruminating wouldn't do me any good. I plopped the can back on the table. As my daughter Zoe would suggest were she here, I counted my blessings. I had so many of them. I had a husband who loved me. Three children who were productive members of society. A granddaughter I adored.

I got up from the table and turned on the heat under the kettle. Outside, two squirrels frolicked up and down the oak tree in the yard. They weren't thinking about growing old and useless. They simply enjoyed the moment. *Why can't you do that, Grace?*

"Because," I answered myself, "it's not enough."

I wanted to feel as if my life had meaning, purpose.

From the cupboard beneath the sink, I took a spray container of homemade cleanser and a rag. I'd done what I was put on this earth to do. I was the best wife and mother I could be. I supported my family at every turn. And they'd turned out well, hadn't they?

Aaron's woodworking business was thriving, and he'd found a lovely girl in Meredith to share his life. Maeve's bakery was starting to take off and her pies had won awards. Zoe had her yoga studio and her aromatherapy business. I still worried about her, though. She tried to pretend everything was okay, but I knew what happened in the city still affected her, even out here where everything was safe and where she was surrounded by people who watched out for her. But she, like the rest of my children, didn't want me to "meddle" in her business.

I sprayed a pantry shelf and let the orange scent of the cleanser fill my nostrils, then wiped it down. I'd worked hard all my life. I'd run a household, managed my family, made things smooth for everyone— organizing, scheduling, loving —so I could be there for them always.

I'd enjoyed my role of wife and mother. I really had. I'd felt needed and wanted. Useful.

But none of my children really needed me anymore. Not

even Maeve and her daughter Neve, who lived a few steps up in the in-law apartment attached to the main house.

The kettle shrilled. I pulled my favorite "Dog Mom" mug from the cupboard— a gift Zoe had given me ages ago when Oscar was still alive —plopped a fresh bag of peppermint tea in the mug, then poured water. The problem was that I wasn't sure how to fill my time. I didn't want to be one of those people who rusted in place, watching TV all day long. I'd never particularly enjoyed TV. I still had *something* useful to give the world, didn't I?

The doorbell rang a cheerful ding-dong, and I let out a sigh of relief. I never liked when my thoughts went down the drain that way, taking me to a scary, dark place. A place that reminded me much too much of my mother's depression while growing up. Her dark moods had my brother Paul and me tiptoeing through our childhood.

Sixty was still young, I reminded myself as I abandoned the tea and the pantry reorganization and headed for the door. I still had a good thirty, maybe forty years left to live. That was too long to feel sorry for myself. I needed to find something that would have me jump out of bed, looking forward to whatever the day would bring.

I opened the door to find my niece, Lark, standing outside, wearing her usual outfit of T-shirt and faded jeans peppered with dog hair of every color. She was the happiest person I knew, so sure in her skin, so grounded in her purpose. Her dark-blond hair was twisted into a long braid down her back that reminded me of the way I used to braid horses' tails before shows when I was a teen, earning pocket change to pay for riding lessons. In her arms, she held a ball of apricot fluff.

"Oh, no, you don't." I tried to close the door in her face, but she stuck her foot inside the door.

"What?" she said, all innocence. "Can't I visit my favorite aunt?"

I grumbled. "If I'm your favorite, why haven't I seen you since Easter?"

"I've been busy. I took over the Stoneley Canine Center. Didn't Mom tell you?"

"I haven't spoken to Kate in a while." I pointed my chin at the creature in her arms. "That's not one of your dogs." Lark bred russet-and-white Cavalier King Charles spaniels, and that ball of fur wasn't one.

"You're right." Her smile widened, so warm and welcoming I almost reached for the dog. "She's yours."

I pulled my hands behind my back, laced my fingers and shook my head. "No, no. I'm not falling for that trick again. I don't want to deal with potty training and obedience training and all the chewing and destruction."

Lark pressed the dog forward. The thing wagged its flag tail, flapped its tongue and turned big molasses eyes with impossibly long eyelashes at me. "She's eight months old. Her family had to leave her behind because of the father's overseas move for his job. They want a good home for her."

"No."

"She's potty trained. Crate trained. She knows basic commands."

"Lark, no." Oscar had broken my heart when he'd died twelve years ago. I hadn't even wanted him. As ugly as he was with his three legs, one eye and chewed-up ear, I'd had to take him in just to stop eight-year-old Lark from sobbing her heart out. Not to mention that even after all those years, my heart still had an Oscar-shaped hole in it. "I'm not ready for another dog."

"It's been a dog's life, Auntie Grace."

"I still miss him."

From my pocket came the tune of "Over the Rainbow." I sighed. "Hello, Maeve."

"Mom, I have a situation at the bakery. Is there any way you could pick up Neve from school?" Maeve sounded stressed. Again.

"Sure." I stabbed the End button. She just assumed I had nothing better to do. I didn't, but that was beside the point. She thought I could drop everything and jump to the rescue. Of course, she did, because I'd trained her that way, hadn't I? The worst part was that I truly didn't mind looking after Neve. But a "Thank you, Mom. I appreciate everything you do for me" once in a while would be nice.

"I have to go," I said to Lark, and grabbed my purse from the small table in the foyer.

"I'll come with."

"You don't even know where I'm going."

"School's about out."

I squeezed through the door and shut it with a decisive slam. "I know what you're doing."

"What?" She acted innocent, but I could lay out the steps of her ploy as if they were a run of Skip-Bo cards.

"You think that if Neve sees this cutie—"

"Aww, you agree she's cute."

"—that I won't be able to say no."

Lark smiled. "Me? I would never do such a thing. I respect your decisions. I just haven't seen Neve in a dog's year."

I gave her "the look," but instead of withering like my children once had, she laughed and filled the air with bubbles of joy.

I sighed and let her tag along as I drove to Neve's school. The pup did seem well behaved, sitting in the back seat quietly enjoying the drive. But Lark was wrong. A pup wasn't going to fix what was wrong with my current situation. It would cause more work, and I was tired of picking up after everyone.

"What's Kate up to these days?" I loved my brother's wife like the sister I never had.

"Since she retired, Mom's always busy juggling fifty

projects. I'm not even sure what she's into these days." Lark retrieved her phone from her back pocket and punched an icon in her contacts. "Mom, I'm with Aunt Grace. She says she hasn't seen you in forever. When are you free? Uh-huh." She glanced at me. "How does tomorrow morning sound for coffee? She's coming into town to run errands."

A visit sounded like something to look forward to. "Perfect. I'll see her at my place when she's done."

Lark looked much too satisfied with herself as she slipped her phone back into her jeans pocket. "There."

"I'm still not taking the dog."

"I know. I respect your no."

At the elementary school, we waited by the side door, the pup sniffing and twirling around our ankles, the silky fur against my shin softening something inside me. Nope, I wasn't going to fall for it. I kept my gaze glued to the brown metal doors.

Finally, the bell rang, and children exploded from the doors, carrying a year's worth of belongings. Neve came running out, all elbows and knees, dark brown curls flying around her like a flock of wings. I couldn't miss her with the neon-green T-shirt she wore over purple shorts with white polka dots. Her pink bookbag flapped on her back. Her gaze zeroed in on the dog. She squealed, dropped to her knees and let her armful of stuff scatter around her like snow. She reached for the dog, who wiggled and jiggled, trying to get closer to Neve.

"Who's this?" Neve asked, giggling.

Judging by the manic licking of Neve's face and my granddaughter's love giggles, it was instant adoration on both sides. I closed my eyes and reminded myself to stay strong. I did *not* want a dog. I would *not* bring this dog home.

"Her name's Snickerdoodle," Lark said. A sea of children parted around us, looking for parents or school buses.

"Snickerdoodles are my favorite kind of cookies," Neve said between joyful laughter.

"Not very original," I muttered. "And a mouthful for such a small dog."

"My client's kids named her. They call her Snick for short." Lark showed Neve how to hold the leash, while I stuffed as many of Neve's belongings into her backpack as I could. "She's a mini Labradoodle. Sweet, friendly, doesn't shed. Won't get much bigger than she is now, which is just shy of twenty-three pounds."

Papers refused to stay put in Neve's backpack, poofing out as if on springs. "Don't get any ideas."

Lark's only answer was a knowing smile.

"I don't need a dog." I herded Neve and Snick toward the car.

"If you say so."

Neve and Snick skipped ahead as if they'd known each other forever.

"Neve's going through a tough time right now," Lark said. "So is Snick."

"How do you know that?"

"I have my ways."

Kate always said her daughter had inherited her dog-matchmaking skill from Kate's grandmother, who'd been a well-known matchmaker in her day. This time, Lark was wrong. A dog would just complicate things for everyone.

"Snick is heartbroken. She really misses her family. The little girl was Neve's age."

"Don't, Lark. Just don't."

Lark mimed zipping her mouth shut.

Neve had perked up around the dog in a way I hadn't seen since her best friend moved last March. She and Riley had known each other from practically birth and had been inseparable. And Neve was having a tough time making new friends.

Between that and that ridiculous diagnosis of ADHD and Maeve turning into the food police, Neve *had* been through a lot. Our girl didn't run around like a madwoman, disrupting everything. She could sit for hours and read or work on one of her art projects. I hated that Maeve had allowed the school to label her. It would make her life more difficult. Didn't Maeve remember what that was like from her own school days? How the label of "difficult" had prejudiced her teachers before the school year even started?

When we reached the house, Neve and Snick tumbled in. Lark attempted to leave with a wave.

"Oh, no, you don't." I grabbed her wrist and pulled her inside. "You are not leaving without that dog."

"How about I make us a cup of tea?" She didn't wait for me to accept her offer. She headed straight for the kitchen where Neve and Snick dropped to the floor.

Lark took in the mess of cans and boxes on the counters and table. "What's all this?"

"Spring cleaning."

"I see. I think we arrived just in time."

Neve's happy laughter rang, striking a chord in my heart. She needed a friend who would love her unconditionally.

"Lark—"

"Auntie Grace."

I flopped into a chair, already writing up a mental list of things to pick up at the Country Store.

4

MAEVE

I elbowed my way to the front of the line forming at the truck's window. "What are you doing?"

Luke, wearing a ridiculous pink apron with "Donut Squad" emblazoned in white on the bib, said, "What does it look like? We're setting up shop."

"You can't do that here!"

He pointed a pair of pink-handled tongs at a piece of paper taped to the wall that looked like a town sales permit. "That says I can set up anywhere I want."

"Hey, Maeve," came a voice from the back of the line that I recognized as Jeb Cannon's squeak. He strutted around calling himself a reporter for the *Tri-Town Times* and was even more of a dinosaur than the newspaper on its last leg. "Do you mind? I have to get back to work."

"Like writing up notes about the Board of Selectpersons' meeting is life and death."

"I'm a man of the people. And here I've got the scoop not only on donuts but Luke Saunders. That's news."

"More like gossip."

"Dani, give the man a donut." Luke's gaze narrowed at me. "On the house."

Dani, eyes wide, ping-ponged her gaze between us, unsure whether to give Jeb a donut or not. Luke popped a fresh-out-of-the-fryer donut into a pink paper bag and lobbed the grease-stained thing to Jeb.

Jeb caught the bag, then tipped the straw hat over his bald head. "Thanks, man!"

"This is the last time I do anything nice for anyone," I muttered.

He dropped donut dough into the fryer, making the oil sizzle. The rolling sugar filled the air with the scent of cinnamon. "As I recall, you're the one who refused to play nice."

I snorted, jamming it with all the scorn threatening to make me lose my short hold on control. "This is because I don't have time to babysit?"

He ignored me and pointed his tongs at Dani. "Let's keep the line moving. We don't want to disappoint customers."

"But Luke—" she started, holding a clean paper bag to her chest like sorry armor.

He hummed "Take Me Out to the Ball Game" loud enough to drown out his sister's protest.

He thought he had me, but he knew nothing about small towns and how they worked. I looked up at Dani. "No worries. I've got the home team on my side."

Keeping an eye on Luke and his antics at the fryer, I stepped away from the truck. I leaned on the brick storefront next door to the bakery, pulled my phone out of my pocket and dialed.

I hated having to ask Mom for help yet again. She disapproved of all the hours I worked. And that disapproval made me feel like a bad mother. But without the bakery, I couldn't support Neve. And taking care of my girl was my number-one priority.

Mom broke off the connection before I could thank her. I frowned at my phone. It wasn't like her to be so short.

I shook my head and dialed again.

"Regina Buchanan," came the regal voice of our illustrious chair of the town selectpersons that always made me think I should curtsy.

"We have a problem," I said as Dani handed grease-stained pink bag after grease-stained pink bag of donuts to greedy hands.

"Then you've called the right person."

The line at the truck kept growing as if no one in Brighton had ever seen a donut before. This was ridiculous. "There's a stinking donut truck parked in front of my bakery." I tried to appeal to her civic pride. "It's a blight on our beautiful village. And he refuses to move."

"Luke Saunders is here?" Regina sounded much too pleased with herself.

I frowned. "You know him?"

"I invited him."

"How? When?"

"When he inquired about the baking contest."

Luke autographed a donut bag with a flourish and, with his signature smile and some sort of story, handed it to Mabel Byrd, who practically swooned right over her bedazzled teal walker. I rolled my eyes. She was old enough to know better. This was going from the ridiculous to the outrageous. "Get him to move somewhere else."

"He's a celebrity," Regina said as if that explained every-thing. "A baseball star of some sort."

"Why can't he flaunt his celebrity somewhere other than right in front of my bakery?"

"Brighton needs all the exposure it can get."

With Regina, it was always Brighton first which, most of the time, worked in our favor. "I need my customers to be able to get into my shop safely."

"You don't sell donuts."

"So? I don't want my customers hijacked by donuts and not come in for muffins or pies. Besides, the line's clogging the sidewalk and my door. It's a fire hazard."

"It's only for a few weeks, Maeve."

I pushed away from the brick storefront. "A few weeks! Are you trying to shut me down?"

Regina tutted. "I would have thought you'd have more confidence in your baking skills."

"Have you ever watched a baseball game?" I asked.

"Oh, heavens, no! But I'm told he's handsome and charming."

I blew out a raspberry. "Oh, well, then let's excuse him everything."

"Maeve—"

I drew in a lake of air, trying really hard not to yell at Regina. "So, you're not going to help."

"He'll have people coming to Brighton just to meet him. I've arranged some meet-and-greets and some baseball clinics. It's money in the bank, Maeve. For Brighton. For the Festival Fund. For the sports programs at both the high school and the town leagues."

"What about the bakery?"

"The good of the many," she said with a cluck. "He can park wherever he wants." The period at the end of her sentence was final.

"Thanks for nothing."

I jabbed the End button and stared at the truck. The line moved like an ant colony invading a picnic.

Just as the odor of burning cookies reached me, I noticed a detail that drew a wicked smile.

I placed another call. "Hey, Colton. I need a favor."

COLTON STOKES STRODE through the bakery door, looking dapper in his pressed navy firefighter uniform. "Rumor has it you set the bakery on fire again."

The town seemed determined to never let me forget how a batch of gingerbread people had gone up in smoke last Christmas. They seemed to forget an oven explosion had caused the fire, not a teenage-Maeve escapade gone wrong. He leaned an elbow against the oak counter, most likely going for carefree. His eyes went moony. His undisguised interest amused me, but he was too young, too sweet for me.

"Rumor, as usual, is exaggerated. Just a batch of burnt cookies." Burnt because I had to deal with Luke and his donuts, and Kayla had been busy taking a phone order from someone who couldn't get in the shop. I downed the coffee I'd just poured.

"You needed a favor," he said with such hope.

Still holding on to the mug, I leaned forward on my elbows. "What's the rule on parking near a fire hydrant?"

"According to Statute 265:69, you can't park within fifteen feet of a fire hydrant. Why?"

I chucked my chin in the direction of the donut truck. "Don't think that's fifteen feet."

He frowned. "Oh, yeah?"

"I have a tape measure if you need one." I reached under the counter and brought out a retractable measuring tape, forgotten here after the fire clean-up last December.

He patted his utility belt. "Got one."

Striding with purpose, he headed outside. Colton and Luke, dueling with charming smiles, exchanged a few words like a burgeoning bromance. The truck rolled back ten feet. Not nearly far enough. Colton accepted a donut bag with a nod and came back inside.

"Need anything else?" he asked.

I growled. "You were supposed to make him go away."

"Ah, well, you could've been a bit more specific."

I flicked two fingers at the bag in his hand. "Traitor."

"You've gotta admit they smell good." He dipped his hand into the bag and brought out a cinnamon-scented confection, that really did smell heavenly. I was doomed. Colton had a soft spot for cinnamon.

"Probably uses oil filled with trans fats." I brought my coffee mug up for a shoring sip and found it empty.

"Yum, yum, yum. Best donut ever!" Colton's eyes rolled back as he swallowed half the donut.

"That truck's a fire waiting to happen."

His gaze measured the line as if he was calculating how long he'd have to wait for a refill. "Good thing I'm here to keep an eye on it."

"All that sugar will rot your brain." As I'd learned from reading one too many of the nutrition books Neve's therapist had recommended.

He just smiled like he had me right where he wanted me and left.

"Kayla!"

She poked her head out the kitchen door.

"I'm leaving," I said, glaring at the truck. "Make sure you lock the door when you leave."

"When haven't I?"

Never, but I didn't want to give Luke half a chance of sticking his nose in my business. I grabbed my purse from my office, located my keys on the floor, and left through the back door.

I had to get home before Mom stacked up too many saint points I could never pay back. I loved her, but I hated that I needed her help, that I depended on her so much.

And I had a plan to hatch.

I OPENED the door to my apartment to find a pile of bills on the counter, my mother at the kitchen table, sipping tea and reading a novel and Neve stretched out on the fake-wood laminate floor, giggling while a dog licked her face.

"What's this?" I plopped my purse on the counter on top of the bills but couldn't seem to let go of the strap. This wasn't going to be good. I could just feel it in my bones and wanted nothing more than to run away. I'd reached overload. Coffee, I needed coffee.

"Snick," said Neve, giggling like a spring brook. I hadn't heard her giggle like that since Riley moved.

"A present from Lark," Mom said, not even looking up from her novel.

I found just enough grounds left at the bottom of the bag for one pot of coffee. "You should've called before accepting."

"You sounded stressed."

"And this is going to help?"

"According to Lark."

I dumped the grounds into a filter without measuring, then filled the water container. I jabbed the Brew button.

The headache that had started soon after Luke Saunders and his truck had shown up and had throbbed in a slow pulse all afternoon, now flared like fireworks.

"You need to cut back on caffeine." Mom tutted, closed her book and got up. "It's not healthy."

Book under one arm, she waltzed to the door separating our apartment from the main house. "I should get dinner started before your father gets home."

"Aren't you forgetting something?"

She tried for innocence as she looked around the kitchen, but guilt swamped her face, even as she shook her head.

I tapped a toe toward the pumpkin-colored dog now playing high-five with Neve. "*That* is going home with you."

"It's a gift. From Lark."

"Who knows better. You said yes, so it's yours."

"Maeve—"

I pressed my hands on my temples, willing the headache to die. "I've had a day, Mom. I really can't handle one more thing." I attached the leash snaking on the counter to the dog's collar. Purple, I couldn't help but notice. Neve's favorite color. I closed my eyes for a moment and swallowed a groan. I couldn't, I just couldn't. With a determined inhale, I handed the leash to Mom, but she refused to take it.

"Mommy, no!" Neve tried to snag the leash away from me. "I want Snick to stay here with me!"

"We don't have any equipment to keep her safe and happy."

"Me and Grandma went to the Country Store and got a bunch of stuff."

Of course, they had.

"I managed fine with three kids and a dog," Mom said, her smile smug.

"I don't want your life, Mom." At least not right now.

"What's wrong with my life?"

Now, I'd gone and hurt her feelings, which was always a tight rope to maneuver.

But I wanted something... bigger. I was supposed to be traveling, learning baking secrets from all over the world. Not stuck in my parents' home, barely making ends meet. I retrieved the leash and plonked the handle in Mom's hand. "It's going home with you."

"Mommy!" Neve wrapped her arms around the dog's neck. Fat tears rolled down her cheeks. The dog licked them as if telling her not to worry.

"You can visit it at Grandma's." I didn't want to deny Neve a friend when she needed one so badly, but I just couldn't add one more thing on my to-do list, especially not a puppy that would require too much of my time.

Her sobs hiccupped. "I c-can?"

"Of course. You know Grandma loves to have you visit."

My mother launched me her famous "look," and I had to admit it found its mark. I tipped my head in a fair-is-fair look. Then I turned my back on the whole scene and attacked a small spill of water on the counter with a sponge.

As Mom reassured Neve that she could visit Snick at any time, as Neve cried broken-hearted tears, I reached for the cleaning spray in the cupboard under the sink. The spray filled the room with the scent of lemons. I had the appalling thought that my mother had the same habit, that I *was* living my mother's life, minus the supportive partner.

"Can I go to Grandma's now?"

I nodded, defeated. "I'll come get you for dinner."

The three left in a clatter of barks and laughter and clomps down the five stairs separating our units.

I needed to get out of here. I needed to find my own space.

I pitched the sponge into the sink. Butt leaning against the counter, I clicked on the Zillow tab on my phone, willing the little cottage on Hummingbird Lane with its cardinal-red Adirondack chairs and wild English garden to still be available.

5

GRACE

On Friday morning, Kate arrived as the mantle clock in the living room chimed ten. She carried a pink paper bag with a bloom of grease stains on the bottom. The scent of cinnamon, cooking oil, and something else I couldn't identify drifted in delicious waves.

"From the new donut truck," Kate said. Like Lark, Kate had a happy-in-her-own-skin look. Her eyes sparkled with laughter and her sprite-like body was almost always in motion. She favored colorful utility pants with lots of pockets— today's were a bright emerald. She wore a white embroidered peasant blouse that she somehow made look elegant. "Thought we'd give them a test drive."

"Don't let Maeve see you with that. She's already not happy with the Eamon clan as it is."

A cheerful bark echoed from Maeve's apartment. What were those two up to?

"Mind going to the dog park?" I asked Kate, wanting nothing more than to fall into a chair, having already used up a day's worth of energy trying to wrangle Neve away from the dog and into clothes. She'd ended up in a red-and-gold Wonder

Woman T-shirt and pink-and-purple shorts. She was dressed; that's all that mattered. "Neve, and the dog your daughter foisted on me, need to run off some energy."

"No problem."

"You could at least pretend you're surprised."

Kate lifted her shoulder in a what-can-you-do shrug. "She always seems to know."

"This time, she got it wrong." I called up the stairs, "Neve! Let's go!"

She and Snick pounded down the stairs as if there were a dozen of them. I somehow fit the harness on the dog, but that was all the stillness Snick seemed to have in her. She danced around my ankles, and I had a hard time hooking the leash's snap to her harness.

I scooped up the backpack I'd packed with snacks and water bottles. We managed to get dog and girl out the door and strolled past the sports field, where two chain-linked-fenced spaces stood— one for big dogs and one for small dogs. Each had an oak for shade, giant blue plastic tubes, a tractor tire standing on end, and wooden seesaws and plat-forms for the dogs to entertain themselves. A scattering of wooden benches dotted the top of the spaces for owners to watch their fur babies scamper. I just hoped no one else came, so the madness that was Snick could have a side to herself.

The left side already held a golden retriever, playing fetch with a pig-tailed girl that looked about Neve's age and seemed, with her red shorts and orange top, to have the same love of clashing colors. I tried to place her but couldn't. Where had she come from? Why was she there with no adult supervision?

On the small-dog side, Snick took off, running in circles, chugging like a train. Neve raced after her.

"Do you know that girl?" I asked Kate as we settled onto a bench on the small-dog side.

"Irene Lambert's granddaughter. She's here for the summer."

"Shouldn't Irene be out there with her?"

"Irene isn't a morning person."

"Still."

Kate broke out the donut bag and offered me one. The cinnamon-sugar coating melted against my fingers. "Apple cider. That's what I couldn't place."

"Remember when we used to go to that orchard outside of Keene? Before kids."

"We ate our weight in apple-cider donuts. There's no way I could do that now." I bit into the donut, my memory falling back to those carefree days. "Getting old sucks."

Kate tipped her head. "You don't seem your usual cheerful self."

I wrinkled my nose. "I'm fine."

"You forget who you're talking to."

I broke off another piece of donut and chewed it. "That dog isn't helping anything."

"All that just because of a dog? Come on, spit it out."

"The dog was just the last straw." The donut bite went down hard. "I'm frustrated." Frozen. Stuck.

"About?"

"I'm not sure. The birthday, I guess. Big milestone and all that. Worse even than fifty, and I didn't think that was possible."

I wrapped the remaining half of my donut in a napkin and stuffed it in Neve's backpack and took out a water bottle. "The kids don't need me anymore. Ansel's busy with his job and all his volunteer work. It feels..." *As if I'm superfluous.* So unneeded that I often fantasized about getting away, somewhere, anywhere.

"How many times have you spring cleaned your house?" Kate asked.

I hiked a shoulder like it didn't matter and took a slug of

water. "I have everything I've always wanted— a home, a family, a close community. I like my life. I have nothing to complain about. But—" I touched the intertwined heart pendant at my throat, the one Ansel had given me for our twenty-fifth anniversary. "It feels as if my life has no meaning anymore. I don't know what to do next."

Kate tutted. "You've just forgotten, that's all. It's a tough time, Grace. But driving yourself into physical exhaustion isn't the answer."

She did know me well. "I'm just angry all the time these days, and I'm not sure where it's all coming from. And I don't like it."

Kate nibbled on her donut, taking quick, tiny bites like a mouse. "How are things going with Maeve?"

I'd spoken to Kate many times about the ways Maeve managed to press all my buttons. The way she seemed to disapprove of everything I did for her, yet still expected me to care for Neve. Of my three children, Maeve and I had the most contentious relationship. "She wasn't happy about the dog."

"The dog is meant for you."

"I don't want a dog. The only reason I kept her is because of Neve."

Donut gone, Kate licked the cinnamon-sugar coating from her fingers. "You need to talk to Maeve and let her know how you feel. She's not a mind reader."

"She's so sensitive, though. If I say anything that even hints at a reproach, she takes offense and flies off the handle. I don't want her to move out and keep Neve away from me." I did love having them so close.

"Do you really think she'd do that?"

I shrugged. Yes, I did. She knew that was the best way to hurt me. And there were times when she wanted, maybe even needed, to hurt me. I didn't understand why.

Kate reached for the upcycled-jeans tote bag at her feet. "Don't you think it's hard for her to be so dependent on you?"

"Hard on her? I make life easier for her. And she doesn't even appreciate all I do for her."

Kate chuffed like she had an inside scoop on my psyche. "Martyr much?"

"Wow, I thought you were my friend." Wanting a little appreciation for the things you did was normal, wasn't it?

"You're kind of laying it on thick."

"Maybe." She was right, of course. I was too sensitive when it came to Maeve. The truth was, I needed to take care of her as much as she needed my help.

Snick slowed down and trotted over to the fence. The dogs sniffed noses through the fence, tails waving like friendly flags, Snick backing away and coming back as if she wasn't sure if she wanted to play, fight or flee. Well, didn't that just sound familiar.

"Hiding the truth from yourself isn't going to help," Kate said.

"I could do without the judgment right now."

"Not judging, Grace. I know what it's like to have to, as the kids say these days, pivot."

Kate had worked as a pediatric nurse and gotten burnt out during the pandemic. One day, she just up and quit. "How did you handle it, after you retired?"

"Not well." She took a skein of mint-green yarn and a crochet hook from her tote bag. "I had a tough time for a few months. After years of chronic stress, I didn't know how to relax anymore."

"You never let on." I noted that Neve had circled closer to the redheaded girl. "I would have been there for you."

"I know." She switched yarns to a pale pink. "The holidays are tough for everyone. After that was over, I made Paul take me on a long vacation. I do my best thinking in the car. The trip gave me time to think about what I wanted, unplug and relearn to relax." She chuckled. "And a captive audience."

They'd driven to Florida last January and spent three weeks wandering from place to place. I could imagine my brother squirming in the driver's seat all the way down I-95, not knowing what to do with all of Kate's emotions. We Eamons were not big on facing feelings. The thought of Paul's deer-in-headlights look made me smile.

"Ansel is a homebody." I doubted I could get him to go anywhere for three days let alone three weeks.

"Where do you do your best thinking?"

"Vacuuming." The back-and-forth motion soothed. Plus, a vacuumed room looked neat and orderly, which settled me. Pathetic.

"While Paul drove, I took stock of my situation. I made a list of what made me happy, what I could control and what I couldn't. Of my resources."

Since March, Kate had become a garage-sale queen, buying junk for next to nothing, then turning it into show-worthy treasures. From tables to chests to trunks, but her specialty was chairs. "How did you land on fixing up junk?"

"By accident." She laughed and worked her crochet so fast that her fingers blurred. "One of the kitchen chairs needed fixing. After I'd glued the leg, it seemed like a good time to repaint it. And if you're going to do one chair, you might as well do the whole set."

Kate had turned her dark, old-fashioned kitchen chairs into bright modern pieces. She'd stripped off the varnish, painted the seats teal and the frames and legs cream, then stenciled a teal Celtic knot along the top rail. Then she'd done the same to her kitchen table, brightening the whole kitchen. She'd always been good at making something out of nothing that I'd never even questioned this was a new direction for her.

Kate racked up rows on the lap blanket. "I happened to

drive by a sale one Saturday and there were six mismatched chairs that called to me."

She'd transformed those broken chairs and sold them to finance her next project.

I tipped my chin at the blanket on her lap already taking shape. "There's no way I could do that or refurbish furniture."

"You don't have to. Creativity comes in all shapes. You have a lot of talents, Grace."

"I'm good at waiting." Not that it fulfilled me in any way. "I wait for Ansel every day. I wait for Maeve. For Neve." I waved at Snick, tail up in alarm, staring across the chain link fence at the golden. "And now I get to wait for that thing to do her business every few hours. I've never seen a dog sniff so much or take so long to pick a spot."

"The way you set up your Sunday dinners," Kate said. "That's creative. The way you concoct your cleaning sprays. By the way, I'm out of the tea-tree-oil-and-lavender bathroom spray."

"I'll make you more."

"The way you find all those fun projects to do with Neve."

I pooh-poohed the comment. "According to Maeve, I'm doing everything wrong when it comes to Neve."

"Maeve has a lot going on right now."

"Not that she's sharing."

Kate opened her mouth, but I stopped her with a hand.

"I know. I never shared anything with my mother. But, as you very well know, I'm nothing like my mother. And yes, I do realize that running your own business isn't easy. Neither is raising a child as a single parent."

Kate switched yarns to a soft yellow. "You know Maeve needs your approval, right? She wants you to be proud of her."

"I am proud of her." I was proud of all my children.

"She needs to hear it."

Hadn't I shown her in a thousand little ways? My gaze

sought out Neve, who had made it all the way to the fence. "Neve starts art camp on Monday."

And that would leave me with empty days again. Where was all the wisdom that was supposed to come with age? I shook my head and focused on Neve staring at the Lambert girl across the fence. Maybe this girl would make a good friend for Neve, even if only for the summer.

"Maybe she can teach an old grandma a new trick and get you to draw. You used to love making those fancy pop-up cards when the kids were small."

I jabbed my elbow into Kate's ribs and laughed. "Who are you calling old? You're two and a half years older than me."

"You could enter the baking contest at the Strawberry Festival."

I shook my head. "Baking is Maeve's thing."

"Is she entering?"

"Not that I know of." On and off went the water bottle cap. But she should. She was sure to win. Her baked goods got rave reviews from the day she opened the bakery.

"Then, why not? You bake a decent pie. Your maple apple pie was always a hit at Thanksgiving. Never a crumb left."

"I haven't baked since Maeve took over making desserts in her teens."

"Then practice. See if it's something you want to do again. It seemed to bring you joy."

I grunted. Had it brought me joy? Or had it been more of a sense of expectation? After all, it wasn't Thanksgiving without pie. Did I want to bake? "Did you know the school made Maeve have Neve tested for ADHD?"

"Lark mentioned something about that."

I hiked my chin in Neve's direction. She stood next to the fence, listening intently to the Lambert girl, whose hands moved as fast as her mouth. "Does that look like a child who's out of control?"

"ADHD comes on a spectrum, Grace. There are seven different kinds, including without hyperactivity."

"She's not impulsive."

"But she is forgetful and disorganized unless she's interested in the subject."

I thought of her room that constantly looked as if a tornado had stormed through. "That doesn't mean there's something wrong with her."

"No one said there was. Her brain just works a little differently. The school's trying to help her."

"By putting a label on her?" The same thing had happened to Maeve with her rebellious streak. She'd been labeled as "difficult" and had come to believe that meant she was bad, which had led to some bad decisions. I'd fought so many battles with the school to have her treated as a person and not the label they'd slapped on her. If it hadn't been for the baking, I shudder to think what would have happened to her. I certainly wasn't able to reach her. Not then. Not now.

"By giving Neve the extra help she needs to build her self-confidence." Kate dropped her hands to her lap, stopping her crocheting. "But all this isn't about Neve, is it?"

"You know, in the olden days, the elders of a community were revered."

Kate chuckled. "It's not easy, Grace, finding a place when the world tries to tell you that you're past your prime and no longer useful."

"You've found your thing."

"You will, too." She picked up her project once more. "You just have to keep testing and looking. Start with a list of things you enjoy. I'm not talking about what other people think you should do, but what *you* think. What brings *you* joy?"

"It feels like being a teenager all over again, trying to decide what to study and be for the rest of your life." I tsked. "If only

I'd known back then how little it mattered, I wouldn't have stressed so much."

"See, you're already halfway there. It's not what you do that matters, it's that you find joy in it. I drive for Meals on Wheels twice a week to give back, and because it gives me a chance to check up on neighbors who have no one. The upcycling of furniture reminds me that even old, useless things can find new life and purpose. Plus, it's fun. It brings me joy."

Kate was back to joy again. Did I even remember what joy was? I'd spent so many years focused on others that I barely remembered who I was.

I glanced up, expecting to find Neve and Snick still by the fence. But the small-dog side of the dog park stood empty. How had they gotten by us? Head on a swivel, I scoured the area until I spotted Neve outside the large-dog area and the Lambert girl opening the gate, golden retriever nosing out ahead of her.

Snick's tail went straight up and waved like a mad road-construction flagman. As the golden eased out of the gate, Snick jumped up, made a 360-degree turn in the air like a ninja, snatching the leash right out of Neve's hands.

I shot up but was too late. Snick launched herself at the golden, missed and hit the Lambert girl, knocking her backwards into the gate. Cries— of surprise or pain? —erupted from the girl on the ground. I raced toward the downed girl. Snick and the other dog tussled, barking and running in circles, Neve running after them, trying to catch Snick's leash.

"Get the dogs!" I yelled at Kate, who was faster than me.

Kate sprinted after the dogs while I checked over the girl. "Where are you hurt?"

A run of tears rolling down her cheeks, the girl rubbed at her chest.

This was my fault. I should have paid more attention, seen Neve leave. That was what I got for wallowing in my own neediness.

Just because I couldn't see bruises didn't mean there weren't any blooming under her skin. I reached for her hand. "Let's get you up and get you some water. What's your name?"

"Ch-Charlie."

I dusted her shorts and T-shirt, then led her to the bench and made her sit down while I dug through the backpack for water. "There you are. Snick is scared of big dogs for some reason."

Charlie guzzled some water. "Yeah, Sunny likes to jump on people, too. But I'm ready for her."

"Sunny is your dog?"

She nodded and used the tail of her shirt to wipe her face. "Well, Grandma's dog. She's mine while I'm visiting."

When had Irene gotten a dog? I usually knew everything that went on in town.

Kate had caught both Snick and Sunny and was leading them back toward me, Neve skipping behind her. The dogs trotted and batted at each other, tails wagging, having a grand old time.

"I hear you're here for the summer," I said to Charlie, trying to distract her.

She nodded and perked up. Her red pigtails bobbing. "I'm going to baseball camp." She narrowed her gaze and simulated a throw. "I'm going to pitch in the World Series one day."

"That is a grand goal." She'd have to break a lot of glass ceilings, but I was rooting for her.

"Grandma, can Charlie come over for lunch?" Neve folded her hands at her heart and rose on her toes. "Pleeeeease!"

She'd made a friend. I couldn't say no.

"Why don't we go ask Charlie's grandma if it's okay?" And drop off one dog. I could handle two girls and a lunch, but I wasn't sure I could handle two girls and two dogs.

The girls squealed. I hadn't seen Neve this excited since Riley moved. Charlie seemed none the worse for wear after her collision with Snick and the gate. She grabbed Sunny's leash. "Let's go!"

"With that," Kate said, handing me Snick's leash, "I'll get back to my day. There's an estate sale I want to check out on my way home." She hugged me tight. "This was nice, Grace. Let's do it more often."

I hugged her back and rolled my eyes. "Tell Lark I'm still mad at her."

"Which reminds me...." Kate dipped into her jeans tote bag and brought out a brochure for the Stoneley Canine Center. "She said you might need this."

A class schedule. Lark had known all along Snick needed training. "Afraid to give it to me in person, was she?"

"Make a list, Grace. It helps." With a smile and wave Kate headed back to the house and her silver SUV.

I managed to catch up to the girls and dogs, grateful Charlie was okay. That Neve had found a friend brought me joy.

Dealing with dogs, on the other hand, was definitely *not* going to make the "joy" list.

6

MAEVE

"Your boyfriend's back," Kayla teased as she ambled through the front door of the bakery on Friday morning. Only an hour late today.

Arms crossed, lurking at the edge of the picture window, I stared at the donut truck and Luke handing out bag after bag of greasy donuts. The grease stink permeated the street and my shop. My own aunt had stopped by the truck to buy donuts and hadn't bothered coming into the bakery. If you couldn't count on family to support you, who could you count on? Of course, I knew the answer to that: nobody. "He's not my boyfriend."

"You're legit growling," Kayla said, swirling the dribble of coffee at the bottom of the pot, shaking her head at my caffeine consumption.

"With good reason." I shifted to get a better look, then wished I hadn't. Pink shouldn't look that good on a guy. Those well-defined biceps had no place peeking from a T-shirt that read, "Donut Worry, Be Happy." I reminded myself he was a spoiled sports star with the depth of a wooden bat. "It's bad enough he's parked right in front of my shop *and* serving his blasted donuts. Now he's offering coffee. Nobody has a reason to come in here now. We're losing money, Kayla. If this keeps up, I'm going to have to close the store."

"A little dramatic, no?" She measured out grounds, fitted the filled coffee filter into the machine and pressed Start.

"Not as much as you'd think." I rubbed at the newest burn scar on my left hand, still red and smarting. I blamed it on Luke Saunders and his donuts for the new addition to my collection, keeping half my mind out of my kitchen.

Kayla's hands stopped in mid-air. "Just how bad is business? Do I need to start looking for another job?"

The coffee machine gurgled as fast as my thoughts. "I'm going to have to donate everything I baked today." Well, I could freeze some of the cookies and cupcakes. But still, the rest— that was money out and nothing coming in. You couldn't refreeze more than once without affecting the taste. And I'd have to bake again tomorrow on the off chance someone did come in. "If no one comes in tomorrow... more money out the door."

"It's something new." Kayla handed me a steaming mug of coffee. "They'll get bored in a couple of days."

"Let's hope it's sooner than later." Coffee in hand, I pushed away from the window frame. Stewing wasn't going to change anything. "We need to do something."

"Like what?"

I downed the coffee like a shot and the caffeine reenergized my stalled brain. If I was going to have to donate the food, might as well offer a discount. At least I'd make some of the cost back. "A sale."

"Sounds like a plan."

I handed Kayla the empty mug. "Where's the sandwich board?"

"In your office. Somewhere."

I found it under a pile of folded bags, wedged between the filing cabinet and the wall. I really needed to do a spring cleaning in here. A quick sponging gave the board new life. Using an array of colorful chalk I found scattered on my desk, I drew a big-topped muffin and slashed the price in half, offering a free small coffee with it. Then I stuck the sign outside the door where the donut seekers would have to see it on their way to the head of the line. The offer lured in a few people tired of waiting for their sugar rush, but not enough.

With a flurry of chalk and nonchalant look over his shoulder, Luke matched my offer, and the line at his truck buzzed like hornets in a nest. He had *not* just done that! The ego on him.

Smiling that press-conference confident smirk, he arrowed my gaze in challenge. Growling, I grabbed the board, wiped it clean and changed the offer to buy-one-get-two. *Take that, Donut Guy.*

With a guileful smile, Luke crossed out his discounted price and above it wrote, "3-for-1." He couldn't even use real words. And didn't he realize that was the same thing as buy-one-get-two?

I couldn't let him win. I just couldn't. I crossed out my offer and wrote, "Pay what you like," knowing full well that some town cheapskates would take that as free.

He nodded in a you-win way that somehow failed to make me feel as if I'd won. I didn't trust that he'd leave it at that. I narrowed my gaze, staring at Luke, showing off for his fans. What would he cook up next?

At noon, the truck's side door closed, and I breathed a sigh of relief. *What does he have up his sleeve?* another part of me wondered and worried. But I couldn't let him get to me. I couldn't let his maybe-plans derail the reprieve he'd just given me. The lunchtime crowd wouldn't have a choice; they'd have to come into the bakery for their shot of sugar. I had to upsell like my life depended on it.

To my surprise, Dani was the first person through the door.

She wore a denim-colored "Glazed Anatomy" T-shirt that tented over her shaggy-hemmed jeans shorts.

"Does your brother know you're fraternizing with the enemy?"

"He's gone to a meeting." She moved with tentative steps toward the bakery display, eyeing the strawberry cheese tarts I'd made earlier. "He'll be gone for a while."

I went to the other side of the counter and waited for her to speak again.

"I'm sorry," she said, perusing today's offerings. "What Luke's doing? It wasn't my idea."

"I'm well aware."

She continued to troll the bakery case. "Can I have one of the tarts, a purple-velvet cupcake— what did you use to turn it purple? It's too subtle to be food coloring."

"Purple sweet potatoes."

"Really? Wow."

"I try to use natural coloring and flavors whenever possible." Something I focused on even more since Neve's diagnosis.

"Makes sense." Her gaze never left the bakery case. "A funfetti-cake truffle. And a lemon crinkle cookie."

"That's it?"

She offered me a shy smile. "For now."

"For here or to-go?" I snapped open a blue Brightside Bakery bag. "Given how your brother feels about me, I suggest to-go."

She gave a vague nod, drew some sweaty bills from her shorts pocket and passed them to me. The money had no doubt come from donut-buying customers, and I handled it like it was dirty. She took the bag with a thanks, then sat at one of the tables by the wall, eating each dessert as if she were a sleuth uncovering clues. After each mouthful, she scribbled something in a composition notebook with donut stickers on the cover.

Part of me was dying of curiosity about Dani's notes, but I wouldn't give her the satisfaction of letting her know.

A few of the old regulars shuffled in for their usual favorites — a lemon bar for Mrs. Holt (the first-grade teacher who'd already been sour and ancient when I went through the school system), a brownie for Clyde Moran (a sweet retired state trooper who still drove a beat even though he wasn't on any payroll), and the muffin of the day— lemon blueberry —for Cecilia Jennings, a treat she would share with the sable teacup Chihuahua in her purse.

After the geriatric brigade had left, Dani studied the cookie from all angles and asked, "Did you use zest as well as lemon juice in the crinkle?"

"Trying to reverse-engineer my baked goods?"

"Is that a problem?"

Her knowing what I used to bake my goods wasn't going to hurt me. And it wasn't her fault her brother played dirty. "Both zest and lemon juice from real lemons."

"I thought so. It's very lemony. In a good way."

"I chill the dough overnight to bring out the flavor."

"Thanks!" She scribbled a note in the book. "These funfetti truffles, they're so much tastier than any cake pop I've ever had."

"Everything's homemade, not from a mix, and I used good-quality white chocolate, not those fake white chocolate chips."

"I'm starting to get that quality ingredients make a huge difference."

"You get out what you put in." One reason my profit margins were so low. If I was going to bother to bake, I wanted it to taste fantastic, and that meant using the best quality ingredients I could find. Not the best policy in a market trending downward.

"I'm sorry," Dani said again, staring at the paper remnants

of her dessert feast. "Luke's wrong and he's stubborn. But he's not a bad person."

"It's not your fault." I nodded toward the truck. "But you should probably go before he comes back."

She glanced at the muffin-shaped wall clock and scrambled out of the chair, scooping up her notebook and pen. "He's going to be so mad I didn't get the cleaning done."

Just as Dani hurried out, Colton walked in, wearing baggy khaki shorts and ridiculous-looking slide sandals rather than his firefighter uniform. He held the door open for her, admiring her backside as she disappeared around the truck.

"Who was *that*?" Colton asked, a wolf whistle in his voice. "She smells like heaven."

Colton and his cinnamon fetish *would* glean on to Dani's cinnamon-sugar donut scent. I tossed a parchment-wrapped cinnamon-pecan Danish his way. "Trouble, that's who."

Before I could say more, the squeal of brakes and a sickening bump came from out front. Abandoning the Danish on the counter, Colton vaulted into action. I followed and pushed to the front of the crowd.

"I didn't see him!" Olivia Ryan stood, hands on her face, sobbing and shaking like an earthquake beside her orange Smart car. Dani and Colton knelt beside Jeb Cannon, who lay on his back like a beetle in the middle of the road, arms and legs flailing. "I didn't see him! I didn't see him!"

I took the short and usually sassy Olivia by the elbow and led her to the sidewalk, all the while checking on Jeb. No blood stained the asphalt. He looked surprised but unhurt. "The truck was blocking your way. You couldn't see."

I said it loud enough so Luke, who limped toward the accident, would hear. I was hoping it would fill him with guilt, although I suspected guilt wasn't in his emotional arsenal.

Luke knelt next to Dani and Colton, handling the situation with calm and care.

Darn, why did he have to look genuinely worried about Jeb? *Don't let Luke's compassion fool you; he just doesn't want to get sued.*

"Look, Olivia," I said. "Jeb's fine." He'd eaten enough of Luke's donuts over the past twenty-four hours to have the small car bounce right off his padded middle. "He's getting up."

By the time Micah Shepard, our one full-time police officer, had sorted through what happened, Jeb sat on the curb, eating more donuts, courtesy of Luke, Olivia was sent home, and the donut truck was ordered to move around the corner, away from Main Street where it couldn't block traffic.

I couldn't help it, I gloated, and let Luke see it. Finally, business could go back to normal.

Sweet victory didn't last long. Now Main Street was empty. And, for the rest of the day, I got even less foot traffic than before.

I stared at the mostly untouched bakery case.

I needed a better plan.

7

MAEVE

That night, Neve picked *Ella Enchanted* from the toppled pile of library books, then snuggled into her bed with me and her nest of stuffies. A fan blew a cool breeze and drowned out the sound of rain outside. Which made me think of gray skies, which brought up a picture of Luke's eyes. I swallowed a groan and sank deeper into the mattress.

I opened the book to the first chapter. "Haven't you read this book a dozen times already?"

"I like it." Neve burrowed into my side, tucked her favorite bunny under her arm and motioned for me to read.

Reading out loud wasn't my favorite thing. Reading wasn't my favorite thing, period. I'd always had a hard time with it at school. Still did. Which often made me feel like a failure. And now a bad mom because I hadn't read to my baby as much as I should have. Not that it had curbed her thirst for stories. "'That fool of a fairy—'" I started reading.

"Mommy?"

"Yes, honey bunches?"

She twirled her index finger through a hank of hair. "I don't want to go to art camp."

Just what I didn't need right now. "How come? You've been looking forward to it for weeks. We bought you new supplies and everything."

"I know. But I can draw any time. Maybe I could go later."

"You begged me to sign you up for art camp." I'd had to clean out a chunk of my savings to pay for the full ten weeks. But that wasn't for her to worry about.

She turned her dark, soulful gaze toward me, eyes so much like Patrick's that I found myself melting. "I really want to go to baseball camp."

"Baseball?" Since when had Neve even had an interest in baseball?

"My friend Charlie's going, and I really want to go, too."

"Who's Charlie?"

"The girl from the dog park. She has a dog, too. Her name's Sunny and Snick likes her. Grandma made us a picnic lunch and we ate it outside in the yard."

"That was nice of Grandma." Mom hadn't mentioned any of that when I'd gone down to get Neve for dinner.

Neve nodded. The softness of her hair, the silk of her skin and the strawberry scent of her shampoo were my definition of cozy.

"What did you have for your picnic?" I shuddered to think what my mother had included in that lunch. She deliberately went against my wishes, called the diet the therapist had suggested too extreme.

"A tuna sandwich." A Neve favorite. "Charlie likes them, too." No wonder they'd bonded. Not many kids liked tuna fish. "Chips, strawberries and cookies."

I noticed the plural. I'd have to have another talk with Mom about sugar and the importance of this diet for Neve's success next September. No wonder it had taken me so long to wind my child down for bed.

"I've never heard of Charlie." I put the book down on my knees.

"She's staying with her grandma for the summer."

Neve had made a friend. My throat worked, already dreading Charlie's departure and the hole she would leave in Neve's already fragile emotional fabric. Right before school started, too. I drew her closer and sniffed in her little-girl smell deeper, wanting to protect her from all the heartaches of this world. "They're expecting you at art camp on Monday."

"I know, but I really want to play baseball with Charlie."

I ran my fingers through her hair. "You've never played baseball."

"At gym, I did."

"Did you like it?"

She shrugged like liking baseball wasn't the important part of the equation. "I got a home run."

"Hey, that's fantastic!"

"So, can I go?" She twirled her hair again, a sure sign of stress.

Neve didn't ask for much. And her therapist had suggested more exercise, something art camp wasn't going to provide. On the other hand, the Friday night before camp started wasn't the best time to switch things around. "It's not that easy. The camp might already be full."

"Oh." She sounded resigned, and I hated seeing her that way. I loved her spunk, the creative way she looked at life, even if, to everyone else, it seemed like too much. "But can Charlie come play after camp?"

"Tell you what," I said, kissing the top of her head. "I'll make some phone calls and see what I can do to switch camps."

Neve squealed in my ear and hugged me tight. She plucked

the book from my lap and scooched me out of bed. "Goodnight, Mommy. Love you!"

"Love you more."

OF COURSE, making calls after nine was not gaining me any popularity. But if Neve wanted baseball camp with Charlie, I would do my best to get her baseball camp with Charlie. Especially given all I was asking her to change to manage her ADHD.

Finding the information for the baseball camp took longer than I expected. Finding out Coach Mac, my old high school softball coach, was in charge was a stroke of luck. Good thing I'd been one of his best players— no, make that his best player. Even better that he owed me.

"Do you know what time it is, Carpenter?" His voice still boomed even though he had to be pushing seventy. I'd heard through the gossip grapevine that he now worked as the Athletic Director at Hopewell College.

I paced the kitchen floor, trying to keep my voice steady and firm. "I do. I wouldn't have called unless it was an emergency."

"An emergency? You haven't played for me in over a decade. How could you possibly have an emergency that I could answer?"

"My daughter, Neve, needs to be on the roster for your baseball camp on Monday." I blurted out the words so that they almost ran one onto the other.

"Needs?"

I pulled in air, straightened my shoulders. This *was* a need, not a flight of fancy. It was for my daughter's wellbeing. "She's had a really tough year, and she's finally made a friend who's going to your baseball camp. Starting Monday."

Some sort of comedy with canned laughter played in the

background of Coach's home. "There's already a waitlist a mile long, Maeve."

"Out-of-towners or locals?"

"Both. Luke Saunders offered to run a series day of clinics while he's in town for the next few weeks. And suddenly my camp is the most popular thing in the state."

The mention of Luke Saunders's name had me gritting my teeth. He wasn't going to mess up Neve's summer as well as ruin my business.

Time to bring out the ammunition.

"I played senior year. Because you asked me to." I'd have much rather been home baking or out with Patrick, planning our future. "We won State," I reminded him. And we'd won because of my pitching arm. "You got your banner."

"Maeve..."

"Coach."

He sighed, resigned, like he'd had so often when I played for him. "Let me see what I can do."

"Thank you!"

"No promises."

"I won't take no."

He groaned, but the edges held laughter. "Don't I know it."

Ten minutes later, Coach called back. "I used a loophole to make a space for Neve."

"Thank you! You were always my favorite teacher."

"Cut the blarney, Carpenter! Monday morning. Nine sharp."

"We'll be there." I hung up laughing, so pleased I'd pulled this off for Neve. My emergency fund would take a hit having to pay for two camps for two weeks, but I couldn't wait to tell Neve that she would get to go to camp with her new friend Charlie.

But as I made my way to the pull-out bed in the living area, my step faltered. Would Luke treat Neve differently because I'd refused to help Dani?

8

GRACE

Maybe I *was* getting old because spending the day entertaining two girls and a dog had worn the stuffing out of me. By the time ten o'clock rolled around, I could barely keep my eyes open. I slipped on my pajamas then went back downstairs with a handful of treats to lure Snick inside her crate in the living room for the night.

"Goodnight." I closed the crate door and tried not to think about how much it sounded like a jail door. Lark had insisted Snick was crate trained, that it was good for her to sleep in her crate. A fake sheepskin cushion lined the bottom, and she had a chew toy and her comfort puppy stuffed toy to keep her company. She would be fine.

I returned to the bedroom, holding my breath. Last night, none of those comforts had soothed the wild beast. I'd ended up spending the night on the floor because, otherwise, the mutt whined, and Ansel had to go to work the next morning. Friday was always a busy day for him.

I rolled my shoulder and rubbed at my hip. My bones couldn't take another night on the floor.

I stood in front of the dresser, removing the sea-glass

earrings I'd forgotten to take off earlier, ears perked to the living room. Just as I thought I was home-free and could relax, that we would have a quiet night, the whining started. A low, tentative note at first, quickly followed by more and louder ones until the house reverberated with the plaintive sound of Snick's wails. Hands flat on the dresser, I closed my eyes. If I did nothing, maybe she would stop. As if she'd heard my thought, she redoubled her effort.

Ansel came out of the bathroom. "What's wrong with the dog?"

What wasn't wrong with her? She had none of the training Lark had promised. "I don't understand what possessed Lark to bring me a puppy."

He gave me a kiss. "It was sweet."

Snick chose that moment to loose a particularly mournful cry.

I groaned, deep and long. "I want to strangle her."

"Lark or the dog?" Ansel asked, undressing for bed.

"Both."

He chuckled and the sound of it vibrated in my chest, warm and tender.

"What's wrong with me?" I asked the woman in the mirror.

He came to stand behind me and wrapped his arms around my middle. "There's not a thing wrong with you. You are still the most beautiful woman I know."

"You don't have your glasses on." I scoffed in a half-hearted way and leaned into him anyway. "I have everything I ever wanted, and I'm not happy."

"Having the dog around will be good for you."

Into the mirror, I gave him a look of incredulity.

"It'll give you someone to fuss over. You love taking care of people."

I swiveled around until I faced him, hands splayed over his chest, his arms still wrapped around me. "You're wrong, though. That's why I quit all those festival committees, stopped volunteering at the community center, and left the Friends of the Library. I was tired of it, of always taking care of the details no one else wanted to."

"Do you think that, with everything you've let go, maybe you have too much time on your hands?"

I'd been so busy for so long that maybe he was right, maybe I didn't know how to relax. "I just don't know who I am anymore."

"You are Grace Eamon Carpenter. A woman of many talents with a heart so big, it puts the rest of us to shame." He kissed the top of my head, let it linger. "In two years, I'll retire—"

"Hah!"

"Okay, maybe not retire all the way, but slow down, and we can do some of the travel you've wanted to do."

"That thing—" I jerked my head toward the living room "—comes with at least a ten-year life sentence."

"The kids would take care of her while we're away, if you asked."

I jostled my head in a maybe. Asking for favors wasn't easy.

"Where would you like to go?"

I had dreams of going to an Austrian Christmas market, on a European river cruise, an Australian adventure, even an African safari. But Ansel had zero interest in any of those destinations. "I'd settle for a long weekend away from home. No kids. No dog. Just you and me."

"You've got it." He padded over to his side of the bed. "What have we here?"

I craned my neck over the foot of the bed at the mess on the floor. Somehow, Snick had managed to empty all the socks from Ansel's bottom night-table drawer and shaken them out as if she planned on using them as a nest.

"Looks like a lesson," I said, loosing a real belly-jiggling laugh for the first time since the mutt had arrived. When had

Snick had time to trot upstairs and redecorate? "Maybe you'll close your drawers all the way next time."

This mess was the latest in a series. The dog was a ghost. She moved on silent paws with speed, stealth and precision, leaving destruction behind her. She'd shredded the girls' lunch napkins into a thousand pieces I'd had to retrieve halfway down her throat. She'd reorganized the bathroom's waste basket contents all over the floor. Thankfully, she hadn't eaten any of the refuse. In her haste to bark at the mailman, she'd knocked over and broken the three pots of succulents on the living room's windowsill. She'd hidden the girls' sneakers in the curves of her bed in the kitchen. Not to mention all the water I'd had to mop up due to her beard drips. Note to self: Time to make a grooming appointment.

Ansel scooped up the mess of socks and dumped it in the drawer. And that was how they'd stay until I got around to refolding them, which the way I was feeling probably wouldn't be until next laundry day. He had no clue how much work this mutt was creating for me.

"So, what's the verdict?" he asked as he settled into bed.

"About?"

"The dog."

The concert of her cries sounded like a diva's aria from a tragic opera. The mutt had pipes.

"I'm not spending another night on the floor."

The crate was too heavy for me to carry, so I went to the kitchen and retrieved her daybed— a fiber-filled, anti-anxiety donut covered with plush that was supposed to remind a dog of its mother's fur. The label had promised it would calm and soothe any dog. I dumped it on the floor on my side of the bed, then went back down to the living room. As soon as I arrived, the whining cut off and her tail beat a tattoo against the metal sides of the crate. "Don't think you've won."

I scooped her up before she could get the thought to

wander around the house and cause trouble or disturb Maeve and Neve. Upstairs, I placed her in the bed, then slipped between the sheets and turned off the light.

The next thing I knew, two paws dipped the top of the mattress and a wet nose poked at my cheek. "That's where I draw the line," I told the dog. "I don't want ticks or fleas in my bed."

Not that she had either, but you never knew. She had spent the day outdoors, romping with the girls. Which reminded me, I needed to take her to the vet and see about a flea and tick regimen before the end of the month.

I pointed a finger toward her bed. "Bed!"

In the shadows of the room, her silhouette glanced from me to the bed and back at me. "It's that, or back in the crate."

Snick dropped to the floor, hopped into her bed, twirled three times, then plopped down with a huff.

Ansel hummed, "You've Got a Friend."

I elbowed him in the ribs and bit back a smile, wishing dealing with Maeve was this easy.

9

MAEVE

With the bakery closed on Monday, I had time to cook some eggs and make a berry salad for breakfast for Neve, pack her a lunch (without sweets), and help her gather all she'd need to start camp this morning. Every week, I forgot how frustrating getting her going was and how I ended up wanting to pull my hair or growl. Today—both.

That dog of Mom's complicated things because Neve kept wanting to go down to visit. And once she got something in her head, distracting her was like trying to turn a giant cruise ship in a small river. Finally, we got going, only to realize I'd forgotten my travel mug of coffee on the counter, which was not doing wonders for my mood.

The sports field at the north end of Brighton Lake, just off Main Street, buzzed with activity. The remnant of last night's rain dewed the grass. The scent of chalk filled the air as well as a sense of excitement. Girls and boys of all ages milled around, waiting for camp to start. So did parents and babysitters. All these fans had shown up, not for their children's sake, but because they were hoping to catch sight of Luke Saunders before rushing off to work or back home for a kid break.

Certainly didn't take much to impress people.

Neve spotted Charlie, who arrived with her grandmother.

"Mommy? Can I?"

"Sure." She started to run, but I stopped her with a quick hug. "Have a great day, honey bunches. I'll pick you up at three. Remember, we have your therapy right after."

Neve nodded, extricated herself from my hug and she and Charlie greeted each other like long-lost friends. Even though I'd made half a dozen people mad trying to change Neve's camp, I'd made the right choice. Having a friend was as good as therapy.

Coach Mac marched out of the equipment shed. Shaped like a powder keg, he still looked as stern as ever, eyebrows low over his eyes, deep lines bracketing his mouth. The tuft of white hair poking out of his red ballcap shocked me. Last time I'd seen him, the hair under the ballcap had been russet. The man was getting old. How would he handle all these kids?

He stood on a chair, reached for the whistle hanging around his neck and blew it, causing an instant quiet. "Welcome to the Brighton Baseball Camp." His voice carried as if he were using a megaphone. "By now you should have received your team assignment. When I call your team's name, head toward your coach."

Coach Mac glanced down at his clipboard and barked out team names. "Blue Jays!"

From the field, a lanky young man wearing a Blue Jays T-shirt waved. A dozen kids jogged to his side.

"Red Sox! Yankees! Orioles! Tigers! Angels!"

Hand in hand, Neve and Charlie skipped toward their coach, a tall girl with an infectious smile and a high ponytail sticking out the back of her red ballcap.

Thanks, Coach, for putting them on the same team!

I headed to the stands, where half the town seemed to sit, to watch for a bit. Not on the off chance I'd get a glimpse of Luke Saunders, like the rest of these easily impressed people, but because I wanted to make sure Neve settled in okay with so many people around. Noisy situations tended to make her irritable. Not a great way to start a camp after Coach Mac had done me a favor. Sitting next to Charlie, she looked as if she was already having a great time.

Claudia Catherine Bass, nee Boone, sidled up to me and sat. She pushed her Marian-the-librarian glasses up her nose and tucked the edges of her dirt-brown skirt around her knees. She had a son a few years younger than Neve. "Saw Patrick at the brewery last night."

I detected a note of gloat in her voice. Why bother with hello when you had juicy gossip? And just what was Little Miss Perfect doing in a pub on a Sunday night?

She'd been petty since high school— prim and oh-so properly perfect with China-doll features and her starched drab clothing. On the outside, anyway. She'd tried more than once to seduce Patrick. But, back then, he never had eyes for anyone but me.

His last visit happened right around Christmas. He'd promised Neve the moon and left without even giving her stardust. Just last week, he'd called and promised a visit, but not set a date for said visit. Pretending I knew he'd arrived, I said, "He just flew in."

"He looked real chummy with Amy Tucker wrapped around him."

Saying anything would be a mistake, given C.C.'s bent for gossip that usually ended up like a bad game of telephone— every word scrambled to cause maximum drama.

She tsked like a schoolmarm. I half expected her to draw a ruler from her skirt pocket to rap on my knuckles. "I saw them leave together."

Everything in me wanted to grab Patrick by the throat and shake him— *how dare you!* —but I couldn't let C.C. know her barb had found its mark. "Uh-huh."

"Was he at your place last night?"

"His brother's." At least that's where I hoped he'd spent the night. I got up suddenly needing to move. "It's been nice as always, C.C. See you later."

"Oh, you will." Her lip-glossed smile was so big, it shone like a clown's. She was loving having something on me.

I headed toward the blue bakery van as if I didn't have a care, all the while feeling smoke pressure my ears. Why hadn't Patrick called me? Instead of the usual anticipation swirling in my veins at one of his visits, I found I wanted to yell at him until his skin blistered.

I— or at least Neve —should have been his first stop. I shoved the van in gear. I'd been patient. I'd been supportive. We deserved an explanation.

Instead of heading to the bakery and taking care of the mound of paperwork waiting for my attention, I wound through the streets until I reached the trailer park at the northern edge of town— on the other side of the proverbial train tracks. Past the entryway with its two yellow-brick pillars holding nothing, I followed the too-familiar dirt path to Patrick's family's dilapidated single-wide trailer. I parked and cut off the engine.

Nope, nothing had changed. The sides looked more yellow than white. The once robin's blue of the door was now scratched and dusty gray. Two of the three metal steps needed shoring. Unlike the cared-for postage-stamp front yards of the other park's inhabitants, this one had no grass, no bushes, no flowers— just dirt and weeds. Pretty much this family's history.

I'd thought Patrick with his plans and ambition was different.

I shook my head to clear the gathering dark clouds. What

did it matter if he'd gone home with Amy Tucker? Except that we were engaged, and an engagement was a promise. I wasn't stupid. I knew he sometimes cheated on me while he was away. But I'd hoped that he wouldn't do it in Brighton. Ever. For his daughter's sake, if not for mine.

I got out of the van and knocked a little too hard, making me wonder if the door would fall off its rusty hinges.

The door opened with a squawk and Patrick's close-cropped dark head appeared.

At least he wasn't at Amy's.

"Maeve!"

That deep bass never failed to send a zing through my core. That smile practically melted my resolve. Those bad-boy good looks, even with their professional neatness, made me want to ditch my obligations and play hooky like we used to do back in high school.

I used to be fun.

And a whole lot of trouble.

But now I was a mom, and Neve came first.

"Patrick." I tamped back the unwanted sizzle, reminding myself I was mad at him. His presence in Brighton most likely meant another fly-by visit with Neve where he would shower her with impractical gifts and me with memories of my rebel self. His visits were like sugar highs— then both Neve and I had to deal with the inevitable crash. "I heard you were in town."

"Got here this morning."

Liar! But I bit my tongue and said nothing, wanting to hear what tales rife with holes he would spin. I didn't want to get caught up in another one of his whirlwinds. I didn't want a reminder of the girl I used to be. Not this time. Neve needed him. I needed him to step up and finally take responsibility.

"I was just about to go find you at the bakery," he said.

"We're closed on Mondays." As he should know by now.

He pressed against the door, inviting me in. "We need to talk."

I stayed planted where I was. "Derek here?"

"Asleep."

More likely passed out drunk. Patrick had somehow resisted his family's fondness for the bottle that sent both his parents to an early grave. Maybe because he really did love his corporate flight-attendant job and took that, if nothing else, seriously. "Let's walk."

Like well-rehearsed choreography, we took the path we'd strolled over a thousand times into the woods to our favorite bluff where the whole of the valley spread out beneath us. The spot where Neve had been conceived on a spectacular spring day. With each step, rebel Maeve reawakened. I had to remind her I had a hurting child who really needed her father's support.

"What brings you to Brighton?" I asked once our legs dangled over the thirty-foot cliff.

"I'm home." He waggled his eyebrows at me and flashed his slow, sexy smile.

My skin flamed, but I pulled my gaze back to the valley with its miniature houses, ribbon roads and pencil river. I couldn't let him walk all over me. "You can stay with Derek."

"Aw, come on." He tapped his elbow into mine. "I'm *home*, Maeve. To stay."

In spite of my doubts, my heart picked up speed, my blood all but sang. He was finally coming home. I knew how that sounded. Like I was stupid for holding on to that dream for so long. Most people would have given up and moved on. But a promise had to count for something, didn't it? And when someone saw you, the real you, and still loved you, that wasn't something to blow away; it was something rare and precious. I understood that fear made him keep his distance. Fear he'd end up caged like his parents. That was why I'd given him the time and the freedom to see that we were different. And it had paid off, hadn't it? He was here to stay.

"I'm so happy to hear that," I said, smiling at him and reaching for his hand.

Twining his fingers with mine, he lifted my hand and kissed its back. "I quit my job."

His corporate flight crew serviced private jets, flying millionaires and executives all over the world. We'd had it all planned. We'd work together, him as flight crew, me as onboard chef. We'd see the world. A far cry from coming back to Brighton with my tail between my legs, single and pregnant, and never leaving the state, except for a few baseball games a year with Dad. Patrick loved his job, had chosen it over me, over Neve.

Home. He said he was staying. "Why did you quit?"

He shrugged. "It's time."

But I knew Patrick intimately, knew his tics, knew his tells. That he was working so hard to keep his face still told me he was lying again. I just couldn't figure out why. "What are you going to do?"

"I'm not sure yet." His heels kicked against the granite of the cliff, a kerplunk-plunk that rang with warning. "I'm exploring my options."

"Is one of those options stepping up and being Neve's father?"

He pulled his hand from mine and stuck it in his jeans pocket. "Maeve—"

"Don't Maeve me." I didn't know what to do with my hand, so I picked a dandelion and twirled it. "She needs you now more than ever."

He looked at me, face worried. "Why, what's wrong?"

"I've told you!" I growled. Didn't he ever listen? "Her ADHD."

"Oh, that." He dismissed the problem with a wave of his

hand. "That's nothing. Half the kids these days have it." His dark gaze studied mine. "You turned out okay. She'll be fine."

"Me? I don't have ADHD!"

His brows rose. "Why do you think you got into so much trouble at school?"

I glared at him. Was he serious? "You! That's why I got into so much trouble. Following you!"

He held up his hands in surrender. "Hey! No need to bite my head off. Everybody knew."

Everybody? Knew what? "I was never diagnosed."

His head tilted and his grin skewed as if something awful filled his mouth. "Your so-perfect parents probably couldn't stand the thought of a less-than-perfect child. They certainly never thought I was good enough for you."

I stared at the slow-moving waters of the Candle River, remembering Mom's outrage when Patrick accepted a job with a company based at Teterboro Airport. Dad had sat me down and made me put together a financial plan— starting with getting a job so I could support my baby. Aaron had offered to go beat up Patrick and drag him back home to take care of his responsibilities. "You did leave me alone and pregnant."

No, not alone; I'd had my family. But definitely pregnant without a partner.

"Even before."

How had this conversation gone from concern for Neve to taking care of Patrick's emotions again? "This isn't about us. It's about Neve. She's been through a lot this year. She needs you to be there for her, not fly in and disappear again."

"She has you. She doesn't need me."

"You're her father. She loves you. But she also needs stability right now."

He stared down at Stoneley spread out at our feet. "Okay."

"Okay, what?"

"I'll be there. What do you need me to do?"

The flicker of hope sprang into a flame.

"Take a ride with me. There's something I want to show you."

I DROVE the van around the far side of Brighton Lake and onto Hummingbird Lane, where the rutted dirt road made the van rock from side to side. I slowed around the curve and stopped in front of a cottage— *the* cottage.

A stone pathway curved to the front door, painted the same cardinal red as the Adirondack chairs, past the morning glory archway that led to the lakefront. Bird songs lilted from the pines along the sides of the property. A riot of red, pink, and white flowers dotted the front yard in a way that never failed to cheer me up. I rolled down the window to take in the scent of pine and lake water and flowers. It smelled like home.

"What do you think?" I asked.

"About what?" Patrick shifted in his seat as if he had some place better he wanted to go.

I jutted my chin toward the cottage. "This place."

He tossed the cottage a cursory glance. "Looks like it needs a lot of work."

It did look much sadder in real life than in the photos on Zillow. The roof needed work, the paint updating, the gardens weeding. "I want to buy it."

I'd been putting a little money aside every month for a place of my own for over a year. Still, it was nowhere near what I needed for a down payment. And paying for baseball camp had made the balance dwindle.

"So, buy it," he said as if it were that easy.

I opened the tab on my phone that showed the cottage's listing.

Patrick whistled. "For this?"

"I can't afford it. But we could."

"We?"

"You said you were staying, that you wanted to be part of mine and Neve's lives. We can't live in my parents' house forever. Don't you want a real home? Just the three of us?"

He looked away from the cottage toward the choppy waters of Brighton Lake. "I thought the bakery was doing well."

"For a bakery." We'd talked more than once about the low profit margins. Did he not listen to me?

"Raise your prices."

"It's not that simple. I have to keep my baked goods affordable."

"Tourists don't care. They'll pay premium prices if they think they're getting something special." He swiveled his head my way. "What you need is a way to draw attention to you like all those times you got your shop in the news with your Best Pie wins." He drummed the console between us with his fingers. "The baking contest," he said, his face taking on the animation it always did when he was hatching a plan. "You need to enter and win. I heard WMUR was going to film the finale for their *Chronicle* show. That would bring you a whole lot of publicity."

I glared at him as he fell into a hole in his story. "I thought you just got in this morning. How are you so up on local gossip?"

"Derek."

He tossed his brother's name in an offhand way that made me sure the information had come from another source. "The same Derek who's sleeping off a night of drinking as we speak?"

He turned in the seat to face me. "Think about it, Maeve. The prize'll make a mighty fine down payment. We could live here. As a family."

His enthusiasm, the fire in his eyes had me believing again. "There's the slight detail of the thousand-dollar entry fee."

He whistled again. I waited for him to take the first step on his promise to be there for us, to make the offer to pay it himself.

"Can't you ask your parents?"

"They're doing too much already." The last thing I needed was one more debt to my mother.

"Aaron?"

"He's getting married and buying a house of his own."

"Zoe?"

"She makes less than I do."

"There has to be someone who could lend you the money until you win."

"A win isn't guaranteed."

"Here?" He scoffed-barked. "Of course it is."

His belief in my talent should make me feel good. But the way he'd said it somehow diminished both my skill and the win — as if just about anyone could take the prize. "Plus, I don't have the time. I have to get my booth ready for the festival. I'm nowhere near having enough hand pies."

Subtle hadn't worked, so I took out the metaphoric hammer. "What about you? It's not like you've been paying child support."

"That's low, Maeve. You know I would have if I could have. Living on the road isn't cheap."

"You must have some savings."

He sniffed. "It's invested."

"In what?"

"A project."

"The 'options' you're exploring?"

He nodded. "It's going to be big."

"Yeah?" I said, not quite keeping the skepticism out of my voice. "How big?"

"I can't really talk about it until all the pieces are in place."

The joy I'd expected at Patrick's return, at his promise to stay home, somehow didn't shine as brightly as I'd expected. As if a puffy cloud had drifted across the sun, a chill went through me, but I brushed it aside.

Pivoting took time, I told myself. He didn't know how to be a partner, a father. He'd quit his job to stay near us. I had to help him out. I couldn't give up on our family just as it was finally coming together. "How long are you planning on staying in Brighton?"

"I hope for a long time."

Hope? "Are you going to be there for Neve?"

He let out a long breath that sounded like exasperation. "What do you want me to do?"

I shouldn't have to spell it out, but for Neve, I would. "We have therapy this afternoon. But why don't you start by picking her up from baseball camp tomorrow and spend some time at the park with her?"

A trial run to test the waters of fatherhood.

He turned his gaze back to Brighton Lake and nodded without much enthusiasm. "Okay."

I put the van in gear and headed back toward the trailer park. I didn't know what I expected, but this empty feeling wasn't it. I stopped the van in front of his family's trailer.

"Camp gets out at three." I released the door lock. "Don't be late."

He got out and dared to look me straight in the eyes. "Maeve, I'm trying, okay?"

Trying wasn't good enough. Trying was expecting to fail. But trying was the best I could expect from Patrick right now until he got used to playing his role in Neve's life. And that had hot tears prickling. This homecoming wasn't what I'd dreamed of on so many lonely nights. "Okay."

I sped out of the trailer park. When I got to the bakery, I set an alarm on my phone to remind Patrick of his promise.

10

MAEVE

After a frustrating day of dealing with paperwork, supply orders and taking a stab at better planning, I arrived at the sports field early. I'd hoped to get the chance to see Neve play. What greeted me instead was half the town filling the stands, gawking at Luke Saunders who stood in the middle of a baseball diamond, demonstrating an infield skill to what looked like the older half of the kids.

I shook my head. They wouldn't be there if it was just their kids. Toss in an ex-major-league baseball player and they all turned into summer-camp baseball fanatics.

Neve and the rest of the younger kids ran drills at this end of the field. She looked so fierce, focusing on catching the ball Charlie launched at her.

Without permission, my gaze crept back up Luke's way. Even with his limp, his body— those wide shoulders, that narrow waist, those sculpted muscles—had an ease and grace that made every move look like poetry.

What is wrong with you? I thought, fanning myself with an envelope I'd forgotten to drop off at the post office. The hot sun after spending the day in air conditioning had scrambled my brain. He wasn't art; he was a pain in the side of my business. One I couldn't figure out how to deal with. I forced my gaze off Luke and back onto Neve. She had a wicked arm, and Charlie had to hustle back to catch the throw.

Coach Mac blew his whistle, called the kids in for a debrief then sent them on their way. Shouting and laughing, the kids scattered in all directions, their milling bodies reminding me of a living Spirograph design.

Neve and Charlie skipped hand in hand toward me. Irene Lambert, with her floppy cream sunhat, long-sleeved yellow T-shirt and poppy-covered maxi skirt even on a hot June day, came to stand next to me. The scent of sunscreen and frankincense drifted my way. That combination reminded me of my grandmother and brought back fond memories of learning to bake pies in the tiny kitchen that was now mine.

"I'm so glad Charlie made a friend," Irene said, looking at her granddaughter. "It's going to make a tough summer easier on her."

"What do you mean?"

"Her parents are divorcing."

"I'm so sorry."

Irene worried the edge of her shirtsleeve. "It's for the best, really. But it's never easy on the kids, even when it's amicable."

The repercussions echoed to more than just two. "I'm glad she and Neve hit it off. Neve's had a hard time making friends since Riley left."

Irene laid a soft hand on my arm. "We'll have to plan play-dates for the weekend."

"That would be great."

Neve and Charlie separated. Neve threw herself at me, offering me one of her patented whole-body hugs— the best stress remedy ever invented.

"Hey, honey bunches, how was your day?" I asked, hugging her back.

"Fantastic! Coach Cassie said I had a great eye and a good arm."

"She said I was a real speed demon," Charlie said, mimicking pumping her arms, sending her red pigtails flying.

I loved this Coach Cassie already for making these girls feel good. I high-fived Neve, then Charlie. "Wow! I can't wait to see you girls play."

"There's going to be a practice game for everyone on Friday," Neve said, her gaze widening in question. "Then a real game with umpires and everything next week."

"I'll be there, even if I have to close the bakery. I'll even bring my megaphone."

Neve groaned. "No, Mommy, don't embarrass me!"

"Didn't you know?" I wrapped an arm around her shoulders and turned her toward the van. "That's what moms are for."

She rolled her gaze to the sky, then cranked a look over her shoulder to wave at Charlie. "Bye!"

"See you tomorrow," Charlie said, fitting her hand in Irene's.

Neve looked up at me, batting her eyelashes. "Bring cupcakes for my team for the practice game Friday?"

The little monster knew just how to manipulate me. Could I make healthy cupcakes? Was there a way to cut sugar way back and still make them appealing to kids? I foresaw experiments in my future. "Of course."

"DAD'S HERE," Neve said as I parked the van at the clinic in Hopewell. The mustard-colored brick building sat on the same campus as the Hopewell Hospital, and the parking lot went on forever. Of course, this late in the day, the only spot available seemed like a mile from the door. As I focused on parking between two crooked cars, I thought Neve meant Patrick was here in the parking lot, but then realized she meant in town.

"I know, honey bunches."

"He waved at me during lunch."

"That's nice." Had he even bothered to talk to her? Hug her? Tell her he loved her?

"When do I get to see him?"

Nope. None of those. Part of me wanted to say, "Never" just so she wouldn't end up disappointed ever again. "Tomorrow. He said he'd pick you up from camp. Won't that be nice?"

"Uh-huh." Her hand tightened around mine even as she skipped for a beat. He'd taught her not to expect much from him, and that made me want to cry for her. Zoe was right; this wasn't good for her self-esteem.

We walked in silence for a bit, the slap of our sneakers hitting the pavement in unison. What was going on in her head?

"Do you think Dad will still be here on Friday?"

That, of course, was the perpetual question. She was used to his surprise pop-ins and his sudden disappearing acts. But he'd promised he'd stay this time. I put on a cheerful smile and opened the clinic door. "Ask him when you see him tomorrow."

A blast of arctic air swamped over me, raising goose bumps. I reminded myself to send Patrick at least three reminders so Neve wouldn't look out for someone who wasn't going to show.

ONCE AT THE therapist's office on the second floor, I had Neve sit down with a book and asked Lauren Sutton, her therapist, to talk for a few minutes.

I sat at the edge of the lavender egg chair, fingers picking at the peeling paint on my travel mug, staring at the blue flecks peppering my lap. "Someone said something to me today, and it made me wonder..." I curled my lips inward, holding them tight with my teeth as if speaking the words out loud would make them true, "...if I have ADHD."

"How did that make you feel?" Lauren had a gentle air about her. Maybe it was the ringlets framing her face. Maybe it was the flowy skirt in pastel colors like a Monet waterlily painting. Maybe it was her soft voice. She made you feel as if you could say anything, and she wouldn't judge.

"Hurt," I said, fingers tight against the sides of my travel mug. "I run a business. It's doing well." Ack, I sounded like my mother when I'd told her about Neve's diagnosis.

"Adults who've lived with undiagnosed ADHD tend to have a whole toolbox of coping mechanisms," Lauren said. "Your business, it's something you enjoy?"

I shrugged a shoulder as if I didn't care, but really the bakery and Neve were my whole world. "Most of the time. I love the baking and the creativity. I don't enjoy the business part, but I can get it done." Eventually. That part made me feel inadequate. It all sounded so basic when Dad explained it, but executing the principles got lost somewhere between thought and deed.

"Do you leave that to the last minute?" Lauren asked.

I pursed my lips. I was lucky Dad took care of the books for me or they'd be a total mess. I was also lucky that Kayla ran the front of the shop. She was way more organized than I was, even if she wasn't always dependable. "Doesn't everybody, though?"

"How often do you lose your keys?" Lauren asked. "Your purse? Something important?"

I swallowed hard, thinking of the letter I forgot to mail sitting in the van, of how I'd spent ten minutes looking for the van keys I was sure were on my desk and found in the bathroom instead. "Doesn't everyone who has kids?"

She smiled as if she got the inside joke that wasn't a joke

and tipped her head. "Did you have a hard time making friends when you were younger?"

I sighed. I'd tried so hard throughout school to make friends, but girls just didn't like me, and I could never figure out why. I never knew what to say to them, or how to approach them. I had a knack for hurting girls' feelings without understanding why. And, even though I'd loved playing softball, I'd dreaded the bus rides to away games and team parties where I felt like an outsider. I probably should've gone out for cross-country running. There, you only competed against yourself. In the end, I just gave up. Even today, my few friends were guys. "I mean, I'm not an easy person to get to know. Never was."

"How was school for you?"

I chuffed, remembering the daily distress that was school. "Teachers used to tell me I was smart and that, if I'd just apply myself, I'd be successful. They called me lazy." Like that was going to help make me feel better. Or comparing me to Aaron and Zoe. "What they didn't get was how hard I tried."

"I'm sorry that happened to you."

I tucked a hank of hair behind my ear. "I survived."

I'd jumped for joy when I got the packet accepting me to culinary school. Finally, a chance to start over. Nobody knew me in New York City. I could reinvent myself.

Then, of course, I got pregnant, screeching all those reinvention dreams to a halt.

Lauren let the silence grow for a beat, then asked, "How about your feelings? Would you say you got your feelings hurt more than most kids?"

I chipped off more paint, fascinated by the way the flecks turned my blue shorts to crocodile skin. "My mom tells me I'm oversensitive."

"How often do you feel anxious?"

I took a slug of my coffee, noting the buzzing in my chest right now. "Almost all the time."

"Do you have a hard time reading a book or watching a movie?"

Both activities were torture to me. "Sometimes. But Neve doesn't."

"There's a whole range of symptoms, as you know."

I motioned for her to go on.

"Do you use food or alcohol or something stronger to help you cope?"

"Not really. I mean I do own a bakery, and I have to taste..."

She nodded at my travel mug, nearly bare of paint and empty by now. "What about caffeine?"

"I have to get up really early. Coffee's the only way I can stay on track..." I blew out a long breath. "Okay, so yeah, coffee helps me cope."

"Do you get sidetracked easily?"

"Depends. At work, it's easier to focus than at home. But at home, there's Neve." I thought about the load of laundry I'd put in the washer two days ago and forgot about. Again. It would be musty by now, and I'd have to rewash it. Again. "So do I have ADHD?"

"The questions I asked aren't a diagnosis. They're more of an exploration of symptoms. We can set up testing for you, if you'd like. But it's my experience that if a child has ADHD, it tends to show up somewhere in the family tree."

My child was broken because of me? "It's hereditary?"

"There's some evidence that it is."

I ran through each of my family members and couldn't think of another person like me. Both my siblings had done well in school. Mom and Dad both had their lives together, juggling business and family as if it were easy. I'd felt different while growing up, broken, bad— like an outsider in my own family.

"Neve being the way she is—" I frowned at my lap and shrugged a shoulder, "—it's my fault..."

"It's not your fault. It's not anybody's fault. It's just the way the brain's wired. You just need to work on skills that help you maximize your beautiful brain." She reached forward and placed a comforting hand on my knee. "You know what works for Neve. Eat well. Get enough sleep. Find ways to manage your time, tasks and space that work for you. Practicing mindfulness to handle stress. And having support— both in people and in systems –those will all help make life smoother for you."

I stared at the galaxy of blue paint chips on my lap. I couldn't see myself sitting still long enough to meditate. That would add to my stress, not relieve it. When did I have time to exercise other than all the walking I did in the kitchen? I had a kid to take care of. I did the best I could with sleep and food. Meredith, my sister-in-law-to-be, had helped me set up a few systems in the kitchen after the fire last Christmas. They were helping. "Thanks."

"ADHD isn't a curse, Maeve. It can be a gift. Your baking awards prove that."

Sure didn't feel like a gift right now.

As I sat in the waiting room while Neve went in for her session with Lauren, a whole lot of my life suddenly made sense. School. Friends. Forgetfulness. I wasn't a rebel. I wasn't bad like those teachers had told me. My brain just wasn't wired correctly. And yet, that miswiring had allowed me to create flavors that had put my bakery on the map and made it successful.

Maybe Patrick was right. I'd turned out okay in spite of that misfiring brain.

And I had to make sure that Neve would, too.

I had to find a way to pay for all the coaching and nutrition-counseling bills that would help her thrive once school started again in September.

Maybe Lauren was right, too. My bakery, my baking, they were the best parts of me. They were how I kept Neve's world safe and secure. And Luke and his donut antics were putting that livelihood in danger.

He was leaving me no choice. Since the second I found out about Neve, her well-being had been my number-one priority. Winning the baking contest would set our future on a solid footing. Maybe even leave enough to put a down payment on that cottage by the lake.

I took in a breath and held it while I typed the URL for the Brighton Village page on my phone.

Thumbs flying over the keys before I changed my mind, I filled out the online entry form.

"I'm sorry, Dani, but you can blame your brother for this." He could afford to send his sister to culinary school. I couldn't afford to lose my bakery. "If he hadn't declared war on my shop, I wouldn't have to enter this stupid contest just to keep it alive."

I hit Send. Take that Luke and Mom and all those teachers who called me lazy and stupid and unmotivated.

Then my stomach plummeted.

I was doing this. On top of taking care of Neve and running the bakery. I was really doing this.

I was entering the contest.

Now, I just had to win.

I had three days to find the entry fee.

And ten days to come up with award-winning recipes.

ON TUESDAY, I had to send three reminder texts before Patrick deigned to answer me. Even then, I didn't quite trust him and made a stealth visit to the ballpark to make sure he would show up and not leave Neve stranded. I breathed a sigh of relief when I spotted him in the stands. After the coach released the kids, he scooped up Neve and twirled her around and her laughter ran around the field.

She was so happy to see him.

A father was something special in a girl's life, wasn't he? Mine certainly was. He was always there for me, ready to protect me even now that I was all grown up. I didn't want to deprive her of that unique relationship.

Patrick said he was staying. He was trying. I had to give him a chance to make things right by Neve.

But could I depend on him to be consistent?

11

GRACE

When Snick and I got to the Stoneley Canine Center on Wednesday afternoon, I parked at the far end of the lot where half a dozen cars already occupied spaces. That looked like an awful lot of people—dogs. Snick did okay with most people, but the sight of dogs, especially big dogs, turned her into a Ninja helicopter that had already made me have to apologize to too many people on our daily walks.

I opened the car's rear door, clipped Snick's leash onto her harness and unclipped the seat belt. "Come on, out you go."

Eyes bugged out as if I were taking her to the gallows, Snick dug in her feet and refused to get out of the car. "It'll be fun."

Words weren't going to work, so I riffled through the pocket of my capris and brought out a handful of treats. "Want one of these?"

The tip of her tail flapped, and she licked her lips. But she didn't move. Yelling at her wouldn't help, but it sure would help release some of the steam building inside me.

"Come out," I said in as sing-songy a voice as I could. "And you can have the lot."

But even her favorite stinky salmon bites weren't enough to lure her out. I had to crawl onto the back seat, grab the handle on her harness and lift her out. Good thing she wasn't Sunny's size. This wasn't a great start to our training session.

Once on the ground, Snick shook herself like an old dust rag. "I wish I could do that, too. Oscar wasn't half as stubborn as you are. Sometimes you make me so mad, I just want to scream." Of course, comparing dogs, like comparing children, wasn't productive. They all had their own personalities and frustrations. And Oscar was— had been —a one-in-a-million dog.

"Let's go!" I dangled treats in front of her, but still had to half drag her to the front door, which wasn't doing much for my relaxation.

The Stoneley Canine Center consisted of a box-like building. The beige paint sported black pawprints alongside the door that had "Welcome" written on a bone-shaped sign. A series of happy barks greeted us as we entered. From behind a metal gate, a mutt of some kind called out to Snick.

I held on tight to the leash while Snick scrambled back toward the door, tail between her legs, pulling on her harness so hard she half dragged me with her.

"Auntie Grace! You made it!" Lark rounded the desk and crouched down to greet Snick, who transformed into a tail-wagging, face-licking maniac. "We're about to start."

"I thought you said this dog was trained," I said, a little jealous at how easily Lark could make Snick do what she wanted.

"I said she had some basics. She needs boundaries. Don't you, pretty girl?" Snick redoubled her face licking.

"Well, I can't exactly sit down with her and have a chat now, can I?"

Lark smiled and rose from her crouch. "That's why you're here."

"I'm too old for this." Snick went back to cowering behind my legs.

Lark took the leash and the traitorous Snick followed, if not happily, then at least willingly. "You've raised three kids. The same principles apply. You'll see." Lark opened a door that led to a fenced-in yard where three other dogs waited. "You'll do just fine."

"I need to get out by 2:30 so I can pick up Neve from camp."

"No problem." Lark held the door opened for me and handed me Snick's leash. "Go on in. I'll be right back."

Standing as far away as I could from the other dogs in the yard, I took in two puppies frolicking next to their owners— a cute black dog with a white patch on its chest and a beige pug. The third dog, a beagle mix, sprawled at its owner's feet. Two of the owners looked about Maeve's age and the third like a teenager, which made me wish I was anywhere but here.

"Looks like we're both the old ladies here," I told Snick and sat down on one of the wooden benches along the solid wood fence that would keep puppy distractions to a minimum.

Snick pawed at my knee.

"What do you want?"

Before I was ready, she jumped up into my lap and burrowed into me. This did not bode well. If it wasn't for Neve, I'd sneak out while Lark was out of sight, and leave Snick behind. That would show her.

"Anyone have a trick for cleaning up pee messes?" the teen with the bad skin and greasy hair asked, holding on to the hot-pink leash of the black pup. "Jazz happy piddles everywhere. The vet said she'll outgrow it, but she's five months now and shows no signs of stopping."

I didn't want to burst her bubble and tell her that Snick, who was three months older, still happy piddled.

"Otis seems to think that the bathmat is for his personal

business," said the woman with the beagle mix. "He hates going outside."

At least Snick had the going outside part down pat. Other than the happy piddles when she saw Neve, she hadn't had a single accident.

"You're lucky it's just one spot," said the woman patting the pug. "Milo's a stealth pee-er. The whole house stinks, and I'm not even sure where all he's peed."

"Get a black light," I said before I could stop myself. "Turn off the lights, then shine the black light around the floor. The urine will glow a dull green or yellow. Then use an enzymatic spray to get the old stains out."

They all looked at me as if I'd come from another planet. "I worked for a cleaning company for a few years," I said. "I know all the tricks."

"What's an enzymatic spray?" the teen asked.

"Something that breaks down the stain. If it's been there for a while, I suggest volcano spray."

"Where do I get some?"

"You make it. Take two cups of vinegar and two cups of lukewarm water in a spray bottle. Then have baking soda handy. Spray the stain with the vinegar mixture, then spread a thin layer of baking soda. Put a bowl over the area until it's dry. Then vacuum." I lifted one hand. "Ta-da! Stain gone. The vinegar breaks down the stickiness and the baking soda takes care of the smell. Together, they make a pet-safe carpet cleaner."

"Does anyone have paper?" the teen asked, lifting her phone. "My phone's dead."

Pug Mom looked through her bag. "Shoot, no!"

Beagle Mom found a small notebook in hers and ripped out two sheets. "Can you repeat the recipe?"

They all looked so eager as they scribbled down the recipe that something inside me warmed. "For Otis and the bathmat, you might want to try a cup of vinegar mixed with a quarter cup of peroxide and a teaspoon of grease-cutting dish soap, then fill the rest of the spray bottle with water. If you want to make it smell nice, I can recommend some pet-safe essential oils."

"Yes, please!" they all said.

It felt good to be wanted, even if it was only for my expertise at cleaning pee.

I walked Snick over to the ballfield to pick up Neve from baseball camp, hoping the mutt would run out of energy and lie low the rest of the day. And because the thing had a nose that wouldn't quit and had a stubborn streak— so much for the training in today's class —we were late. Only Neve, her coach, Charlie and Irene remained on the field.

Snick yanked the leash out of my hand and jumped right up into Neve's arm, who somehow caught the dog on the fly.

"Good hands!" said Coach Cassie, whose bouncy step reminded me of Maeve in high school.

"Thanks for staying with her," I said to Irene and the coach, noticing how Irene had had no problems getting there on time even with Sunny in tow.

"They've been having a good time, getting extra pointers from Coach Cassie." Sunny wagged her tail, but seemed to know who was boss and stayed at Irene's side.

Having finished licking Neve's face, Snick jumped back to the ground, play-bowed and helicoptered in front of Sunny. The golden wagged her tail and looked up at Irene, who petted the dog's head and kept her in place.

"They're great girls," Coach Cassie said, scrubbing both girls' heads. "I love having them on my team. You'll be there for the game Friday?"

"With bells on," I said, injecting cheer into my voice. I'd always hated going to Maeve's softball games. I'd had to listen to books on tape just to get through the sheer boredom of seven impossibly long innings. But I'd gone to every single home game. Something I was sure Maeve wouldn't remember. "Minus the dog."

"Great! See you then!" The coach trotted off toward the parking lot.

"Can Charlie come over?" Neve asked, eyes wide and beseeching while Snick leaped around her, looking for attention.

"Why not?" My day was already shot. I wasn't going to get anything productive done. "Want to come over for tea, Irene?"

"I'd love to." Irene smiled in a way that hinted at gratitude. Her husband had died last summer. She was lonely with Stan gone, and I really should invite her over more often, especially now that the girls were friends.

Then I remembered that I had nothing to offer to go with the tea. And I certainly wasn't going to stop at the bakery just to have Maeve chide me like a child about sugar and its evil qualities. "Let's stop by the new donut truck for a snack."

"Yay!" Both girls jumped up and down, setting Snick to barking and Sunny to dancing in place.

BETWEEN THIS AFTERNOON'S dog training and the walk to and from the ballpark, Snick seemed to finally run out of energy and sploofed on the kitchen floor like a bear rug next to Sunny.

The girls disappeared to the apartment while I lit the burner under the kettle and placed eight of the dozen donuts I'd bought on a plate, saving the rest for Ansel.

Irene and I sipped tea and talked about plants (her hobby) and the Strawberry Festival that would start next week and how we needed to take the girls together. I was dying to ask why Charlie was spending the summer with her, but I'd let her bring up the subject. The girls came scrambling back down the stairs, giggling in a way that made me think they were up to something. Charlie plopped into a chair and reached for a donut. "Can I have some milk, please?"

I got up and poured her and Neve a glass.

Neve placed her chin on the table and studied the plate of donuts. "Can I have a bowl?"

I was too tired to care why and grabbed two bowls from the cupboard. Concentrating on the task, Neve tore two donuts into pieces and into the bowl. Charlie followed suit with two of her own donuts. Neve jumped up and plucked two spoons from the cutlery drawer. They dug into the donut pieces as if it were a bowl of cereal.

Of course, that was when Maeve came home. She called down from the apartment. "Neve? Mom?"

"In the kitchen." I glanced at the donut-filled bowls, resigned. She'd disapprove and all I'd tried to do was give the girls a small treat after a tiring day at camp. I couldn't clear the donuts before Maeve arrived. And sure enough, her gaze narrowed, zeroing right in on the bowls.

"What's going on?" she asked. The dark circles under her eyes and the limp state of her hair made me wonder if she was getting enough sleep.

"Snack," Neve said, licking her spoon with great relish.

Maeve's face transformed into a lightning storm. "Mom?"

Irene got up. "Charlie, sweetie, let's go. I need to run to the store before dinner. I didn't realize it was so late already."

"Aww, can I stay?"

"You'll see Neve in the morning," Irene insisted, all but lifting Charlie from the chair.

Charlie's pout drooped so low, I had to pinch myself not to

laugh, because Maeve would think I found the drama she was about to unleash funny, and that would escalate everything.

I walked Irene and Charlie to the front door. "Sorry about that."

"Trust me, I've had many of those conversations with Charlie's mom. Thanks for having us over." She gave me a quick hug and a conspiratorial wink. "Next time, let's meet at my place."

I lingered at the front door as long as I dared then sighed. Better to rip off the bandage.

In the kitchen, Maeve scraped the remains of the donut bowl into the garbage, banging the spoon on the bowl with emphasis while Neve cried and tried to grab the bowl.

"Go upstairs," she told Neve. "I'll be up in a bit."

"But Mo-om!" Neve fisted her hands at her side and stamped one foot.

"Now!"

With high-pitched squeal worthy of a racoon kept from a garbage can, she stomped away. Snick followed her upstairs, tail wagging.

Maeve shoved the garbage can back in its cupboard, then rounded on me, hands on hips. "I've told you and told you that I don't want you feeding Neve sugar."

"It's just a donut." I busied myself cleaning up the teacups. She was making a big deal out of nothing. One donut never hurt anyone. Except maybe a diabetic. "A treat while we had guests over."

"You're not the one who has to deal with her sugar high."

"You know there's no scientific data that proves sugar makes kids high." I'd read up on it after Maeve's ban of all sugar.

She rolled her head back, drawing in a river of air. Her jaw flinched in quick succession. "It worsens her ADHD."

I placed the remaining two donuts on the plate into the grease-stained box and closed it to keep them fresh. "If you keep treating her like she's defective, she's going to think there's something wrong with her."

"There is something wrong with her. Something I can lessen by keeping her off sugar."

I rammed the box on top of the bread box. "Don't you remember what it was like at school when teachers you'd never had before already believed the label of 'difficult?'"

"Yes, Mom, I remember. That's why I'm trying so hard to control Neve's ADHD before school starts. So that she won't be treated any differently. So that she can have a good year."

We squared off like two boxers in a ring. "So, you're asking her to be different from all the rest of the kids at camp instead."

Maeve glared at me, eyes like green fire. "This isn't camp. This is home. Where she should be safe and cared for and loved."

"You think I don't love my only grandchild?" I gasped.

"I don't know, Mom." Her arms flailed in a dramatic arc. "How can you say you love her and give her something I've told you is going to hurt her?"

That she could even think I would hurt Neve on purpose cut deep. To keep tears from leaking, I reached for a sponge.

"I'm sorry," I said, wiping the table clean. "All I've ever tried to do was make life easier for you." To make sure Neve wasn't raised by strangers but by her own family while Maeve worked to support her child. To give Neve the same loving environment Maeve herself had had. "From now on, I'll do as you wish."

Her nostrils flared as if she'd expected a longer fight. I just didn't have it in me right now to rehash our well-worn argument. If she didn't think I had Neve's best interests at heart, nothing would change her mind. "Did you know there's a baking contest at the festival? You should enter."

"I wasn't going to." She yanked a cloth from the stove's handle and crouched down to pick up the crumbs she'd spilled in her zest to get rid of the donuts.

"Everybody raves about how good your desserts are." Which was the irony of ironies, considering her newfound hatred of sugar.

"I actually signed up on Monday." She turned gray as if the thought nauseated her.

"That's great!"

"It's not." She turned back to the sink and shook the cloth with enough vigor to dislodge the world's supply of germs.

"Why? What's happened?"

She jammed the cloth back on the stove's handle and jerked it into place. "Donut Guy."

"I don't understand."

"He's stealing my business. I don't have the time to enter *and* bake for the festival *and* keep my business afloat. Everyone's gone gaga over his blankety-blank donuts. So, I don't have a choice. If I want to keep the bakery open, I have to enter. And win. Not to mention I have only one more day to come up with the thousand-dollar entry fee."

Was business as bad as she made it out to be, or was she making mountains out of dust motes again? Given how she wasn't usually so verbose, maybe business was bad. At least, I could help with this tiny hurdle. "I'll give you the entry fee."

She went still, her spine stiffening. "I can't ask you to do that."

"You're not asking. I'm offering." Maybe that could soften the after-camp treat situation.

She turned back to me, eyes roiling with fury. "So you can be my sainted savior again?"

Where had that come from? "I'm just trying to help." I launched the sponge into the sink where it landed with a splat. "You were always like that. I swear your first words were 'I do it.'"

"'Get your act together, Maeve,' isn't that what you're always telling me? Well, I'm trying, okay? I'm trying to juggle all the balls. And keep them in the air."

"Maeve—"

"But they're all crashing around me."

I could hear the tears in her voice, so I gentled mine. "You have a whole network of people ready and willing to help you. Why won't you let them?"

She snorted as if I'd just said the most ridiculous thing. "You taught me that if you want something done, you have to do it yourself. You can't count on anyone."

"You are so stubborn." I'd put my life on hold to help her out. I'd gone out of my way to make life easier for her. How could she even think that she couldn't count on me? "I'm just trying to help."

"I don't need that much help!"

That's when Snick came trotting in, so proud of herself, a pair of Neve's socks in her mouth, flopping like dead prey with each bounce of her step. The cap to a perfectly rotten afternoon.

"Fine, then." I did a handwashing motion. I'd had more than enough. I was tired after a long day. I needed a vacation, or at least a nap before starting dinner. "Do it your way."

Then I stormed out of the kitchen and went to my room where I slammed the door. If she wanted to do everything herself, then she could do everything herself.

From now on, I was focusing on me.

12

MAEVE

The fight with my mother yesterday still circulated on an endless loop in my mind. She just didn't get how important it was for Neve to eat properly, how that helped balance the chemical composition of her brain.

I hadn't slept well. Even looking at the cottage online hadn't settled my brain enough to sleep. The tornado-siren alarm on my phone and the backup across the room rang much too early, leaving me feeling as if I hadn't slept at all. At least the coffeemaker had brewed up a pot by the time I reached the kitchen. I kissed my sleeping daughter, left her a love note on the kitchen table, filled my travel mug and hiked over to the bakery.

I loved this time in the morning when no one else was out and about. The air smelled different this early, fresher somehow. With the summer solstice less than a week away, at four the sky already had brushes of pink and purple and birds already twittered in the trees.

As I stepped into the bakery, the aroma of yeast surrounded me. My bread baker, Natalie Beausoleil, had Debussy's "Clair de Lune" playing this morning. Natalie not only talked to her dough as she kneaded it but believed that playing classical music coaxed the dough to rise. She might be on to something because her bread had a special taste that had customers lining up first thing in the morning to get a loaf before they were all gone and buying more the next day. That was the one thing that hadn't changed since Luke's donut truck had turned my business upside down; the regulars still came for their daily bread.

I slogged through the darkened shop, trying not to bump into any of the white tables or blue chairs, to my cramped office. My Mary-Poppins purse dropped on the desk with a thud, all but obliterating the paperwork that needed attention yesterday. I headed for the coffee machine behind the counter to start a pot.

"Don't ever leave me," I called to Natalie, who was hard at work shaping loaves on the long table. She laughed. I had to blink a few times to see her outline against the cream-colored walls. With her white pants and coat and her drab-brown hair hidden by a white kerchief, she all but disappeared.

"I am happy here," she said in her French-accented voice.

"That is the best news I've had all week."

I returned to my office while the coffee brewed, fully intending on at least sorting through the paperwork. I fell hard into the desk chair. Like I'd done every day since Monday, I opened the business app and scrolled through the entries to find somewhere I could skim the entry fee. The numbers were already so tight. I didn't want to skimp on quality, but for right now, maybe I could cut back on quantity. Which brought me to baking for today. Would anyone actually show up to buy anything? What could I bake that wouldn't break the bank?

I should have a plan, an agenda, a strategy for each day's offerings, but I never seemed able to organize myself ahead of time. I picked up my phone, planning on scrolling through a few of my favorite sites for inspiration. Instead, Instagram sucked me in.

I wasn't sure what made me stop at the photo of a hawk eating a mouse.

"Do you have an ex you'd like to feed to a bird of prey?" read the caption. "Then the Best Revenge Fundraiser is for you. For a second year, The Hopewell Raptor Recovery Center is offering a Summer Solstice Special. For $10, we'll name a frozen mouse after your not-so-special someone and feed it to one of our recovering hawks. For another $100, we'll include a personalized video message to your chosen recipient."

"The event was such a big hit last year that we decided to run it again this year," said Priscilla Walsh, the Center's director. "We had five hundred donations last year and, so far this year, we're on track to break our record. That goes a long way to help us save these beautiful birds of prey. You can watch the daily feedings online at the Center's site from June 21—July 4. So, hurry and get your nominations in before the twenty-first!"

My gaze went back to the photo of the Cooper's hawk with its black cap, reddish barred chest and fierce red eyes.

You can't, I told myself.

You have to. If only for your sanity.

Before I quite knew what I was doing, I added Luke's name to the list of not-so-special someones and paid the entry fee. Even my tight budget could afford a one-time splurge of ten dollars. My receipt came with an ecard of a hawk devouring a mouse with the name Luke penned on its side. I printed it and tacked it to the corkboard above my desk. Luke would never see it, but I'd have the satisfaction of knowing frozen mouse Luke would feed an ailing hawk.

"You deserve it," I told the mouse Luke.

Well, that was fun. Also, the inspiration for today's special — a white chocolate covered dark chocolate truffle that I would shape into a mouse. Those would last several days before going stale.

Natalie appeared at my office door and leaned on the door-jamb, arms crossed over her chest. "Who deserve what?"

"You know why I hired you?" I asked, sketching the truffle mouse in one of the spiral notebooks I bought by the dozen and listing the ingredients I would need.

"For my charm and wit and excellent breadmaking skills," she said.

"That, and also because I love your French accent."

Natalie quirked an eyebrow in a dramatic way I couldn't emulate if I tried.

"I was going to go to France, spend a year at *L'École Nationale Supérieure de Pâtisserie*. You're as close as I'll get." I could easily blame Neve. If I hadn't gotten pregnant, I'd have gone to pastry school in Paris. Patrick would have stuck around. We'd be together, traveling the world.

Yet, Neve was the bright light in my life. I didn't for a second regret having her, and I would do anything to see her happy, even if it meant never moving out of my parents' house.

Natalie shook her head. "*Oy, yoy*. You are even more lost than I suspected. First, I am from *Québec*."

I ripped the page out of my notebook and stood. "Still French."

"Second, why can you not go to France if you want?"

I squeezed by her, tasting the recipe in my mind as I went. Maybe a touch of orange zest with the chocolate? "Daughter. Bakery."

Natalie followed me back to the kitchen. "Pah! Excuses."

"Says the woman who has not once come to family dinner even though she has a standing invitation. I never see you around town."

Natalie didn't talk much about herself, but she had a way of getting me to talk about myself that sometimes made me uncomfortable. She made her bread and went home. Which, naturally, made me curious about her past.

I laid the paper on the table, now cleared and cleaned. Boules and baguettes lined trays in the proofing cabinet, waiting for their time in the oven.

"I came to tell you that the bread was ready, and that I have written the baking schedule down for you." She tipped her head toward the blackboard next to the oven.

"That's great. Thanks." The visible schedule allowed me to bake the bread in time for the early morning regulars. The boules would go first— as soon as the oven reached 450-degrees.

One hand on her hip, she stared at me as if she could see through me. "Why does the mouse in your office say Luke?"

Was it bad to feel both a little bad and a lot exhilarated by the thought of frozen Luke becoming a meal? "A little private revenge."

"Um." She dipped a hand into the gray tote bag, hanging on a hook by the door, and brought out an envelope. "This is better."

"What's this?"

"The entry fee for the Strawberry Festival Sweet Spot Baking Contest."

I pulled my hand back as if the envelope would singe my fingers. "I can't take this!"

"Why not?"

"You're my employee."

"I consider it an investment in my future employment."

I shook my head and stuffed my hands in my pants pocket. "I can't accept."

"You must." She pushed the envelope toward me. "The entry fee must be in by three today, *non?*"

I nodded and pulled both dark and white chocolates from the staples shelf.

"You are an excellent baker, *non?*"

"I am." There was no point in being modest. I *was* an excellent baker. It was possibly the only thing I did well. This kitchen was the only place where my "rebellion" was acceptable. That rebel streak had created my most famous pies— ones that had gotten me voted "Best in New Hampshire" five years in a row; three for Brightside Bakery and two for Shirley's Sandwich Shop.

"Then you must enter the baking contest."

I yanked the fridge door open and pulled out heavy cream. "I've already signed up."

"I did not see your name on the list of participants."

I said nothing as I hunted through the molds for an oval silicone one.

"Do you know the prize is $100,000?" she asked.

Where Regina Buchanan, our illustrious town leader, had found that much prize money for a small-town baking contest still astounded me. "I'm aware."

"Then why you not let me help you?"

My cheeks burned three-alarm hot. "What if I don't win, Nat? There's no way I can pay you back."

"Pah!" She batted my comment away. "Jake Cunningham from the Elfin Bakery in Manchester and Delia Horton from La Vie en Sucre in Concord would be your biggest competitor. I have tasted both of their pastries. You have a better palate."

She had? I may have won for best pie in New Hampshire, but Jake Cunningham had won for just about everything else. And Delia Horton was the "it" girl in pastry right now with her gluten-free offerings that tasted as fine as any regular baked goods.

"Still doesn't guarantee a win."

"*Oy, yoy yoy. Mais, comme tu as la tête dure!* You have a hard head. Why do you fight yourself so hard?" She dropped the envelope on the table. It landed with a splat. "Think about it."

She grabbed a gray sweater from behind the kitchen door and stuffed it in her tote bag.

"I don't want to gamble your hard-earned money on an entry fee that may not pay off."

"It is my money to do as I wish, and I wish for you to enter." She hiked the tote bag's handle over her shoulder. "I will be your assistant."

I blinked twice. The rules allowed each baker to have an assistant help them with their bakes. I needed Kayla at the shop, so I'd planned on going solo. "You will?"

She laughed as if I was being ridiculous. "You are a silly woman. Of course!"

If I wanted the cottage, if I wanted to give Neve all she deserved, I needed to let go of my stubborn pride. And having Natalie there during the contest would help me stay organized. Systems and support. If I wanted Neve to accept them, as her therapist suggested, I had to set an example. "I won't let you down."

"Win or lose, you could not let me down. You have already showed me more kindness than I can repay." With that, Natalie left, the heels of her white clogs clacking on the shiny navy-and-white floor. Her voice echoed through the shop. "I expect a new oven when you win, not one that work only when it want to. My music can charm only so much out of the dough."

"Deal!" Hope filled me. I was going to come up with prize-winning recipes. I was going to win that contest.

One step at a time, I reminded myself. That was how I'd handled everything since my dreams fell apart. And just like I'd done back then, I'd work through preparing for the contest one step at a time.

First step, bake muffins for the possible breakfast crowd. Strawberry-lemonade muffins always sold well in the summer, and the weatherman had predicted a triple-H day— hot, hazy and humid. Although I hadn't needed the weather report as unruly as my curls were this morning before I wrangled them into a low bun. The plan: make the muffins, then make the mouse truffles. After that? I'd see what business looked like.

Somehow, I needed to bake the hundreds of hand pies to fill my festival booth, keep the bakery going until the contest, and come up with new fantastic recipes to wow the judges.

And win.

13

MAEVE

A t the bakery's sink, I scrubbed mixing bowls as if industrial waste clung to their sides. Neve's practice baseball game started at three, and I would be there. I would *not* be late. She would have at least one person cheering for her. I'd promised, and I would keep my promise.

The shop's front bells jangled, and I gritted my teeth. *Go away!* Not that I could afford to turn away a customer, even a last-minute one.

"Hey," came a timid voice from the kitchen door.

I looked up from rinsing a bowl to find Dani, with her pink-tipped hair and eyebrow rings, melting into the doorjamb as if she could disappear into it.

"When the wolf's away the mice play?" I teased.

"Isn't it when the cat's away?"

"Usually."

"Luke's not that bad." She hooked a thumb over her shoulder. "There's no one out front."

"Yeah, my help didn't show." Again. Another reason for my less-than-stellar mood.

"I can man the counter, if you like."

I jammed the bowl into the drying rack. "No point. I'm closing."

"Oh, okay."

I took in a breath and softened my tone. Maybe I *should* cut back on caffeine. "Everyone's going to be at the baseball games this afternoon."

"Luke's already there."

My pulse kicked up. Too much caffeine, I told myself. Or anger. I was mad at Luke and his business-stealing tactics. That those tactics had forced me to enter a contest I didn't have time to prepare for. I reached for the next bowl and scoured hard.

Dani came into the kitchen with tentative steps, dragging fingertips along the counters and taking in the space as if she were taking pictures to study later. She peeked into the row of cup-size glass containers along the back of the counter.

"Flavored sifting sugar," I said, reaching for the stack of measuring cups.

"Sifting sugar?"

"It's an easy way to fancy up a dessert." I nodded toward the containers. "Go ahead, sniff."

She did. "Wow!"

"The vanilla one is the secret ingredient on my hand pies." One of them anyway— and the easiest one to figure out. I wasn't giving away state secrets.

She sniffed again and smiled.

I hated that I liked Dani, that I saw so much of my teen self in her. Transferring my anger at her brother to her wasn't fair. "Why donuts?"

Dani studied the spice wall, the one my sister-in-law-to-be, Meredith, had created and organized for me. "My grandparents owned an orchard, and they were known for their apples, their cider, and especially for their apple- cider donuts. People would drive for hours for a Pleasant Valley Orchard donut."

"As in Pleasant Valley, Connecticut?"

She nodded.

"No way! I've been to that orchard!" Dad had driven the whole family to Connecticut on a sunny fall day when I was eleven or twelve. We'd picked bushels of apples and gorged on donuts and cider. I still remembered the pleasant ache in my belly and the unique flavor I'd tried to recreate so many times without success.

"Every Saturday in the spring and summer, my dad would take me to watch Luke play baseball." A soft smile played on her lips as if she was back there once again. "We'd always stop and get donuts first." She worried the hem of her sunshine-yellow "Sprinkle Happiness" T-shirt that showed a donut sparkling with multicolored sprinkles. "It's a good memory, you know."

Food triggered memories, all five senses. I couldn't look at an apple pie without seeing Grandma Carpenter roll out pie crust and showing me how to handle it as if it were something tender and precious to bring out the dough's flakiness. Without smelling the cinnamon and apples or tasting the phantom flavors. Without hearing her bell-like laughter tinkling through the kitchen and echoing in my heart. "I get that."

"After my parents died..." Dani said, and looked away.

As much as my mother drove me crazy at times, losing her or Dad would hurt unbearably. "I'm so sorry for your loss."

She nodded and swallowed hard. "I got into *a lot* of trouble." She shrugged a shoulder. "Luke can't cook worth sh— beans. He somehow manages to burn boxed mac and cheese. After— well..." She shook her head as if the memory hurt. "To make myself feel better, I baked. Finding my grandfather's secret recipe, well, it saved my life."

I got that, too; I wouldn't have survived my teens without baking. Rolling out pie crust soothed. Mixing a cake relaxed. Scooping cookie dough comforted. During my teens, baking had become my therapy.

Which suddenly made me feel bad I'd taken away Dani's chance to win the contest. Not that a newbie had a chance against Jake Cunningham and Delia Horton. But my entering wasn't personal; I liked Dani. I needed to save my bakery. "Listen—"

The alarm on my phone filled the kitchen with the sound of a tornado siren— the only sound that could wake me up at four in the morning.

"Shoot!" I hit the Cancel button. "I have to go."

Dani nodded.

"Want to come with?" I handed her the insulated bag with the boxes of cupcakes for Neve's team. I hurried to my office and grabbed my bag, Dani following with uncertain steps. "Unless you move the donut truck to the ballfield, you're not going to get many customers, so you might as well."

Her smile lit up her face. "Thanks."

FINDING parking proved next to impossible, especially with the van. People just couldn't seem to park straight and used up more than their fair share of space. I left the cupcakes safely in the van and would retrieve them later. By the time Dani and I reached the stands, the only seats available were high up along left field. My parents, Zoe, Aaron and Meredith were all there, scattered across the stands. That Neve would have a whole cheering squad for her practice game, made me happy for her.

And there, close to the protective fence along the third base line, Patrick paced. He'd remembered. That made my heart sing. Neve would be so happy to see him there.

Looking up at the one free space on the last tier, I groaned. "We're not going to see anything from up there."

Dani gave a mischievous smile and took my hand. "Come with me."

She led me to the equipment building where she stopped and crouched. "Hurry!"

She raced into the building, then up the narrow stairs to the small attic littered with dust and broken equipment. She tiptoed across the plywood floor to a window that just happened to face the field on which Neve would play.

I crowded in next to her and took in the perfect view of the bench below and the field. "How did you find this space?"

She lifted the window open, and the sounds of chatter from the crowd and the scent of popcorn and hot dogs from the canteen filled the room. "I got bored when Luke came to talk to Coach Mac after we got here, so I explored. I come up once in a while to check on Luke."

"He needs checking?"

She leaned both elbows on the windowsill. "It's been hard for him, too."

"Losing your parents?"

She nodded. "It's been a mess. And I didn't make things any easier for him."

Worrying about the people you loved was normal. They were lucky to have each other.

"Neve's not going to see me here." I didn't want to disappoint her. "She's going to think I didn't make it."

"Wait here."

Dani sneaked back downstairs and came back up a few minutes later with a straw. She ripped off the paper, made three pea-size balls with it, then aimed one at Neve's back. I doubted it would reach her, but somehow it did.

"That's some pair of lungs," I said.

"High school marching band. Sousaphone."

"Sousaphone?" I glanced at her, wondering how this mouse of a girl could power a sousaphone. "Really?"

"Nobody else volunteered, so I always had a spot." Dani laughed and launched her second and third missiles.

Frowning, Neve turned around, rubbing her neck. I waved like a madwoman. She grinned and waved back.

Dani dragged over a sawhorse. We balanced our butts on the narrow back and settled in to watch the game.

Luke and the coaches gathered the kids around in a huddle. They all rammed their fists toward the middle of the circle, and yelled, "Go Angels! Go Blue Jays!"

He stood off to the side at home base, out of the way of the play, but close enough to offer coaching tips to both sides. He looked way too good in his Brighton baseball uniform— one I noticed sported the number thirteen —the same one he wore when he played for the Gulls.

A lucky number, until it wasn't.

Reluctantly, I had to admit that he handled the kids well. I didn't think that many of these younger kids knew or cared who he was, just that he was fully focused on them.

Neve's turn at bat came up.

Luke said something to her about hitting the sweet spot. I could only make out the occasional word from my vantage point.

Though I couldn't see her face from this angle, I was sure it was scrunched in concentration.

The pitcher threw the ball.

"Watch for it, watch for it," Luke encouraged.

Neve hit the ball with a satisfying thwack, and it flew right down midfield.

Dani and I cheered as did the spectators. Loud above the others, came Patrick's, "That's my girl!"

Since when? the nasty thought popped in. I shook it away. He said he would try, and he was trying. I had to give him a chance.

"Run!" Luke reminded Neve.

Pumping arms and legs, she made it safely to first base. Right foot on the base, she readied to run to second as the next batter stepped up to the plate.

"She's got a good swing," Dani said.

"So her coach keeps telling me." Maybe she'd inherited my softball skills. The thought warmed me.

By the fourth inning— the last one of this practice game — Neve's team was up by one. Neve had struck out twice and I could tell from the stiff lines of her body that she was getting frustrated. She was up at bat again. She swung at and missed the first two pitches.

"You suck, Neve!" a boy lined up to bat said. "Just make the hit, weirdo!"

Neve had come home yesterday, complaining that all the kids on the team were mean to her, except Charlie. I hadn't believed her because how could *all* the kids treat her badly? I'd thought she was blowing things out of proportion as she often did. Now I felt terrible because here was the evidence that some bullying was happening. I'd have to talk to her coach and make it stop.

As Coach Cassie stepped up to have a word with the bully, Neve launched the bat and turned on the boy who'd called her names. Luke stopped her on the fly, dropped to one knee and whispered something in her ear.

She growled and started to talk back, but Patrick interrupted from the sidelines. "Calm down, Neve, and just play!"

Something he used to tell me all the time. He should know by now that no one in the history of the world ever calmed down when being told to calm down. Telling Neve to calm down would just escalate everything. She was already starting to meltdown, and, from experience, I knew things would get ugly fast.

I jumped up, ready to run down. Dani caught my arm. "Let Luke handle it."

"It's my kid out there."

"He's used to this. He has a way with kids."

"My kid," I said again, but out of the corner of my eye, I

caught Luke, a soft hand on Neve's shoulder, an even gentler look in his eyes as he spoke to her. Her shoulders relaxed and she nodded. She picked up her discarded bat and took up her stance at home plate. She glanced back over her shoulder, and Luke gave her a thumbs-up. "You've got this!"

She nodded once and stared at the pitcher, daring him to strike her out. Her demeanor was so fierce, I couldn't help but smile. *That's* my *girl!*

The ball found the sweet spot on her bat and flew all the way to the outfield. The crowd cheering her on, she made it all the way to third base before Luke signaled her to stop.

"Go! Go! Go!" Patrick yelled, windmilling his arm to drive her on. But the ball, on its way back to home plate, would tag her out if she kept going. She took a step forward.

Breath held, fists tight, I urged her to stop.

As if she heard me, she skidded to a halt, stepped back to third base, and checked in with Luke.

He high-fived her and gave her a smile that made my stomach flutter.

Then she looked up at me, so proud of herself that I wanted to hug her.

Luke had done something even I had a hard time doing— he'd spun her mood around from a sure meltdown to a victory.

Now I felt really bad I'd entered the baking contest.

14

GRACE

I woke up with a swirl of possibilities dancing around me.
Even washing the dishes after making a big breakfast of
strawberries, bacon and eggs didn't feel like a chore.
Ansel sat at the kitchen table, reading the *Tri-Town Times,*
our local weekly paper, that came out each Saturday. How he
could spend so much time reading the few flimsy pages never
ceased to amaze me.

"You're chipper this morning," he said as he turned a page.

"It's a beautiful day."

"So was yesterday."

And I really had been in a foul mood the past few days,
thanks to Maeve. "Today is a new day."

"I'm taking Maeve and Neve to the Sox/Yankees game
tomorrow. It's an early game, so we should make it back for a
late Sunday dinner."

"No need to hurry. I'm cancelling Sunday dinner." The decision came to me suddenly as I tossed and turned trying to fall
asleep. As soon as I'd decided, my whole body had lightened.
No planning. No cooking. No cleaning up. A whole day to

myself without taking care of anyone. Just the thought had allowed me to fall into a deep sleep and wake up refreshed.

Behind me, Ansel's paper crumpled and his lasered gaze burned a hot spot between my shoulder blades. "What's going on?"

"Things to do. Places to go." Research, too. That idea had come in the form of a dream. But before I spoke with Ansel, I wanted to know if the idea was viable. I didn't want anyone, well-intentioned or not, to pooh-pooh the idea, to tell me I was too old, to look at me as if I were crazy. I reserved that right for myself. This new project wouldn't come out of need like when the kids were in high school, and my only marketable skill had been cleaning house, but out of want.

"Is everything okay?" he asked, that dreaded worry in his voice.

Big smile on my face, I swiveled around to face him, dripping dishwater onto the floor. "Everything is perfect."

For once.

"That usually means it isn't." His frown grooved deeper lines onto his forehead. "You'd think after thirty-six years, I'd have the wife code down."

I reached for the dish towel, hanging from the stove door, and dried my hands. "No wife code, my darling. I'm just working on something."

He folded the newspaper and laid it on the table. "You know you can talk to me, right?"

"This is something I need to do on my own. When I've made my decision, you'll be the first person I talk to." I waggled my eyebrows at him. "You know how much I love it when you talk numbers."

He laughed. "Numbers, huh? I can't wait."

I placed the towel just so on the stove's handle. "I'm going out this morning. Errands. Then lunch with Kate. Then a training session for Snick."

"Sounds like a busy day. Want me to grill something for dinner?"

This was why I loved this man. I could count on him to give me the room I needed.

"That would be excellent." I kissed the top of his head, then went to find what trouble Snick had gotten herself into. She was much too quiet. And Lark's number-one rule was, "Never trust a puppy."

I found the mutt in the dining room, looking so proud of herself as she shredded my grocery list into a thousand pieces.

I MET Lark at the dog park where we would work on Snick's helicopter-ninja tendencies when she met other dogs, especially bigger dogs with deep barks.

We stopped away from the busy dog park. Snick sat, staring at the other dogs playing. Vibrating with fear— or desire to join them? I couldn't say.

"You could be out there playing, if you were a good girl."

She glanced at me, then back at the dogs.

"There are no bad dogs," Lark said, appearing as if out of nowhere next to me. "Just owners in need of training."

She arrived with a pouch of treats at her waist, three collapsed travel bowls in hand, and a long leash.

"This owner wouldn't need training if someone hadn't dropped off a dog without warning."

At the sight of Lark, Snick stood and danced, tail spinning wildly, pulling on the leash.

Lark crouched, making Snick drop all four paws to the floor before she patted the dog all over. "She needs you as much as you need her."

Even Lark's off-kilter dog-matching couldn't ruin my mood today. "I don't get that reaction, and I'm the one who feeds her."

"You're there all the time."

"True." I could barely go to the bathroom without the dog at my heels. And even then, she sat outside the door, whining until I came back out. "So, what's the plan?"

"We're going to play a target game."

She dropped two of the flattened bowls about six feet apart. She took Snick's leash from me, switched it for the long leash, then tossed a treat onto one of the bowls. Snick raced to gobble the treat down as if she hadn't eaten in a week. Lark lobbed another treat onto the other bowl and Snick raced over. After a few more tosses, Snick caught on to the pattern, and Lark handed me the leash. "You try it."

"What exactly is the point of this?"

"Distraction. Think toddler. Distract and redirect. Distract her from the behavior you don't want and redirect her to the one you want. We're letting her see the dogs, but not giving her a chance to react in her usual way. That lessens the anxiety."

Every once in a while, Lark would move the target bowls closer to the dog-park enclosure. Eventually, she added the third bowl.

A black-gray-and-white mutt barked at us. Snick stopped, tail cranking up like a flag at attention, neck ruff spiking. Lark called her attention back to the game and the treats. Snick hesitated, then went for the treat.

After half an hour of back and forth, getting closer and moving farther away, Snick calmly sniffed the mutt's nose through the fence and play-bowed at him.

Lark praised Snick, gave her more treats, then led her away. We sat in the shade of an oak tree, Snick between us, enjoying double pats. "She did really well today."

"She did, didn't she?" I gave Snick a scratch under her chin.

"You'll need to practice every day, at different places, until she doesn't react anymore."

I gazed at all the well-behaved dogs, playing in the enclosure, their owners barely paying attention to them as they chatted. "Do you think she'll behave as well if you're not here?"

"You've built your trust with her today. If you keep practicing, the bond between you two will get stronger."

As it happened, I foresaw a lot of free time in my future. I would have plenty of opportunities to train the mutt. Especially now that Maeve would take over all my childcare obligations. Maybe Lark was right. Maybe I needed Snick, especially now. I would need something to fill my time.

I still wasn't sure I wanted to keep her. I still hoped that Maeve would give in and take the thing for Neve. But in the meantime, I wanted a dog with manners.

As Snick and I ambled to the car, I realized that this was the first time today that I'd thought of Maeve. And for some reason, the lightness I'd felt all day disappeared.

15

MAEVE

I came out of the bakery kitchen on Saturday morning, carrying a tray of morning-glory muffins, to find Dani at one of the tables, picking at the crust on my variation of a strawberry swamp pie. Her notebook was spread open in front of her. Drawings with lines snaking from them and neatly printed words peppered the page.

The donut truck might have moved around the corner, but the scent of fry oil and cinnamon still wafted into the air on Main Street every morning, enticing passersby into the alley as if the food truck was a speakeasy and the apple-cider donuts were must-have bootleg.

"Good morning," I said, putting down the tray of muffins on the counter.

She startled, twisted her torso to face me and smiled as if she'd been caught in the act of doing something naughty. Today's purple "Donut Queen" T-shirt featured a crown with donut jewels. "How do you get your piecrusts so flaky?"

"It's a Grandma Carpenter secret." Grandma, with her arthritic hands, couldn't manhandle the dough, so her touch was light and gentle.

"Oh." The single word contained a world of disappointment. Her expression deflated and she turned back to her plate.

What had happened to that girl to make her believe what she wanted didn't matter?

I stacked the muffins under a glass cloche. "Who's manning the donut truck?"

"Luke's at the ballpark for the second half of the practice games. He doesn't get that I need to work up my recipes for the contest."

No wonder I'd had a steady stream of customers this morning, keeping Kayla busier today than all last week. "How's it coming?"

She tick-tocked her head. "I don't know. I keep changing my mind. It has to be special, but with the time limits, I can't get too fancy. And I'm not sure how long it's all going to take me. On the other hand, I don't want to be too plain and not catch the judges' eyes."

I didn't see how Dani could practice baking a cake or a pie in the truck. Not without an oven. And enough guilt stirred up at having entered the contest that my mouth spilled out an invitation before I could quite think it through. "I'm about to start a batch of hand pies."

She lifted an eyebrow in question.

"Come on back, if you want."

She stilled like a mouse in a hawk's line of sight. "Really?"

"Better hurry before I change my mind."

She scrambled, getting out of the chair and stuffing her notebook in her "Life Happens, Donuts Make it Better" tote bag.

I'd made the dough earlier and took it out of the fridge. I tipped the bowl and the wrapped discs of dough rolled out onto the table. "Get out your notebook."

She blinked at me twice, then fumbled into her tote to retrieve her notebook.

"Because you're a beginner," I said, unwrapping a portion of dough. "I'd add a tablespoon of white vinegar to the flour before you add the water. Keep the bottle in the fridge so it's nice and cold."

"Vinegar?"

"It keeps the dough from forming gluten and keeps it tender. It takes a while to learn the right touch."

She scribbled furiously.

"To keep the dough light, you want to leave the fat in bigger pieces. Like walnut halves instead of peas."

Her eyes grew wide. "Really?"

I chuckled, the lightness of it taking me by surprise. Had I been that eager, standing at Grandma's side while she imparted her knowledge? "And if you want your dough extra-flaky, you want to add a couple of lamination folds. That's where you roll butter onto the dough, then fold the dough and chill it."

"I've heard of lamination for croissant dough. But for pie?"

"For pie." I dusted flour onto the table. "You want a light dusting of flour because you don't want your dough to get tough or dry. Flakiness is all about hydration levels."

"How do you know if it's too much flour?"

"You want just enough flour so that the dough doesn't stick to the table or rolling pin." Another skill that came with practice.

She had a thousand questions as I rolled dough, cut out circles, filled them with my secret strawberry filling, folded it into a half-moon, crimped the edges and set them on a baking sheet.

I had to admit that sharing my tips and tricks with someone who got baking felt good. I wasn't arguing with Mom. I wasn't fighting over food with Neve. I wasn't thinking about Patrick and why he wasn't around if he planned to stay home for good. I was in my element.

Maybe I could add some baking classes to earn extra money

for the shop. Then I half-snorted and tried to cover it up with a yawn. When? I was already spending too much time away from Neve.

Dani stopped mid-question, looking like a deer who'd just noticed a wolf on the edge of a clearing.

I turned, following the direction of her gaze.

Luke stood, shoulders owning the doorway, dirty blond brows all but hiding the storm in his eyes.

"Luke," Dani said, tripping over her words, "I'm sorry." She drew a large X across her chest. "I swear I didn't ask. She invited me."

Still, he said nothing, gaze going from his sister to me in a slow arc as if the equation wouldn't balance.

"I didn't expect to find you here." His voice held no malice.

"I'm sorry." Dani dropped her notebook as she tried to stuff it into her tote. It hit the floor sounding like a revolver going off. "I'm going." She grabbed the top of the tote with both hands. "Thanks, Maeve. This was a lot of fun. You're a good teacher."

"Any time."

He let Dani scramble past him. "What happened to no time to babysit?"

"Someone stole my customers." I lifted my floured hands in a ta-da move. "No customers equals time. You got your wish."

"Listen," he started, then stopped, the hint of pink creeping up his neck. He crossed his arms over his chest and let his chin drop. "I'm sorry. I never meant for things to go this far."

I snorted in a way that said I didn't believe him and lifted another filled tray of hand pies onto the rack with a little too much force. That man could raise my anger faster than proofing yeast. "Anything else?"

"I—" He shuffled his feet as if he were nervous and that made me wildly curious. Luke Saunders, nervous? About little old me?

"You..." I urged, noting the vulnerable bent of his neck.

What would it feel like to kiss that spot? My mind was utterly ridiculous. I didn't need more complications.

He pursed his lips as if the words to come tasted sour, then puffed them out. "I want to offer a truce."

I stilled, not sure what he was up to. "And what would this truce look like?"

"Like me moving the truck to the festival grounds and not opening again until the festival starts on Thursday."

"Why?" With a scraper, I gathered the scraps of dough and raked them into the garbage can.

"Sometimes I get focused on outcomes and forget to take what's going on now into consideration. I wanted to give Dani the best chance she could to win. She needs a win. It's a long story, and I don't want to bore you. I just got fixed on the wrong goal."

A story definitely lurked there. A story that made me curious. But I wouldn't ask. And I got that he cared for Dani. I'd do the same for Neve or Aaron or Zoe. For anyone I loved. But I didn't like the softening in my gut for him. He'd cost me a week's worth of profit. I tucked the rolling flour bin under the counter. "There's a lot of big players participating this year because of the size of the prize."

"I get that."

"There's not much chance an amateur will win."

He tipped his head in acknowledgement. "I just thought I could give her a leg up. Especially because she admires you so much."

"You didn't have to do it like a bull in a bakery." As I stowed the leftover strawberry filling in the fridge, his gaze followed me around the kitchen, making me feel like taffy being pulled.

"I said I was sorry, and I mean it." He put a hand over his heart. "Truly, Maeve, I am."

"You should know" –I said, attacking the floury table with a sponge— "that because business was so bad, I entered the contest. I can't back out because of the entry fee." I owed Natalie's trust in me to try my best.

"I understand." But the lines crimping his forehead and the brackets pulling his mouth into a straight line said he didn't.

I turned away, took the dirty tools to the sink and cleared my throat. "Thanks, by the way."

"For what?"

I snapped on the hot water. "The way you handled Neve yesterday at the game. She was on the edge of a meltdown, and you talked her down."

"That was your kid?"

My love for her bloomed into a smile. "That was my bundle of contradictions."

He gave an appreciative nod. "She's got a good eye and a strong arm."

I squirted soap into the water and bubbles roiled, filling the air with the scent of lemons. "I hear a 'but' in there."

"I don't think team sports are the best option for her."

No kidding. I reached for a scrubber and scoured the bowl. "She was supposed to go to art camp, but she wanted to be with her new friend, Charlie."

"Charlie stands up for Neve. She's a good friend."

That was good to know. That little girl had strength and courage, and I was glad she was Neve's friend. "Neve mentioned that everyone was picking on her."

"It's the age," he said, shaking his head. "Kids are trying to figure out how they fit. And sometimes it comes out as cruel."

"She has ADHD." It sounded like a defect, even though I still thought of her as perfect. "She has a hard time being in a group."

"I'll keep an eye on her."

My hand stopped scrubbing. "You would do that?"

"I know what it's like not to fit in."

"I find that hard to believe." He'd been a baseball star for so long, and stars always belonged, didn't they?

He pushed away from the door frame. "We'll be out of your way in less than half an hour."

He turned to leave.

"Hey!"

He half swiveled my way, eyebrows raised in question.

"Dani needs to practice her bakes. Without an oven, the truck isn't going to cut it. Come by later, and you can use the bakery's kitchen."

He stared at me for so long that my insides went all jittery as if I'd chugged five cups of coffee. "You'd do that?"

I shrugged as if the offer was no big deal. "I have to practice anyway. Bring your own supplies, though."

His smile flashed like sunshine on water. "That goes without saying."

I handed him my phone. "Put in your number. I'll text you once Neve's asleep. We have five days to get ready. Tonight, we can work on pies."

He punched in his number and handed me back the phone still warm from his touch.

"See you later," I said, voice sounding strangely rusty.

He nodded, gave me one last long look, and strode away, leaving me with an odd feeling racing through my veins. As if I couldn't wait for later to arrive, to see him again. Which was ridiculous. This wasn't for him. It was for Dani because she was a sweet kid. And it was my kitchen, so I needed to be there.

Plus, if I was going to have any chance to win this baking contest, I needed to practice, too.

And that meant swallowing my pride and asking Mom to watch Neve tonight.

~

AFTER MAKING sure that Kayla had everything in hand, I jogged home, stopping by the main house first. Dad stood at the kitchen counter, a bowl of hamburger meat in front of him, peering through Mom's spice cabinet.

"What are you looking for?" I asked.

"Your mother's secret hamburger spice."

I reached into the cabinet and brought out a shaker of Montreal Spice.

"That's it?" He looked doubtful.

"That's it."

"I thought she made her own."

"Oops, didn't mean to spill her secret."

He shook some spice blend onto the hamburger. "I've been meaning to talk to you about your numbers."

I swallowed a groan. *Not now, please!* I had too much on my mind already. "I'll make an appointment."

"Soon, okay?"

"After the contest." I plucked an apple from the fruit bowl and leaned my butt against the counter. "Where's Mom?"

"Not sure." He focused on seasoning the ground meat as if he were working up a balance sheet for the perfect burger.

The bite of apple went down crooked, and I chuffed out a cough. Mom always made sure someone knew where she was. She wanted to be available to save the day. "What do you mean you're not sure?"

He added one more shake of seasoning before capping the jar. "She had things to do, and she's out doing them."

Since when? "Do you know when she'll be back?"

He crouched down to the container cabinet and riffled through its contents. "Not till later. I'm grilling burgers tonight."

"She's not answering her phone." I'd tried her on the way home and my call had gone straight to voice mail.

He made a noncommittal noise and pulled out a patty mold.

"Do you think she'd watch Neve tonight?" I asked, a sinking feeling like dud biscuits in my stomach.

Dad's glasses rose along with the lines on his forehead. "I'm not getting in the middle of this thing between you and your mother."

"What thing?" I went for innocent, but couldn't quite get there, the escalation of our fight heating me up all over again.

"Whatever she's mad at you for."

"Mad at me?" I was the one who had the right to be angry. She was deliberately ignoring my request not to feed Neve sugar. "Where's Neve then?"

"She's with Charlie at Irene's."

Mom had never been this mad at me before. What if she really stopped taking care of Neve? How would I make sure Neve was safe while I was working? How could I possibly run the bakery? This was bad. I had to figure out a way to make things better.

"Would you watch Neve tonight?" Something I didn't really want to depend on. He tended to let Neve do whatever she wanted, which wasn't good for her routine-loving brain.

"Can't. It's poker night with the guys."

Dad with his sharp mind for numbers and patterns loved a good poker game.

"About the game tomorrow," he said, dumping a quarter pound of seasoned burger into the mold, then pressing the meat. "I'm planning on leaving before lunch."

I'd forgotten all about our annual jaunt to Boston. "Oh, I'm sorry, but I won't be able to go. I have to practice for the baking contest. I haven't even started putting recipes together, and the contest starts Friday."

His face couldn't hide his disappointment. I was breaking tradition; the one thing that was just mine and Dad's. I worked up the day in my mind, trying to figure out if I could do it all. And concluded I couldn't. I only had so much of me to spread around, especially lately. "Take Charlie instead. Neve will love having her along."

With his clean hand, he reached over and pulled me into his side— his version of a hug. "I'm going to miss having you there, sweetness."

I hated disappointing him. I hugged him back. "Next year, I promise."

Maybe I could surprise him with tickets later in the season. If I won the contest, I could easily afford great seats. One more reason to practice.

On the way back to the bakery, I tried calling Patrick, but his phone went straight to voicemail. I left a message but couldn't count on hearing back in time. I growled at the phone. "Where are you?"

Good thing he was home to stay, I thought with a derisive snort. Neve had seen him exactly twice in the week he'd been back. He always had the same excuse: his next great thing was coming along. Not that he bothered to share what that was. I was running out of patience.

And he was running out of chances.

I closed my eyes and took in a long breath. That wasn't fair. He couldn't know I needed help.

I stepped into the bakery and Zoe stood in front of the counter, concentrating on picking out pastries. No one else was in the shop this late in the afternoon.

"Zoe, just who I wanted to see!"

"That's what I was about to say." Zoe pointed at the cherry crumble squares. "A dozen, please," she said to Kayla, then to me, "Mom says you're entering the baking contest."

"Seemed like the best way to save the bakery. When did you talk to Mom?"

"This morning. Business that bad?"

"Getting there." So, Mom was talking to Zoe. I gritted my teeth. Mom was being petty on purpose. "Did Mom say where she was going?"

"Nope."

Listening to Zoe's reason for being here seemed the right thing to do before I asked for a favor. "Why did you want to see me?"

Zoe asked for a dozen brownies. "Are you still going to be able to do Mom's birthday cake now that you'll be in the contest?"

"I've already made the base. I'll decorate it on Saturday night, and you can pick it up on Sunday morning— all in time for her party Sunday night after the contest ends."

"Are you sure? It seems like a lot to do in between all that contest baking."

"You can depend on me."

"A dozen of those." Zoe pointed to the oat-chocolate sandwich cookies. "What kind of cake did you make?"

"Mocha with caramel syrup. I'll make a salted caramel frosting."

Zoe wrinkled her nose. "Seems kind of plain."

"Not when I'm done." It would be a work of art. I jutted my chin at her order. "What's with all the sweets?"

"Studio open house tomorrow."

That made more sense than Zoe suddenly developing a sweet tooth.

Kayla went to the register to ring up Zoe's purchase. "On the house," I said, and Kayla raised a dramatic brow. I shushed with a look.

Zoe narrowed her gaze at me. "What do you want?"

Asking for a favor always turned my insides to jelly. "Is there any way, pretty please, that you could watch Neve tonight?"

"Why?"

"Contest practice."

I could see the wheels whirring in her mind, calculating what she could ask for in return. "Sleepover?"

As brave as Zoe pretended to be, she hated sleeping alone. Having her share my bed for a night seemed a small price to pay in exchange for knowing Neve was safe and for the practice time.

Which had nothing to do with Luke. I would show him. I would win that contest.

"That works," I said. "I'll be home late."

16

MAEVE

After feeding Neve and Zoe dinner and having Zoe pinky-swear promise not to give Neve any sugar, I jogged to the bakery. A move I regretted when the day's lingering heat left sweat stains on my blue "Brightside Bakery" polo shirt and frizzed my hair to witch status. I texted Luke to come around the back door. He sent back a thumbs-up emoji. Then I twisted my hair into a bun, put on my focus playlist— a mix of lo-fi music recommended by Neve's therapist for homework —and prepped my workspace to keep busy while I waited.

Usually, stepping into the kitchen at night was like walking into a playground. The colors of the various containers and scents of spices, the sugar, the butter, the flour— all an invitation to play. But tonight, a tightness strung over my stomach. I'd never shared my space that way before and it felt much too...intimate. Like inviting someone to look into my soul.

Patrick liked to test the results of my experiments, but the experiments themselves bored him. The kitchen, to him, was dull and mind-numbing.

I didn't want to think of Luke here in my kitchen, of his big body taking up too much space, of his baritone disturbing my concentration, of his stormy eyes following my every move— something he seemed to know unnerved me. I had to focus. I had to make the best pie of my life —there was $100,000 on the line, not to mention my future.

The stainless-steel tabletop gleamed under the bright over-head lights—a blank canvas waiting for inspiration. I got out Grandma Carpenter's wooden French rolling pin, worn smooth with age and use, the familiar texture grounding me. Bowls, measuring cups and spoons followed, placed in their proper spot. I might not have gone to culinary school for more than a semester, but I had learned *mise-en-place*. I placed a fresh note-book at the top of the table, pencil ready to take notes as I experimented. Then added a big bowl of strawberries, the star of the pie, for inspiration.

I checked my watch. How long did it take to walk the two blocks from the B&B to the bakery? I riffled through my recipes, willing my mind to twist flavors into something both familiar and unexpected. I pulled spices from the wall, sniffing each— cinnamon, cardamom, rosemary. No, no, no. Vanilla, chocolate, coconut. Maybe.

Finally, a knock echoed on the metal back door. "About time," I muttered.

"Sorry we're late," Dani said, barely visible behind the load of grocery bags she carried. "We had to get supplies."

Behind her, Luke lugged more bags. "I think she bought out the store. Hope no one's expecting weekend treats."

I closed the door behind them. "How many pies are you planning on making?"

"As many as it takes to get something special."

I showed them to their half of the prep table. Dani dropped the bags on the table, then reached into her tote for her notebook.

"You've made a kitchen that feels as if magic happens here," Luke said, taking in the space as if he'd never seen it before. "I love how it's homey and inviting. I can't wait to see what you two come up with."

Homey? Inviting? I glanced around at my efficient kitchen with its cream walls and gleaming stainless steel. I noticed for the first time that the color-coded labels Meredith had created for me in a feminine font, as well as the various containers I'd collected over the years to display my bakes, did add a layer of cozy charm. He looked at ease, helping Dani unpack her bags. I shook my head.

"No time for chit-chat, Donut Guy." As I made my way to my side of the table, I hip-checked him.

He quirked an eyebrow at me. "Donut Guy?"

"We've got work to do."

He mock-saluted. "Aye, aye. What comes first?"

"First, a plan." I turned my attention to Dani. "What are you thinking?"

"Ugh, I keep waffling back and forth. I want to make something creamy, but it needs like a lot of chilling time, and we've only got two hours. So, um, I thought maybe a tarte Tatin with strawberries." She gave a doubtful one-shouldered shrug. "It doesn't feel special enough, you know. Then there's the puff pastry."

"There's always a way to zhuzh up anything. You can do rough puff."

A slow smile took over her face and her eyes lit up. "Okay, let's zhuzh." She turned the page in her notebook where she'd scribbled her recipe. "You're going to show me how to do the rough puff, right?"

I laughed. "Of course." I pulled out a page from my pie book. "So, the rules say that the assistant can assist," I said, though I hadn't asked Natalie to help me tonight. She had to get up so early as it was to get the bread ready, and bread was more important to the bakery right now than her helping with the contest prep. Plus we could figure out our rhythm in no time. She was already a baker, after all. "But he can't do any of the actual baking. You know what that means?"

Dani looked at me, blinked, then shook her head.

"It means you get to boss your brother around. And he has to listen." The idea of bossing Luke around held a certain charm.

A crooked smile gleamed all the way to her eyes, a soft denim blue. "Oh, I like that."

"Don't get used to it, Dani girl," Luke said with a stern glare betrayed by a grin.

Maybe bossing Luke around would help build her confidence.

I reached for an apron and handed it to Luke. "You give your sister the spotlight, for a change, and sit there—" I pointed at a stool next to the table "—till she needs you."

Trying to get the image of how good that apron looked on Luke, how the blue deepened the gray of his eyes, I shook my head, and handed him the rough-puff crust recipe. "On second thought, let's see how good you are at listening. There's a printer in my office. Make a copy of this for Dani."

"You call that a challenge?" He grabbed the recipe and headed toward my office.

I made a give-me gesture toward Dani's book. "Let me see your filling ingredients."

We went over the recipe and discussed how to bring out the flavors. Luke still hadn't returned with Dani's copy.

"How long does it take to make a photocopy?" I muttered, heading to my side of the table.

"He's probably snooping."

Good luck to him. All he'd find would be a mess of bills and boxes and sandwich board. "There's nothing to snoop at."

Just then, he strode back into the kitchen wearing a

dangerous smile, waving the recipe. "Even a has-been jock can make a photocopy."

"You're going to have to move faster than that, Donut Guy." I forced myself to keep my gaze on the page and not turn toward him but lost.

He saluted, a knowing smile still in place. What was he up to?

I didn't have time to wonder at the workings of his mind. I had pie to make. "Do you know what *mise-en-place* is?" I asked Dani.

She nodded.

"Okay, get yourself ready. This is where your assistant could be a great help to you— getting things measured and weighed and set up properly."

Luke was a quick study, using the scale like a pro to weigh out the flour and sugar. He filled the room with laughter, soft, deep—sincere. How could gray appear warm?

Focus, Maeve, focus.

He lost points when he poured water in a dry measuring cup. "That's a dry measuring cup. You need a liquid measuring cup."

"Isn't a cup a cup?" he asked.

"That's like asking if a shortstop's glove is like a catcher's mitt. In baking, like in baseball, it's all about using the right tool for the job."

He hiked an eyebrow. "Look at you, talking baseball at me."

I rolled my eyes. Was he flirting with me? My stomach took a little roller-coaster dip. No, he wasn't. That was just the way he was. "Seems to be the only language you understand."

"Hey, guys. We don't have time for your feud." Dani took out her phone. "I'm going to set a two-hour timer."

I opened my own notebook to the notes I'd made. "Great idea."

I talked Dani through the first pass of lamination while I

worked on roasting strawberries for my entry, aware, always aware of Luke and the space he occupied. It was unnerving. And distracting. And I didn't like it.

Dani was a good student, and Luke turned out to be a good helper, encouraging and supporting her. They made a good team even with the occasional collision when they failed to communicate. I couldn't help the stab of envy, wishing Patrick were here for me the way Luke was for Dani.

You could have asked for help, I reminded myself, and shook my head. *Keep your head on your own pie.*

The kitchen filled with a familiar symphony of measuring cups and spoons, of bowls and whisks. The laughter added a new layer that made the kitchen come to life, making me wish I could afford an apprentice baker. Luke regaled us with stories of his baseball days, like the time the door handle had fallen off the bathroom stall and locked him in before his first major league game. He asked way too many questions, breaking my concentration way too often. I had to keep reminding him to be quiet and let us work.

But, as if he couldn't stand a quiet kitchen, the warning didn't stick.

"Did I ever tell you about the day we haunted the batting coach?" Luke didn't wait for an answer but prattled on, slicing strawberries as he spoke. "The guy was a turd. Mean like you wouldn't believe. I mean, we're tough guys, but this coach was making us all hate baseball. The team was ripping apart at the seams, and it was starting to show in our games. We were losing. Bad."

The Gulls' second season. They were on a demoralizing losing streak, having won zero games in the first half of the season. Announcers were having a great time making fun of the Gulls' Three-Stooges performance on the field. Some even joked that a Little League team could do better.

"On the team bus on the way to Pittsburg," he said with a gleam in his eye, "we hatched a plan."

"We or you?" I asked, rolling out my pie dough, caught up in his story in spite of myself.

The edge of his lips twitched. "The hotel we were staying at had a reputation for being haunted."

"You didn't!"

"He did," Dani said, as if she'd heard this particular story before.

"We did." He handed Dani a bowl of sliced strawberries. "For the first time that season, we worked as a team. We sneaked into his room. Using hand signals we'd perfected in practice, we moved as one. As if we were ghosts, we rearranged his room in an *Exorcist* way. Then we rigged sound effects, and sneaked out as silently as we'd sneaked in."

He stopped like a good storyteller, cleaning up his mess of strawberry caps, leaving me hungry for what happened next. "Go on."

"I thought you wanted me to be quiet."

His lopsided grin had me shaking my head. I was getting lost in the story, forgetting where I was in my recipe. And the more he talked, the closer I wanted to lean in. Which wasn't good. Not at all. I couldn't fail at the one thing I was good at because of a pretty face with a good story. I stuffed my pie in the oven. And yet... "Finish what you started, Donut Guy."

Luke smirked as he placed Dani's pie in the oven next to mine. "Between the sounds of footsteps and the moans and the rearranged room, he ran out screaming like a little girl. Hiding in the room next door, we all high-fived each other, then went back to bed. The next day, the coach looked as if he hadn't slept at all. He couldn't muster up his usual vitriol during warmups. But the exercise gave the team some glue, and we won that game."

And most of the games for the second half of the season. Everyone from announcers to sportswriters wondered what had happened. The batting coach certainly didn't say anything.

"We had to pay a pretty hefty hotel fine," Luke said. "But it was worth every penny."

"Did the batting coach ever find out you guys were behind the prank?"

He mimed a zipping motion close to his lips. "Not one leak. But he knew something was up, and he quit less than a month later."

A team couldn't win with just one good player; it needed all of them to play as a unit. And that was what Luke and his antics had done— brought his disjointed team back together.

I swallowed the sudden knot in my throat. That worked for families, too. My parents had that bond. I would do anything for them, my siblings, or Neve.

I tucked a loose strand of hair behind my ear, fighting the roil of anger in my gut. I didn't want to think about Patrick and his absence, how his team didn't seem to include me or his daughter.

I stepped to the oven and peered at the pie bubbling away. "Looks done."

I pulled it out of the oven, closing my eyes and inhaling the scent of strawberries and flaky dough. Yes, better to concentrate on things I could control.

Dani's pie still had a ways to go and only a few minutes remained on her timer. When the buzzer went off, her face drooped. "So, I don't think that this is going to work because of the cooling times for the crust."

It could work, but she didn't have the experience and didn't have time to gain speed. "It was worth a try."

"Why won't a regular crust work?" Luke asked, butt leaning on the table, staring at the still-baking pie through the oven window like we were.

"Because," Dani said, a definite pout in her voice. "It's not special enough."

"Chocolate and strawberries go great together," I said. "An all-butter crust can be flaky."

She tapped a finger against her lip. "A chocolate crust? Like the one you did with the strawberry chocolate pie?"

"You won't know unless you try."

I got her started with my all-butter chocolate crust recipe. While she and Luke set up for pie number two, I got to work on mine. The cream-cheese filling for this pie would require tight timing— and nothing could go wrong.

"How'd you get into baking?" he asked, breaking my concentration yet again. I glanced over at him, sitting on his stool, waiting for Dani's next order. He focused on me in a way that said I had all his attention, and that made me aware of every little movement I made. In spite of the heat from the oven, a shiver radiated all the way down my spine.

"My grandmother." Just thinking about her softened me. She was a tiny but strong-willed woman. Which was probably why she and Mom didn't get along. But I loved her and loved spending time with just the two of us together. "She came to live with us after my grandfather died. Let's just say she found a way to channel my teenage energy."

"Oh, I want to hear the story behind that." That smile, why did he have to smile that way? It made me want to tell him all my deep, dark secrets.

Right, Maeve, you're too busy surviving to have time for secrets! I shook my head and thought back to the day Grandma Carpenter sat me down at her kitchen table after my latest round of trouble in high school. Patrick and I had skipped school and borrowed my dad's car, because he rarely left his office, and driven down to spend the day at Hampton Beach. On the way home, we got pulled over by the State Police.

Apparently, my dad, unaware I was the one who'd borrowed the car, had reported it stolen.

That episode, on top of the sassing back at teachers, being perpetually late because I couldn't get organized, and the detentions had been the last straw for my parents and for the school.

I'd been suspended for three days.

"You're a smart girl, Maeve." At that time, Grandma was possibly the only person in the world who thought so. "But you're heading down a treacherous path."

As she spoke, she gathered flour, butter, sugar, apples, and cinnamon. "Let's channel that energy into something useful. Everybody loves baked goods, especially pie."

She was right. My baked goods afforded me a certain popularity I would otherwise never have had. My cookies and brownies and hand pies had made people happy. But I didn't want to explain my rocky teenagehood to Luke.

"Another day," I said.

"Why pies?" Luke asked, that stormy gaze probing, making me move too fast and almost slicing off a piece of finger.

"It's the first thing my grandmother taught me to make." I shrugged. "Like grandma said, who doesn't like pie?"

"Luke," Dani said, snorting.

I glanced at him, staring at me as if I were a puzzle. "Why won't you eat desserts?"

Dani made a teasing face. "He's watching his figure."

I couldn't blame him. He did look impressive with those wide shoulders and narrow hips.

He swatted Dani with a kitchen towel. "Hey, watch out or you'll have to look for another helper. And he might not know the difference between a dry measuring cup and a liquid measuring cup."

"Oh, no!" she said in a teasing voice. "That just won't do.

Please, please, Luke, you have to help me." She giggled, brought a hand to her forehead and pretended to swoon like one of his fangirls.

I couldn't remember the last time this kitchen had echoed with laughter. I needed more of that.

17

MAEVE

"Are you hoping to get back in the game?" I asked Luke as I checked my second pie in the oven, attempting to focus on my baking rather than the man taking up so much space in my kitchen.

His face took on a blank expression. "I don't know. Maybe. It depends."

I knew what it was like to burn with desire for something and have it taken away, to have that yearning still there burning. I didn't want to have his stories stir up sympathy. Our stories weren't similar. He had a choice; I didn't because I had to keep Neve top of mind with every decision I made. Something that Patrick had never understood.

Before I could say anything, Dani's buzzer went off a second time. Both our pies were ready. As I pulled out Dani's pie, warmth radiated through the oven mitts. "It looks great!"

I turned too fast, and my knuckles scrapped the edge of the oven, searing the skin.

"Oof!" I struggled to hang on to the skillet and slide it onto the table. "Careful when you turn it over."

Luke jumped up from the stool. "You burned yourself."

"Hazard of the profession." I headed to the sink and ran cold water on the already forming blister.

Luke crowded me. I elbowed him away. "I've got it."

He grabbed my wrist, making the blister pulse with pain. "You sure?"

This close, I could smell his cut-grass, sunshine-and-rain scent, and found it disorienting.

I waved my free hand at him, trying to make space between us. "It's not the first and won't be the last."

He frowned at the scars on my hand but retreated to his stool.

The perfectly caramelized strawberries of Dani's pie glistened. The crust wrapped over the fruit perfectly. The scent of sugar and strawberries filled the kitchen with an enticing aroma. *Focus on that*, I told myself.

"It worked!" Dani looked at me like a hero.

I shook my head. "Don't look at me like that."

"I can't help it. I'm just so happy." She came in for a hug and I stiffened.

Over her shoulder, Luke laughed. "She's a hugger. No getting around it. You might as well just let her."

I backed out of her hug and grabbed a pie server from the tool caddy. "Time to taste the first batch of pies. They're cool enough."

I took a bite of my roasted strawberry pie, turned it over and over in my mouth. "Something's missing."

"How do you know?" Luke asked from his stool, watching us taste the pie as if it were the most interesting show he'd seen in a while.

"It's so good," Dani said, licking every drop of filling from her fork. "I wouldn't have thought that balsamic vinegar would work. But this tastes perfect to me."

I poked the fork at the pie. "This needs more lemon juice. Maybe less sugar. The strawberries were already so sweet."

"Let's do mine."

She watched me cut a piece of the tarte Tatin, examine it on the fork and taste it. Her hands twisted into a knot worthy of a sailor while she waited for my verdict.

"Bake it like this at the competition, and I'll have to watch my back."

She beamed. "Really?"

"Really. Right, Luke?" I pushed a plate of pie his way. "Can't you make an exception just this once and taste your sister's pie?"

Just then, someone rapped on the back door. *Who could that be at this hour?* I headed for the door.

With a hand on my upper arm, Luke stopped me. "Let me."

I rolled my eyes. I didn't need a man protecting me, especially here. "My kitchen."

"What if it's a serial killer?" Dani asked, grabbing her phone, ready to dial 9-1-1.

"Would a serial killer bother to knock?" I inched the door open, Luke hovering over me like some sort of Hulk. "Colton! What are you doing here?"

"Saw the light. The bakery's usually dark at this time, so I thought I'd check it out."

I took in his pressed navy firefighter uniform. "Aren't you on duty?"

"Sandwich run."

"Of course." Colton was always hungry.

"Hey," Dani said, peeking around me. The door was getting crowded. "Do you like pie?"

He looked at Dani and smiled like a puppy. "Do I ever!"

"Let's get him to taste our pies like a judge would," Dani said.

"Why not?" I opened the door and invited Colton in.

We all gathered around the table. I tried to ignore Luke's hip brushing against mine, making my hands shake as I cut four slices and set them in front of Colton. He sat on Luke's stool, taking his taste tester job seriously. "Rank them in order of preference."

Colton gave each pie a fair taste. My second pie came first, followed by Dani's first pie, her second pie and my first pie came in last.

Dani's face sagged. "Well, this isn't good."

Colton's gaze ping-ponged between me and Dani. "I did it wrong?"

"Of course not," I said. "Taste is subjective, and we all know you're a human vacuum cleaner."

"Hey!"

I pointed at each pie. "Mine, Dani's, Dani's, mine. You actually have excellent taste. That's how I would have ranked them."

His chest puffed up. With his fork, he retasted each pie. "This one has the perfect balance of sweet and creamy. The cinnamon in the crust..." He brought the fingers of one hand together and made a kissing sound. "I could eat it all day. The crust on pie two is so flaky, I wanted to keep eating it, too. The chocolate crust is good, and it was really close between these two. The extra flakes gave the other one the edge. And this last one's missing something."

Dani's eyes widened. "That's what Maeve said."

Colton smiled at Dani, then gave a sharp nod as if he had the answer. "Cinnamon."

"Cinnamon is not the answer to everything," I said. "Especially not with balsamic vinegar."

"It is in my book."

"Good thing you don't run this bakery." We'd done most of the cleanup as the second pies baked. "I need to get home and get some sleep if I'm going to do this again tomorrow."

Colton stared at Dani, going all nervous-high-school boy on her. "Can I walk you home?"

She glanced at Luke, who frowned at me. "Is he safe?"

"He's a golden retriever."

"Hey!" Colton said, straightening to his full height as if that would erase the earnestness stamped on his face. "I can hear you."

Luke glowered at Colton. "She better be there by the time I get to the inn."

Dani swatted at Luke. "Don't mind him. His bark is way worse than his bite."

I grabbed a sponge from the sink. "You can go with her. I'll be right behind."

"I'm not leaving you to clean up alone when you were kind enough to offer the use of your kitchen."

"It's fine."

"Just let him," Dani said, wrapping her pies in boxes. "It's easier." She lifted the pie boxes. "I'll return your plates tomorrow morning."

Colton grabbed the pie boxes from Dani and ushered her through the back door. They left, filling the night air with chatter.

The evening had sped by. I couldn't remember the last time I'd had so much fun. After the contest, I had to find a way to have some balance in my life... some fun.

But right now, I was exhausted and wanted nothing more than to fall into bed.

The thought had me picturing Luke falling there with me. My body responding to the image in a way that was wholly inappropriate. Heat raced up my cheeks, and I turned to the sink, scrubbing at the last bowl with more fervor than it needed.

Behind me, Luke sponged the table, making me completely

aware of his every movement, creating an anxious buzzing in my chest. I didn't even like Luke.

Patrick was the only guy I'd ever had eyes for, the only guy who'd ever made my heart leap at the sight of him. This wasn't the same, of course it wasn't. Luke made me nervous because I didn't quite trust what he was up to. I sighed with relief as I rinsed the sponge for the last time. I had to remember he was the competition. Nothing more.

"Well," I said, reaching for my cardigan behind the kitchen door. "Thanks for helping."

"I'll walk you home." Luke made the offer sound like a command.

I scoffed. "You just let your sister walk home with a stranger."

"You said he was a golden retriever. He looks harmless enough."

"So does your average serial killer."

His brows scrunched over his stormy eyes. "Are you saying I should worry?"

"You're missing the point. I've been walking home on my own at all hours of the day and night for most of my life." I changed out of my kitchen clogs into sandals, then grabbed my bag, and headed for the door. "This is Brighton, not Boston, or even Portland."

He took my elbow and the skin there prickled like pins and needles. "Let me anyway. Please, it would make me feel better."

I rolled my eyes like a teenager and took my elbow back. "Because it's all about how you feel."

"Now that you mention it," he teased. He opened the door and let me walk through.

There was something about this time of the night when everyone was asleep that made the whole world feel peaceful. The cover of darkness. The cheer of the stars. The muted light of the moon. The blinking of lightning bugs.

Luke limped beside me, close enough that the heat of his body fanned against my side. I stepped sideways, trying to unhitch from his magnetic orbit. The soles of our shoes echoed in the quiet, my sandals a soft pad-pad and his shoes a bump-slide that seemed more pronounced than usual.

"How's the leg after all that standing?" I wrapped my cardigan tighter around me against both the chill of the night and the waves of his heat.

"It's fine. I just forgot to do my PT exercises today. I'll do them before I go to bed."

I nodded, searching for something to erase the growing tension winding around me like plastic wrap. I told myself it wasn't because of him. That I was tired. And stressed because of the contest. But a small voice called me a liar. "Think you'll be able to stand for three days in a row for the contest?"

"I can do anything I set my mind to."

Of course, he could. For some reason, the thought made me sad. I pointed at my parents' house. "This is me."

"Thank you," he said, sticking his hands into the front pocket of his jeans, thumbs out, "for helping Dani out."

"Not a problem."

The corners of his mouth turned up as he leaned over and whispered in my ear, "The thought of you thinking of me every day is as delicious as I imagine one of your award-winning pies to be."

My whole body stiffened at the soft caress of him leaning so close, of his breath teasing. "What are you talking about?"

He chuckled, a warm, throaty sound that reminded me of a lava cake right out of the oven. "A mouse named Luke."

I tried to breathe in but found my lungs already full. The raptor fundraiser. The thank-you card tacked to my cork-board. I'd forgotten all about it. Heat spread faster than a kitchen fire up my neck and over my cheeks. "I can explain—"

"No need." He took my hand and dropped a soft kiss on the burn on my knuckle.

My free hand covered the spot as if he'd seared my skin with a burning spoon. My mind spun, my body shuddered. This wasn't good. I hated giving him ammunition he could use against me. "It's not what you think."

He had the nerve to bark out a laugh as he waved.

18

GRACE

Sometime after midnight early on Tuesday, I woke up to Snick burfing—a cross between a bark and a soft woof, as if she wanted to sound the alarm, yet not wake me up. Maeve's tired footsteps climbed the stairs. A late night for the third night in a row. This practice baking for the contest wasn't good for her health. And, unlike yesterday when she'd slept in because the bakery was closed, today she'd have to get up in a few hours to get the bakery open.

I growled silently. I hated being such a sucker. Fine, I'd take Neve to camp. But Maeve was on her own for pickup. I flipped the sheet off and headed toward the kitchen. Snick rose from her bed with a yawn and a stretch and followed me down the stairs. Not wanting to ruin my night vision, I didn't turn on any lights, finding my way by feel. Something I regretted when I tripped over one of Snick's chew toys in the kitchen, the sharp shards of Nylabone digging into the tender skin of my arch, and I crashed into the table.

By the light of the microwave-oven clock, I wrote Maeve a note and taped it to her side of the door so she wouldn't miss it when she got up. Then I went back to bed.

You didn't stop worrying about your kids just because they didn't appreciate you and you were angry with them.

Snick's chin dipped the mattress and she stared at me until I cracked my eyes open again. "Nope."

I turned my back on her and resettled into the bed. With a huff, Snick dropped back to the floor and flopped onto her bed.

But it was no use, guilt about Maeve made sure I couldn't fall back asleep.

"How can you make such a mess?" I clucked at Neve the next morning. A sea of clothes, toys, stuffed animals, books and art supplies covered every inch of her bedroom's floor. Somewhere under there, existed a rug.

Neve, sitting on her bed, hitched a shoulder and went back to petting Snick and reading her book.

"You have an hour until it's time to leave for camp. That's enough time to clean up this mess."

Neve didn't look up or acknowledge my request in any way. "Neve!"

She looked up and blinked.

"Room. Clean it. Now!"

With a long-suffering sigh, she flipped the book over on her pillow and stood, surveying the mess strewn about the floor.

"I'm going to make some breakfast."

She nodded, but something about her expression made my heart sag.

Half an hour later, eggs and bacon and buttered toast ready — no jam —I went back up. Nothing had changed. "Neve! Why isn't your room clean?"

"Dunno," she said from the middle of the floor like a boat lost at sea.

With a sigh, I sat on her bed only to hear the ripple of

papers under the covers. Doing the job for her wouldn't do her any good. She had to learn to do hard things on her own. Life would throw her much harder curves than having to clean her own room.

I reached for the paper under the blanket. "Why Your Child's Messy Room is an Abstract Monster," read the title of the article.

It went on to talk about how telling a child with ADHD to clean their room was like tasking them to complete a Rubik's Cube with no help. Well, wasn't that just what I'd done? ADHD or not, she did seem lost looking at the mess. And I hadn't even given her a starting point— something that came easy for me because of my years cleaning other people's messes.

But Neve was just learning.

I did as the article suggested and wrote down Clean the Room at the top of a fresh sheet of paper, then listed all the different facets of room cleaning— books, clothes, toys, art supplies, making her a cheat sheet for the next time. Clothes made up most of the mess, so I started there.

"Neve, honey, reach for the red shorts by your knee."

She did and held them up.

"Are they clean or dirty?"

She sniffed them. "Dirty."

"Okay, throw them near the door, so we can get a load of laundry going."

She giggled and pitched them like a baseball. They landed outside the room.

"Do the same for all the shorts you see on the floor."

She got into the game, Snick playing tag with her with every object Neve put away. Once she had her specific task, she finished it fast. We took every different object on her floor by type and put them where they belonged.

My mind went back to my last training session with Snick where Lark had done something similar to teach Snick to learn to come when called. She'd broken the task into bits and pieces, rewarded Snick when she got anywhere close to doing it and kept narrowing until Snick could do the task. Coming when called was still a work-in-progress but we *had* made progress.

I surveyed the clean floor, taking in the flowered rug. "That looks much better, don't you think?"

Neve nodded, looking proud of herself.

Then I had a horrid vision of me yelling at ten-year-old Maeve to clean her half of the room she shared with Zoe, us getting into a shouting match that ended with Maeve spending a whole weekend in her room, her side still messy on Monday morning. I'd cursed her under my breath and picked up her mess myself while she was at school, sure her stubbornness was pure spite. Then I'd gone and made things worse when she got home. "Zoe's younger than you are and she can get her side of the room clean. Why can't you?"

But, of course, I got it now. She couldn't. Like Neve, she'd needed direction to get started; she'd needed a recipe.

Tears made me blink fast.

"Grandma, what's wrong?" Neve asked, patting my hand. Snick butted her body against my legs, a worried look pinching her brows.

I crouched and hugged them both. "Nothing, honey. I'm just so proud of you."

I noted that the article suggested another one on organizing and vowed to read it before Neve came back from camp. I folded the article and put it in my pocket to look at the link later. "Let's hurry up and eat breakfast, or we'll be late for camp."

I'd done everything wrong with Maeve. I couldn't bear the thought that I'd been a bad mother, not when Ansel and I had sacrificed so much so I could stay home with the kids.

Maeve was working so hard to do everything right by Neve.

I would do better.

SNICK'S ANTICS on the way to drop off Neve at camp provided us with entertainment. She chased a butterfly, preyed on an ant, and tripped over her feet snapping at a bird she had no chance of ever catching. She sniffed everything in sight, including a pile of fluff from someone's dryer that made her sneeze.

She was a little clown in an apricot suit.

Neve safely at camp, Snick and I made our way to the dog park. The park seemed overrun by dogs this morning. The small-dog side contained at least half a dozen with even more on the big-dog side. Had I missed a memo of some sort? Either way, that many people would come in handy.

"Now, you need to behave while we're there," I told Snick as we neared the gate. "I need to talk to these people, and I can't do that if I have to bail you out of trouble every two seconds. Got it?"

Wagging her tail, Snick woofed at me as if she understood. And the second I let her loose, she chased all the other small dogs, stirring them into a frenzy.

"The pups'll be tired tonight!" Ramona Bradley said, her knitting needles working as fast as a machine. She owned the long-haired Dachshund.

"I can call her back," I said, thinking I'd have to wade into the fray to even catch her attention.

"Looks like they're having fun," Ramona said, pausing for a moment to push her glasses back up her nose.

Tails were wagging. For now.

"Grace, I've been meaning to ask you about that spray recipe you gave Alexis Burke," Lynette Dobbs said. She must be working the late shift at the urgent care center today. "She's raving about how good her house smells now. She wouldn't share. Tornado, I think she said."

"Volcano." I told her the recipe and spied several other

people taking notes. Here was my opening. "How do you bathe Rocco?"

Rocco was a Bichon Frisé with a wild mane of hair, almost like a lion. He looked overdue for a trim.

"As little as possible." Lynette laughed. "It's a battle every time. And it takes forever to blow dry him."

"You don't take him to a groomer?"

"A, not in the budget. It costs more than what I pay for a haircut. Ooh, there's an idea. Maybe I should ask Kenzie at the Hair Hut if she'd cut Rocco's bangs. B, I don't have an hour to waste on driving a dog to get a shampoo. Not with the hours I work."

"What if there was a local place you could shampoo your dog yourself with professional equipment— high sinks, dog dryers, grooming tables —for less money?"

"Well, now that would save my poor back and my wallet."

That started a discussion about bathing and who had it the toughest. Chairs shifted on both sides of the dog park until we formed a circle with a fence between us. The dogs' play had slowed down, but they were all still in motion.

"How about your shampoo and cleaners?" I asked the group. "Where do you get those?"

"Online's about the only place," Shannon Sandoval said, pushing the stroller at her side back and forth to keep her daughter sleeping. "The Country Store has a few things, but Dixie's sensitive skin needs fancy shampoo." She shook her head. "The things we do for these mutts."

An hour later, I hurried home, my brain crammed with ideas I needed to write down before they disappeared. Once in the kitchen, to the sound of Snick lapping water, I scribbled as fast as I could— eco-friendly, natural, refills, self-serve.

I had research to do, but it could work. Maybe, just maybe, I wasn't past my expiration date.

19

MAEVE

On Thursday, opening night, the fairgrounds at Candlewick Park swarmed with people and activity. Bright lights flooded the game area and the food court and eclipsed the stars on this clear, warm evening. Barkers pulled in passersby for games and rides. The clashing scents of fried dough, hot dogs and cotton candy wafted in the air. I'd hired a high school girl to man the bakery booth. I'd set her and the booth up, Zoe tagging along for company, and all seemed on track.

I was meeting Patrick and Neve at the gate in a bit, and Zoe and I were headed in that direction.

Zoe took a bite of the strawberry shortcake she'd just bought at a neighboring booth. "Not as good as yours."

"That's a given."

"Modest, too."

As we neared a garbage bin, Zoe reached out to drop her barely touched treat.

"You're wasting food." Something our mother had drilled into us not to do. I shook my head. I really was turning into her.

"Mom is right. You have turned into the food police." She

offered me the bowl. "It's not like they offer tasters. All I wanted was a bite."

I pushed the bowl away. "I can't."

"Why not?"

I sighed. "The profession I love makes people sick."

Zoe raised a brow. "A little dramatic, aren't you? I should dig up that tiara I gave you for your sixteenth birthday. And that Drama Queen sign."

"Neve's therapist suggested a bunch of books on nutrition." I swallowed hard. I'd read them all even though reading wasn't easy for me. "They all agree that sugar is evil."

"There's nothing wrong with a treat once in a while."

"That's the problem, though. It's not just once in a while. For a lot of my customers, it's a daily thing. A daily thing that keeps me in business." I made people sick. And all this time I'd thought I'd made them happy.

Zoe rolled her eyes and threw away the unwanted treat. Maybe she was on to something. Maybe I should sell taster sizes. Maybe selling smaller treats at a lower price would make merchandise move faster. But would customers go for that when what they expected was a hand-size bun, a muffin big enough to feed a family, or a pie a mile-high thick with filling?

"How are your plans for Mom's party going?" I asked her, trying to keep my mind off the constant sugar dilemma since Neve's diagnosis. I hadn't seen Mom since last week. She didn't answer her phone and communicated with notes tacked to my door. I had to find a way to fix this mess between us.

And the situation with Neve, and with Patrick, and with the bakery.

The timing sucked. I had too much going on right now to do anything right, which didn't bode well for the contest— the contest I needed to win to save the bakery and ensure Neve's future.

I would win, I told myself. I had to.

"Merry's got everything under control," Zoe said, hiking her colorful chakra tote bag back on her shoulder.

"Of course, she does." Meredith was nothing if not organized. The town's visitor numbers had gone up since she'd taken over the Tri-Town Tourism Coordinator job. "How long is her checklist?"

Zoe grinned. "A mile at least. Aaron's going to invite Mom to see the house they bought. He'll pretend that they're thinking about the house and ask for her opinion. And we all know how much Mom loves to give her opinion. While they're doing that, Merry and I will set up a cookout in the backyard. How's the cake coming along?"

With everything that was going on, I'd completely forgotten about Mom's birthday cake. "I said I'd have it done in time and I will."

"Just checking." Zoe bumped her shoulder into mine. "Don't look now, but Baseball Hunk is making googly eyes at you."

Yep, there was Luke, with his broad shoulders and stormy good looks, walking with a hitch to his stride as if he had somewhere important to go. My pulse did a little skip. He wasn't looking at me, was he? "Don't call him that. It's rude. Don't you have a class to teach about now?"

"I have a few more minutes before I have to leave."

Luke waved at me, then strode right by, headed toward the food truck court. I wasn't sure if I was relieved or disappointed. As promised, he hadn't fired the donut oil until tonight. I gave him points for that.

"Well, that was not satisfying," Zoe said.

"What do you mean?"

"It's fun to watch the sparks fly between you two."

"What sparks?"

She shook her head, then floated away toward the parking

lot. "See you later. Good luck tomorrow. I'll be cheering for you."

"Thanks," I said, distracted, searching the parking lot for Patrick and Neve.

"Maeve!"

That voice always brought me back to high school, to that fun, free... and foolish girl. I spun around. Patrick strode my way, Neve at his side, picking fluff off a purple cotton-candy cone. I narrowed my gaze at her.

"Mo-om," Neve said with a whine. "Just this once. Please, pretty please."

I gave her Mom's patented, guilt-producing look. I'd been on the receiving end often enough to get it just right.

"Not fair!" With a pout low enough to trip over, Neve deposited the sweet treat in the nearest garbage bin. Arms crossed, she stalked to the other side of her father, as far away from me as she could. I was the bad guy yet again to Patrick's fun parent. That one little thing reminded me I couldn't be that foolish girl anymore.

"Patrick," I said. I tried to let go of all the disappointments, to stay here in the present, but it was hard when I wasn't sure what his intentions truly were. I pasted on a smile. "You're here."

He tipped his head. "I said I would be."

He'd said a lot of things lately, and I had a hard time parsing the truth from the lies. *Stop it, Maeve! He's here. He's trying. Be together.*

"Where do you want to go first?" Patrick asked Neve.

She looked up to her father with stars in her eyes. Even after all her disappointments, she was willing to give him another chance.

"The carousel!" Neve took hold of each of our hands, swinging between us, heading toward the Christmas carousel Aaron had refurbished.

"Want to share a horse?" Patrick asked after he'd helped Neve on hers. His voice purred with heat and longing, melting a little more of my resolve.

"Sure." I settled on a gray with a red bridle. Patrick hopped on behind me, his arms folding around me as he held on to the pole. I leaned against him, letting him support me, waiting for the heat of desire to soften my insides the way it always did.

The music started. Neve looked back at us and giggled. Patrick waved back at her, making her smile widen.

This was what we were supposed to be. What we could still have.

So why didn't it feel right?

~

As we got off the ride, Neve spotted Charlie and yelled over at her. Charlie dragged poor Irene toward us. The girls hugged and jumped up and down. Charlie met my gaze. "Can Neve come with us?"

"Have fun," Patrick said before I could answer.

Neve turned to leave.

"Hey, not so fast, young lady," I said. Irene already looked exhausted. She didn't need another child to look after.

Neve stopped, both eyebrows hiking up in question.

I gave Patrick a what-gives look. "This was supposed to be our family time. Together."

He shrugged as if that meant nothing to him.

"Sorry about that," I said to Irene. "Do you want Neve tagging along?"

Irene let out a long breath. "She'd be doing me a favor."

Neve's time with Charlie was limited. She needed a friend right now. And yet, she needed time with Patrick, too. I glanced at my watch. "Let's meet back here in an hour."

"I can watch her overnight, if you'd like so you can get ready for tomorrow's competition," Irene said. "I know your mom's been busy with her new project and can't help you as much."

What new project? "Thanks, Irene, I would really appreciate that. Are you sure?"

"Absolutely. She can borrow a pair of Charlie's pajamas, and I have spare toothbrushes." She leaned over and whispered, "It's a big help for me to have someone entertain Charlie. I love my granddaughter, but she has no Off switch. I'll drop them off at camp and pick them up."

"That would be a great help." I hated to make a fuss when someone was going out of their way to help me. I had to admit that not having to worry about Neve would make getting ready for Day 1 of the contest tomorrow easier. "Would you mind keeping the sugar to a minimum? Neve's therapist has us trying a high-protein diet."

"Of course, dear. Is buttered popcorn okay with a movie?"

Not much better than sugar, but I nodded. "Thanks, Irene."

"Grandma! Hurry!" Charlie grabbed her grandmother's hand and tugged. "There's a baseball game I want to try."

"Duty calls." Laughing, Irene let herself get pulled away by the girls.

"Speaking of baseball," Patrick said, hooking his arm around my waist and slipping his hand into my back jeans pocket like he used to. He led us toward the bright lights of the games. "Neve's got quite the arm. Do you think she'll be an all-state champion like you?" His smile widened, lighting up his bad boy looks. "She's better than the boys on her team."

Where was he going with this? "Team sports aren't really her thing."

"You coddle her too much."

I stopped and faced him, and his hand slipped out of my pocket. "How would you know?"

He gave me a sad-puppy look. "Let's not do that right now."

I could feel my temper simmering with all the ways he'd let

us down the past nine years. "If not now, when? You haven't been around like you promised."

"You're ruining our evening." Now he was pouting— as if he was the injured party.

"I thought you wanted us to be a family."

"I do." He traced an arc on the dirt with the toe of his expensive sneaker. It felt like a line in the sand, that I was on shaky ground. "Can't I be proud of my daughter's skill?"

I tilted my head. "Of her skill or of the bragging rights?"

"Can't it be both?"

The crowd parted around us like water around rocks. Patrick didn't see Neve the way she was. The sweet girl with the eye for details. The cuddle bug who loved to read. The sensitive child who cared so fiercely. He just saw her skill as his success. It shouldn't surprise me—his mother had treated him that way. And his father, like him, hadn't been around for his kids. But Patrick had to take responsibility for his actions at some point and stop blaming his behavior on his past.

"No, actually," I said, stepping back from him so I could look him in the eye, "you can't have things both ways. You have a choice to make."

His brow furrowed. "What do you mean?"

"What are your intentions, Patrick? Toward Neve? Me?"

"The same as yours." He lifted his arms up as if his goal was obvious.

"Then where have you been since you got home? Actions speak louder than words."

His arms fell back down to his sides. "What do you want from me?"

He'd gotten the fun side of parenting, and I'd had to deal with everything else. "For one, I need for you to start paying child support."

He rolled his head back. "We've talked about this—"

"I know, the big plan that you won't talk about. Family,

marriage needs communication." Something I was doing all wrong with Mom. We had to sit down sometime soon and talk, really talk. "Sharing. What is this big plan? Why is it keeping you from taking care of your own child? I need extra help right now when I'm getting ready for this contest. A contest I need to win."

He shuffled his feet, staring at the ground as if it would give up an answer.

"How can we be a family if you're off by yourself all the time?"

He pinched his lips hard, then said on a long exhale, "I have the chance to get in on the ground floor of a new charter flight company based in Concord."

Concord was a doable commute. Even if he flew as crew on the charters, he could be home often. "Was that so hard?"

"No," he said, his smile reappearing. He reached for me and kissed me. And all I could think about was how dry and hard his lips were. "I should've done this sooner. This could set us up for a great future, Maeve."

He'd wanted to know he would succeed before sharing his plan. And yet...

For the first time in a long time, his promise failed to ignite hope.

20

GRACE

After dropping off the girls at camp on Friday morning, Irene and I drove to the nursery in Stoneley where Irene had offered to help me pick out plants to brighten up the patio in the backyard. Hopefully, she would throw in some upkeep tips because the family joke was that I had two black thumbs. That was the reason my only house-plants were of the succulent variety—they didn't require much care.

We wandered the aisles, the swirling scents of everchanging plant perfumes, soil, and moist mist surrounding us. I pulled a green cart with a squeaky wheel. Irene examined plants, her floppy sun hat bobbing with every move.

Irene sniffed at a pot of daylilies. "What effect would you like to have?"

"My goal for the backyard is to have a place where people feel comfortable. I want it to look nice and inviting. Everything I plant tends to die."

"We'll fix that." Irene put the plant back on the table. "What about bugs?"

"They're not invited."

Irene laughed. "Do you have a problem with them?"

"We have some tiki torches to keep the mosquitoes away. I'm not fond of using them when Neve's running around though."

She picked up a plant and pushed it under my nose.

"Oh, I love lavender."

"It helps keep bugs away." She put several containers on the cart. "So does peppermint."

"I can always use that for iced tea." If it stayed alive.

Irene nodded. "Basil and rosemary repel insects, too."

As she loaded enough herbs to start a restaurant onto the cart, I got the courage to ask her the question that had simmered since we'd dropped the girls off at camp. "Does Charlie have ADHD?"

"She was tested, but no. She's just highly energetic, which is why her parents enroll her in as many sports as possible."

Irene picked up a weedy looking thing. "This is citronella. It's part of the geranium family. They also call it the mosquito plant. You can crush the leaves on your skin and mosquitoes won't land."

She handed me a leaf that I distractedly rubbed on my arm. "I always thought of myself as a good mother."

"Of course, you are. Look at how well your kids turned out." She added two big containers of citronella to the cart.

"I'm starting to realize that maybe I wasn't for Maeve." I pulled the cart behind Irene, who moved on to the next table.

"What do you mean?"

"When Neve was diagnosed, I didn't want to believe it, because I was afraid the label would make her an outsider."

"People label each other all the time," Irene said, weeding through the plants with purpose. "The bully. The smart kid. The class clown." Her eyes crinkled. "The gossip. The snoop. The dragon lady."

True, but that didn't lessen the pain those labels could

cause. "Maeve had such a hard time at school. I didn't want that for Neve."

"But..."

"I'm confused," I admitted.

"About what?" Irene lifted two six-packs of petunias. "Pink or purple?"

"Neve likes purple. What if the ADHD label does get her extra help?"

"That would be a good thing." Irene dropped two six-packs of purple petunias on the cart. "Okay, let's go look at pots."

The pot shed contained planters of all shapes, sizes and colors. I picked up a clay pot glazed in a brilliant red. "I like that."

"Let's get a bunch for the herbs." She loaded pots onto the cart. "The thing you have to remember, Grace, is that we do the best we can with the information we have. You thought you were looking out for Neve's best interest because of what happened to Maeve."

"Except that it turns out I wasn't."

"But Neve isn't Maeve. Times have changed when it comes to ADHD and other developmental issues. Teachers are taught to look out for kids who might need some extra support. They want kids to succeed."

I squeezed my eyes shut for a moment. "I've also come to realize that the friction between Maeve and me is because I—" I stared at the cart, brimming with life and vibrancy. I'd dimmed my own child's sparkle. "Because I couldn't see things through her eyes."

"Oh, Grace." Irene reached an arm over and squeezed me into a hug. It made me want to cry.

I eased out of Irene's comfort, as if part of me felt I didn't deserve it. "When Maeve went on and on about the evils of sugar, I just dismissed it. I didn't take it seriously. How could one cookie wreck all of Neve's life?"

I added a purple-speckled pot for Neve to have a plant of her own. "What if I was wrong there, too? What if sugar does make Neve's ADHD worse?"

"Sugar is a hit to the brain." Irene laughed. "I try to keep it to a minimum for Charlie, too. There are other ways to be the fun grandma."

Irene lifted a sandaled foot, showing off blue paint deep under her toenail. "The other day, Charlie fingerpainted with her toes on this huge piece of paper that had come in a box of dog supplies. I really didn't want to take my shoes off and join her slip-sliding on paint, but she insisted. And we had a great time. For her, it'll be a good memory. Painting barefoot with Grandma in the backyard." She laughed. "Even if the paint never comes off."

"How did you get so smart?"

"The school of hard knocks. I made plenty of mistakes with my boys. Still do. When Tyler said he and Mona were divorcing, instead of being supportive, I nagged him to try to work it out." She headed toward the nursery once again. "Let's go check out."

The overloaded cart squealed in protest. "Turns out they already had." Irene shook her head. "There were things I didn't know. Shouldn't have needed to know to support my son."

As we waited in line, Irene said, "You've taken Neve on all sorts of field trips, so give yourself some grace. You're a good grandma, just like you are a good mom. She'll have plenty of good memories."

I blinked hard, tears surfacing again. "The outings I remember most all revolve around food. Picking out penny candy at the candy store in Stoneley. Tea parties in the backyard with all of Neve's stuffies. Stuffing ourselves with pancakes on Maple Weekend last March at Sanford's Sugar Shack." All the things I'd wished my own grandmothers would've done.

The clerk tallied up my purchases, and Irene nodded

toward the register. "It's about sharing memories, spending time together, not so much about what you do in them."

I pulled out my credit card. "I hope you're right."

I needed to find the courage to talk with Maeve. Soon. Before the situation became irreparable.

21

MAEVE

Today was the first day of the Strawberry Festival Sweet Spot Baking Contest. I woke up with a knot in my stomach, glad I didn't have to worry about getting Neve to camp this morning.

I hurried though my morning routine at the bakery, making sure to pack enough hand pies for my hired help to sell at the booth. Kayla would man the store during the festival. Not that I expected a huge day because everyone would be at the fairgrounds.

"What time do you need for me to arrive for the pie competition tonight?" Natalie asked as she got ready to leave after her breadmaking duties.

"It starts at 5, and we can set up our equipment at 4:30." I placed a hand on my heaving stomach. Why was I doing this again?

"Do not worry," Natalie said, exchanging her clogs for sneakers. "You have me, and we will be excellent."

I drew in a long breath. "I hope so."

"I will meet you here at 4, *oui*? To pack the van." Natalie glanced longingly toward the oven that needed replacing. "I have faith I will use a new oven soon."

"Thanks again, Natalie."

"*De rien.*" With that, she left.

But it wasn't nothing; it was everything. I was used to feeling alone, and having Natalie there to help organize my baking was a huge asset.

Of course, because I'd planned for a slow day due to the festival, the shop's bells on the door never stopped ringing. I'd run over to the sports field in the morning to catch a bit of Neve's exhibition game and to the fairgrounds at lunch to restock the booth and make sure the high school girl I'd hired was all set. I'd barely had a chance to drink coffee, let alone eat anything substantial.

An apologetic Irene dropped off Neve after camp to go to an appointment she'd forgotten about. Part of me wondered if having both girls was too much for Irene, who wasn't used to that much energy filling her home. "I'll be back, I promise."

So many people promising so many things. *Stop being so stubborn! Accept the help people offer you.* But trusting the follow through was hard for me. Trusting usually led to disappointment. And I needed everything to go perfectly today.

I tried calling Mom, but she still wasn't answering her phone. Neither was Patrick. I knew Zoe had a class coming up. Dad was at work. I had no choice but to keep Neve here with me. I sat her in the kitchen with paper and some colored pencils and helped Kayla take care of customers between stocking the cooler and bins for the contest.

Somewhere along the line, Neve got bored because when I came into the kitchen to finish packing my supplies for the contest, chocolate covered her lips. And not just any chocolate but the expensive Guittard chocolate batons I used in my chocolate croissants. The container sat on her lap. She tried to slide it under the baking table where she sat on a stool.

I hadn't had enough coffee for this. "Neve?"

She gave up on trying to hide the box and smacked it on the table. "I got hungry, and you weren't here."

Those words created a mountain of guilt. How often did I have to put the bakery first and ignore her needs? Especially lately with all the contest prep.

"How many?" I asked, trying to gauge the damage.

"Two." But she wasn't looking at me and her heels kicked at the stool.

"How many?"

She sighed the sigh of all sighs. "Fine. Three."

With a fourth melting in her hand.

I took the box and put it back where it belonged, making a mental note to store it higher. I went to the fridge and made her a snack of plain yogurt and strawberries.

She wrinkled her nose at it but ate it anyway. She really was hungry, which of course made the guilt bloom.

Natalie breezed in right on time, and we made short work of packing the rest of the supplies we would need to make the strawberry vanilla cream pie I planned for today's competition. Timing would be everything. I couldn't afford to let this mad day get to me. From the counter, I snatched the travel mug I'd filled with coffee. I'd need it to calm my nerves.

"Kayla!" I yelled from the back. "We're leaving."

"Everything's under control," she yelled back.

Everything, except my thoughts, running an obstacle race, and my nerves, snapping like water in hot oil.

I grabbed the last plastic container and headed toward the back door, Natalie and Neve in tow. "Let's go win this."

EVEN WITH THE COFFEE, the nerves didn't settle as I did my *mise-en-place* with Natalie at my assigned workstation under the big tent where twelve baking stations were set up, each with a long counter, a stove and a cooktop. If anything, the knot got bigger and tighter. I'd let Irene know we were at Candlewick Park. In the meantime, I'd sat Neve in the front row and ordered her to stay there. I dug through my bag and found a small notebook and pen to keep her busy. I gave her a snack pack of nuts in case she got hungry.

I was used to working alone. To folding inside myself when I baked. To letting the rest of the world melt away. Here, a section of VIPs sat in a tent, watching the twelve contestants prepare for the pie portion of the contest. Beyond the tent, milling festival goers could also stop and gawk at the event.

We were bugs under a microscope. Every misstep bound to show up on social media.

Dani and Luke had the station next to mine and Natalie's. I wasn't sure if that was a plus or a minus. I didn't need Luke's every movement distracting me from my task. I *needed* to win.

Dani wore a green "Donut Stress" T-shirt that made me smile. She covered it with a pink apron, then wound the pink strand of her hair around and around her index finger like Neve often did when she was stressed.

"You guys ready?" I asked, going over my recipe in my mind. My thoughts popped from one thing to the next. I needed to settle them and fast.

"As we'll ever be," Luke said. His bad leg seemed stiffer than usual, and it dawned on me that he was nervous, too. This was Dani's big chance, and he couldn't do anything except support her as best he could.

"You'll do fine, Dani. You've practiced and your pie is delicious." I chucked my chin toward the crowd. "And look, there's Colton." He gave Dani a thumbs-up. "He loved your pie."

Dani smoothed a hand over her pink apron and sent Colton a shy smile.

Regina Buchanan, clad in a white, short-sleeved wrap dress

adorned with strawberries and a straw hat with a clutch of strawberries on the side, stepped in front of the crowd of VIPs, mic in hand. "Good evening, everyone! Welcome to the Strawberry Festival Sweet Spot Baking Contest!"

She beamed at the crowd, waiting for applause. The locals knew their cue and clapped.

"This contest will spotlight the area's finest strawberries. Harmony Hill Farm generously provided the strawberries for today's contest." She held up a basket of berries similar to the one at our stations. "Nature's candy!"

I rolled my eyes. *Come on, Regina. Let's get going here.* Before the stress cracked me to pieces.

Regina turned to the baking tent. "Welcome, bakers! Tonight, you are tasked with making a sumptuous pie with strawberries as the hero. You will have exactly two hours to create your dessert."

She paused to hike tension. "Bakers, get ready!" She held up a red handkerchief and with a dramatic hand flutter, let it drop. "Bake away!"

I stared at my station and, for a second, I didn't know what to do. Natalie handed me a cup of flour. "Take a breath. You are the best baker here."

"No pressure, Nat." I laughed and that broke the tension.

Once I got going, I found the zone. The crowd, the other contestants, the world faded away to just me, Natalie and the pie. Natalie and I worked as seamlessly as dancers. We didn't even need words; she seemed to know what I needed just when I needed it.

I could do this. For Neve. For her future.

When the two-hour timer blared, my braid was a mess, my apron was covered with a crime scene's worth of strawberry juice, and my polo shirt was more sweat than cotton. But a gorgeous strawberry vanilla cream pie sat at the end of my station.

"Fingers crossed," I whispered to Natalie, and she waved away my concern.

While Regina prattled on about the sponsors of the contest, I took a first good look around. All the pies were as pretty as mine. I just had to hope my flavors were on point.

Regina called each baker to a table propped between the baking tent and the VIP viewing area. Beside her stood Sarah Mason, a celebrity chef who owned a summer home in the Lakes Region, and Peter Perl, a restaurant critic, of the *Perl's Picks* TV show out of Boston.

The judges tasted and whispered and finally arrived at a consensus. Regina reached for her mic, pumped up her chest and smiled so widely that the people at the back of the crowd could see it.

"Tonight, we will lose six bakers." She put on a sad face and named the six bakers who wouldn't be coming back for the cake competition on Saturday. "Thank you for your efforts."

Dani's eyes went wide, and her mouth dropped open as she realized she was still in the running. Good for her. Luke clapped her on the back, pride glowing on his face. She hugged him fiercely while jumping up and down. I searched the crowd, relieved to find Neve still where I'd sat her, playing with a heart-shaped strawberry-themed piece of fabric. Where had she gotten that?

No Mom. No Patrick. I shouldn't be surprised but it still hurt. How many times would Patrick have to disappoint me before I learned my lesson?

"In sixth place... we have Kenny McDaniel and his Mile-High Strawberry Pie," Regina said, making sure to draw out the announcement as long as she could. Kenny owned Bob's House Brewery and Pub. His pub food was quite good, but I hadn't realized he baked.

"In fifth place, Danielle Saunders and her Strawberry Tarte

Tatin with whipped cream sauce." Luke hooted and hugged his sister.

"In fourth place, Kimberly Kim with her Strawberry Peek-a-Boo Pie. Third, we have Delia Horton with her gluten-free Strawberry Pie with Streusel Topping. Second, Jake Cunningham and his Strawberry Jam Cookie Pie." Regina beamed at the crowd. "And the winner of the pie portion of the competition is our very own Maeve Carpenter with her Strawberry Vanilla Cream Pie! The judges all agreed this is the one pie they couldn't stop eating."

The crowd erupted in cheers. I recognized Aaron's and Zoe's voices calling my name.

Natalie leaned over. "I told you, *non?*"

"You did. Thanks, Natalie. Having you here made everything easier."

Luke reached across his work area and shook my hand, his grasp warm and solid— something you could count on. *Right, Maeve.* Brighton was a temporary stop for him. Come Monday, he, his sister and his donut truck would roll on down the road.

"Congratulations!" he said and meant it. That generosity of spirit had always surprised me during his playing days. I'd figured it as part of the persona he played. But his eyes, so clear and genuine, told a different story. One I couldn't get lost in. Not if I wanted to win.

I nodded and peeked around his broad shoulders. "Good job, Dani."

"I can't believe it." She pumped her heels up and down. "I couldn't have done it without you, Maeve."

"Give yourself more credit."

Regina pretend-whispered into the mic, "Maeve, I'll need three of those Strawberry Vanilla Cream Pies for my Fourth-of-July gathering."

The crowd laughed. I turned to Natalie, but she'd disappeared. I frowned. Where had she gone?

"And a great big thank you to our guest judges." Regina led the crowd in a round of applause.

"Come back tomorrow afternoon at 2 for the cake portion of the competition." With that, Regina put the mic down and circulated through the crowd of VIPs.

One down, two to go. I needed coffee. I needed food.

A crowd mobbed around Luke and Dani, I suspected more for Luke than Dani.

Neve ran to me and hugged me. "You did it, Mommy!"

And that made everything feel better. Winning this prize was, after all, for her.

"Hey, Mr. Luke!" Neve pulled away, gestured for Luke to crouch, and whispered in his ear, "I'm slaying the gremlins."

What on earth?

"That's great, Neve," he said, giving her a high-five.

Then she lifted the pink heart at Dani. "It did make it easier to sit."

Dani gave her a thumbs-up. "Glad the fidget helped."

Before I could process what was going on between the Saunders' and Neve, Luke looked up at me. "Join us for dinner?"

No, I shouldn't. Yes, I wanted to. "The cake competition..."

He shrugged a shoulder. "You've got to eat. I hear they have the best donuts here."

I shook my head, chuckling. Dani and Neve would be there. It wasn't a date. It was a practicality. And Neve and I did have to eat dinner before I went back and practiced my cake for tomorrow. "Let's go hunt down some protein for a hungry girl."

Neve slipped the fabric heart in her pocket and glared at me.

"Hamburger," I said, scrubbing a hand over her head.

She grabbed one of Luke's hands and one of mine. "Let's go! I'm starving!"

I couldn't help wishing that Patrick stood in Luke's place.

22

GRACE

Snick hadn't been herself all day. She'd thrown up last night's dinner before breakfast, so I'd left her home while Irene and I went to the nursery. Since we'd come back, Snick had thrown up some white foam. Then more white foam. She'd moped around, going from bed to couch to sunny patch in the living room.

She'd splayed on the cool slate patio outside while Irene showed me how to plant our purchases and take care of them.

As I ate my lunch, she'd pawed at me, wanting to snuggle. I had to admit that I did love those snuggles. But I was worried about her. She didn't try to sniff out my sandwich or snag a carrot stick. Her usual M.O. was to find as many ways as possible to get into trouble. And she hadn't found one yet today.

After lunch, figuring her stomach might be ready for food, I added a bit of cheese— her favorite treat— to her breakfast kibble, but she just turned up her nose at it. I tried taking her to the dog park, but she wasn't interested in playing or sniffing. She just laid down and watched the other dog in the enclosure frolic. Once back home, she sploofed on the cool tiles of the kitchen floor and laid there like a bear rug.

"Are you missing Neve?" I asked her as if she could answer. Neve had spent the night at Irene's with her friend Charlie. She'd spent a lot of time with Charlie lately. Which was my fault because I'd made a point not to be around when Maeve was home. But the house sure was quiet without that whirlwind of a girl around.

Still, I had to stick to my boundaries, didn't I? I couldn't let Maeve walk all over me when it suited her and ignore me the rest of the time.

Snick licked her lips and gave me sad eyes.

When she still hadn't eaten her breakfast by late afternoon, I knew something was wrong. Snick was nothing if not food motivated. That's when I noticed her nose was desert dry. I checked her water bowl. It was still full. "You have to drink something, Snick."

But Snick turned her head away from the bowl and curled into a tight donut in her bed. She didn't even want an ice cube.

I glanced at the clock— just after four. Was the vet clinic still open?

Win, Dr. Shaffer's daughter and assistant, answered the phone. I laid out the whole situation.

"Mom's busy stitching up a bite. I'll have her call you when she's done."

I paced the kitchen for what seemed forever. I made the mistake of googling Snick's symptoms and found a myriad of horrid possibilities from obstruction to parasites to liver failure. The mutt did like to hide socks. What if she'd ingested one and I hadn't noticed? She also liked to sample everything on our walks. Her favorite forbidden snack: rabbit droppings. What if they were filled with parasites or bacteria? Finally, before my mind spiraled into the possibility of kidney failure if she didn't hydrate, the phone rang.

"It's normal for a dog to throw up once in a while," Ava said after asking all sorts of questions about the vomit.

My grip on the phone tightened. "She hasn't eaten or drank anything, though. All day. And you know how much she loves food."

"Her tummy may be a little sore. Think about the last time you threw up. You didn't feel like eating for a bit."

She was right, of course. But it wasn't as if I could offer Snick some chicken noodle soup and soda crackers. "Is there anything that would help her stomach?"

"You can try a little plain chicken and rice."

I could do that. Doing something was much better than sitting around, worrying.

"But don't force her to eat," Ava said. "She'll eat when she's ready."

"She's not drinking, either. I don't want her to get dehydrated." Especially because the temperature outside was so hot.

"You can try a little broth. Just make sure it has no garlic, onions, or salt."

I nodded, then remembered to talk. "Broth. No garlic, onion, or salt. Got it."

"Keep an eye on her," Ava said. "If she throws up again, or if she's not better in the morning, call me."

I petted Snick in her bed and placed her water bowl within reach. When Ansel came in from work early, I charged him to watch her while I ran to the market for chicken. He wasn't good at picking out groceries even with a list of specifics.

"Maeve's competition starts soon," Ansel said, looking at me over the top of his glasses.

So that was why he was home early.

"That's today?" But I couldn't seem to focus. All I saw were Snick's pain-filled eyes, her lying there in pain. I hadn't felt this helpless since Zoe's kidnapping in college.

He glanced at his watch. "It starts about now."

"Oh." I was torn, of course. Maeve, for all her bravado, needed encouragement. Although never from me. I sighed. "She doesn't need me. Aaron and Zoe will be there. And when I get back from the market, you can go, too."

"She does need you, Grace."

I shook my head. "Snick is sick, and I'm so worried about her."

He chuckled. "Good thing you didn't want a dog."

I didn't want her, but I didn't want her to suffer either. I blinked my eyes fast, but tears still formed. Blast Lark and her dog matchmaking. How had Snick managed to worm her way into my heart so quickly?

Ansel opened his arms to me, and I let him hug me. "She's going to be fine," he said, kissing the top of my head. "We'll take her to the vet in the morning. For your peace of mind."

I nodded against his shoulder. He was a good man, a patient man. I was so glad he was mine. My grip scrunched his shirt at the shoulders, and a truth spilled out I hadn't known was true. "I can't lose her."

After dinner in the food court at the fairgrounds, Neve squirmed in her seat at the picnic table. "I have to *go*."

"Okay," I said, gathering up the detritus of our hamburger dinner.

"I'll take her," Dani said, springing up. "I need to go, too."

"Are you sure?" I scrunched papers and napkins and Neve's bun into a ball.

Dani offered her hand to Neve, who took it as if she'd known Dani forever. Something she rarely did.

"We'll meet you at the Batter Up game," Luke said, dropping his empty water bottle in the recycling bin. Half his mouth quirked up. "I want to win a prize."

"For me?" Neve asked, hope on her face.

Luke gave her a pensive look. "Okay, two prizes. One for you and one for your mom."

For me? My pulse skipped a beat. Why?

Neve gave him a thumbs-up and skipped with Dani toward the porta-potties bathed in orange light from the setting sun.

"Make sure she uses the hand sanitizer," I called after them.

"Mo-om!"

I lobbed the ball of garbage into the can, and it swooshed right in. "So, you're going to win me a prize, huh?"

"You look kind of sad for someone who won a pie contest an hour ago."

I'd actually forgotten. It still irked me that neither Patrick nor Mom had shown up. That I was stuck competing to save my bakery, to pay all the bills for Neve's therapy and coaching, when I just wanted to bake alone in my own kitchen. I'd never been one for the limelight, preferring the kitchen to the front of the store. "I have a lot going on."

With a hand to my lower back, he imprinted a palm of heat that shouldn't feel good on such a hot evening and steered me toward the game area. "Talk to me."

"I don't think so." I couldn't even catch all the thoughts battling in my mind, let alone make enough sense of them to discuss them with anyone. Especially a stranger.

I glanced at Luke, who smiled, waved and nodded at people who called out to him. What did I know about him, really? This could all be part of his game for Dani to win the contest. Charm the competition. Let her forget her goal. I shook my head. If that was his game, I feared it might work.

We found the Batter Up game— an inflated red-blue-and-white mini-field with a cartoon batter waiting for a pitch. A series of holes dotted the back wall. Put three balls through the holes, and you won a prize.

Luke bought a ticket, then raised an eyebrow asking if I wanted one, too.

"Sure, Donut Guy." I rolled my right shoulder. "A pitcher beats a shortstop every time."

He chuffed. "When was high school? You're out of practice."

"So are you."

He narrowed his gaze and negated the intensity of his glare with a smile. "Game on!"

Beeps from other games and shouts from winners and losers and carnival music filled the air. All the bright lights hid the stars in the darkening sky. The scent of summer and food and fun hung like a cloying cloud over the fairgrounds.

We both failed at our first attempt, missing two out of three balls. A whisper went through the crowd and people lined up to watch the action.

"Practice run," he said, rolling his shoulder. "Had to get the lay of the land."

I nodded. "These games are rigged, you know."

"Still gonna win you a prize." Luke bought two more tickets. He got two balls in and missed one. The crowd aah-ed as one.

"Let me show you how it's done," I said. In my mind, I made the center hole three times as big as it was— a trick I'd used when I pitched —and the three balls slid in, one after the other. I knocked my shoulder into his, then took a bow. "And that's how you do it."

He laughed, put on a game face, and bought another ticket. Three balls went in as if pitched by a machine. He turned back to me, quirking a grin. "I didn't want to overshadow you when you were feeling so blue."

"Sure, sure. Methinks it's all those donuts." I poked at his hard abs.

He laughed.

The gathered crowd thinned. A few holdouts stuck around, looking for an autograph. Luke graciously chatted and signed everything from T-shirts to soda cans. While Luke played to his fans, I picked out a stuffed puppy that looked like Snick for Neve.

Luke came up behind me and pointed to a hedgehog, so close for a second, I forgot to breathe. "That one, for my prickly friend."

Friend? He considered me a friend? Or was that something he would have said no matter who stood by his side?

"Hey, who are you calling prickly?" I elbowed him, and he made an exaggerated *oof!*

He presented me with the hedgehog. "I can admit that you have a good arm."

"Why, thank you, sir." I accepted the stuffed animal and cradled it in the crook of my arm along with the puppy, feeling much too warm. After sweating through the contest and with the too-warm evening, I needed a long, cool shower.

Dani and Neve appeared. Neve's gaze gravitated to the stuffed animals in my arms. She beamed up at Luke. "You did it!"

Luke wrapped an arm around my shoulder and gave it a little squeeze before dropping his hold. "We both did."

Neve reached her hands toward me with give-me fingers. "Can I have the puppy?"

"That was fun," Luke said, once we were on our way again, milling through the crowd and the noise.

"It was." I glanced at the clock on my phone. "I need to get this one to bed. And prepare for tomorrow."

"Me, too," Dani said, the happiness on her face turning to concern. Was the stress of the competition getting to her?

"Just bake your cake like you did in practice, and you'll do fine." I turned to Luke. "Do you need a ride to the B&B?"

"Yeah, that would be great." Relief edged his voice. His other choice, given the donut truck was parked in the food truck court for the duration of the festival, was the shuttle to town hall, where he was certain to get cornered by fans. The area's one taxi was bound to require a long wait tonight.

Once at the B&B, Dani hopped out and waved. "I'll see you later."

I waited for Luke to get out, but he shook his head. "I'll see you home."

I rolled my eyes, drove to my parents' house, and parked the van.

"Can I go see Snick?" Neve asked.

Both Mom and Dad's cars were in the driveway. The TV was going in the living room and the curtain showed Dad's outline on his recliner. "Just for a few minutes. I'm going to run to the bakery to drop off my stuff, then come tuck you in."

I watched her go in and join my parents in the living room, then turned to Luke and held up the hedgehog. "Thanks, I had fun."

"Glad to oblige." He climbed back in the van.

"What are you doing?"

"I'll give you a hand with your boxes."

He was stubborn. Almost as stubborn as I was.

I parked the van in the back of the bakery, unlocked the door and reached for the plastic containers.

"Leave that one," I said, pointing to the bin with the stand mixer. "I'll be using all that again tomorrow."

As he hefted the box with the dirty tools and took it to the sink counter, I noticed his leg had stiffened. "You need to take care of that leg, or you won't do Dani any good."

"There's a hot tub at the B&B."

On our second trip out to the van, I said, "Hey, I meant to ask you, what was all that slaying gremlin talk with Neve earlier?"

He slid bins closer to the edge of the van. "Remember when she was about to meltdown at her practice game?"

I nodded.

"When I was in high school, I had a temper." He grinned. I could see how he might have been a handful. "And one of my coaches taught me to play whack-a-mole with my gremlins. I just passed on the tip."

The quirk of his shoulder said it was no big deal, but for Neve it was. She had a tool that was working for her.

"What about that heart Dani gave her?"

"It's a fidget. Something Dani uses to deal with her anxiety.

There's a hard ball in with some herbs and rolling it around her hands helps calm her down."

I'd seen the poppers and spinners kids sometimes used as fidget tools, but they were so noisy they got on my nerves. This one gave her the sensory stimulation without the noise. "It was nice of Dani to share."

He gave another no-big-deal shrug. "Neve reminds me a lot of Dani when she was little. So focused and fierce, yet so anxious and shy."

He'd nailed Neve. Something her own father had failed to do.

On our third trip from the van, I blurted out, "I watched that infamous game."

"Not my finest moment." He hefted the cooler and left me behind.

"Accidents happen," I said, catching up with him.

He nodded as if unconvinced and snapped the cooler onto the table in a way that said *leave this alone.* "I'd just heard that my parents had gotten in a car accident and my mind wasn't all on the game."

"I'm so sorry." The cooler lid creaked as I opened it. "Is that when they died?"

He nodded and his gaze became a roiling storm.

I was sorry I'd taken him to the worst time in his life. Losing his parents and his career on the same day couldn't have been easy.

I pulled leftover cream and eggs and butter from the cooler and placed the items in the fridge. "Why baseball?"

"I was good at it." He leaned against the stainless-steel table, arms crossed over his chest, pensive... vulnerable. "All I ever wanted was baseball. I mean, I knew it had an expiration date, but I didn't want to think about it. Plus, it got me my dad's attention. He traveled a lot, so those games when he was there were priceless."

For every home game I'd played, every school program, every achievement, I'd had my family around. How good it felt to have someone cheering for you. I grabbed my cake recipe for tomorrow's contest and gathered the dry ingredients I'd need. I understood, too, what it was like to lose a dream. "You could still have baseball, couldn't you? You could coach."

He made a face as if the thought was bitter. "I've had it with travel."

And here I was longing for it. I snorted. "That's why you're driving all over New England in a food truck."

He gave a small chuckle. "I don't like the idea of Dani alone in that thing. Not just because it's old and could break down in the middle of nowhere, but there are all sorts of jerks out there, looking to take advantage of a woman alone. And Dani tends to see the good in everyone."

Dani was sweet. No one would dare mess with her with Luke standing beside her. She was lucky. "So, you're going to live her dream for her?"

He tipped his head to one side. "For now. Till I figure out what I want."

"Then what? You'll let Dani go out on her own again and face the big, bad world?" I gathered the refrigerated ingredients and placed them all on one shelf for easy retrieval tomorrow.

"I'll see where she lands, then decide. I promised my parents I'd take care of her."

And, Luke, unlike Patrick, kept his promises. The good mood that had returned dimmed. "She's all grown up."

"She'll always be my baby sister. And I'll always be her big brother."

Someone she could count on.

He and Dani were the competition, I reminded myself. He was as determined to secure Dani's future as I was to secure Neve's. I couldn't let his charm distract me from my goal.

I had to win.

Somehow, that didn't feel as good as it had when I signed up for the contest.

WHEN I RETURNED HOME, I found Dad trying to sweet-talk Neve into pajamas, and Neve trying to sweet-talk Dad into more time with Snick.

"What's going on here?" I asked, too exhausted to deal with another problem today. I just wanted to belly flop into bed and stay there until morning. "Where's Mom?"

"Snick's sick," Neve said with a pout. "Grandpa won't let me help make her better."

"Snick probably needs her rest," I said. The last thing a sick dog needed was all of Neve's energy fussing over her.

"We're going to take her to the vet in the morning." Dad handed me the Wonder Woman pajamas. "Dr. Ava will fix Snick in no time."

"You can visit Snick tomorrow after she comes back from the vet." I turned her around and propelled her toward the bathroom. "Now go put your pjs on and brush your teeth, or we won't have time for reading."

She raced to the bathroom and the buzz of her electric toothbrush soon echoed around the small room.

I walked Dad to the door. "Thanks, Dad."

"You're welcome, sweetness. And, hey, congratulations on your pie win. I'm sorry we weren't there to see it. Your mom had me watching the dog while she ran to the market to get some chicken and broth. Apparently, I'm not to be trusted in a grocery store."

Mom was so lucky to have a supportive partner like Dad, someone who was there, someone who went along with all her crazy ideas just because he loved her and wanted to please her. Did she know it, or did she take him for granted? "It's fine.

Aaron, Meredith and Zoe were there. It's enough to embarrass anyone."

"Good luck tomorrow." He gave me a side-arm hug.

"Thanks." I hesitated, hanging on to the doorknob with more force than needed, then said. "Hey, tell Mom I hope Snick gets well soon. She will, won't she?"

"She probably ate something she shouldn't have. She should be fine in a couple of days." He shook his head in a good-natured way. "But you know you mom..."

"She's going to worry." Worrying was her superpower.

"Yep."

After finishing her nightly routine, Neve fixed her room just the way she liked it, her own little world—fan on, stuffed animals placed just so, herself nestled in the middle of the bed, book at the ready. Today's choice: *Howl's Moving Castle*.

"A moving castle," I said, settling in next to her little girl sweat and mint scent. No time for a bath this late. She needed her rest more. According to her therapist, the consistent bedtime and getting-up time were the key to an even mood.

"That sounds intriguing."

"It's got a witch and a spell and a fire demon."

I exaggerated a frown. She loved all this fantasy stuff, and it didn't seem to bother her sleep. "Won't that give you nightmares?"

"'Course not!"

I cracked open the book and, trying to delay reading, talked about camp instead. I'd managed to get away to watch an hour of her exhibition game that morning. "Great game today."

"Yeah, I got two home runs."

I high-fived her. "I saw. So you had fun at baseball camp?"

She skewed her mouth to one side. "I had fun with Charlie."

"Oh?"

"The other kids were mean."

"I'm sorry about that." I wanted to cover her in bubble wrap to keep her safe forever.

She looked up at me with her big, soulful eyes. "On Monday, can I go to art camp?"

"Of course. They're still waiting for you." That was good news for my savings account. No paying for two camps next week.

She cuddled closer to my side. "Some of the boys said that Mr. Luke is leaving soon."

He'd never meant to stick around. Something I needed to remind myself. "Well, yes, he and Dani are here just for the baking contest."

"Oh." She plunged her hand around her stuffies and came out with the fidget heart. "Dani gave me her heart for when I feel bad."

"Are you feeling bad now?"

She squished the ball inside the fidget. "I'm sad. I like Mr. Luke and Dani. They're nice to me."

"Yeah, they are nice. And it was really good to meet them, wasn't it?" They'd certainly turned my world upside down with their donut truck.

She nodded, pensive. "Boys all have cooties."

"What about Grandpa and Uncle Aaron? Mr. Luke?"

"Well, okay, maybe not *every* boy. But most of them."

I had to agree with her. I was sad for her that "most of them" included her own father.

Neve nudged me with her elbow. "Better hurry, Mommy, or we won't have time to read."

I laughed as she threw back my own words. That kid was the best thing in my life.

Patrick had no idea what he was missing.

24

MAEVE

Saturday was the hottest day of the year yet. This kind of heat would melt icing, curdle cream, and keep fillings from setting. And with the time to produce a finished cake tight, this stage of the competition could prove a nightmare. And, of course, I'd chosen to bake a strawberries and cream cake which was covered in vanilla whipped cream, a family favorite, instead of something new and exciting. Natalie had convinced me that, with my secret spice, the cake was more me than the fancy one I'd come up with. Why hadn't I checked the weather forecast before settling on a recipe? Too late now to change my mind. I made sure to pack some stabilizing gel.

Neve was safe with Irene and Charlie. Mom's dog was still sick, so she probably wouldn't be here again. It was fine. She was still mad at me. I thought I saw Aaron and Meredith earlier. Maybe they'd stop by. Natalie was here, helping me set up. It was all going to be absolutely fine.

I had to concentrate on baking the best cake I could. I would deal with Mom after the contest.

By two o'clock, just standing had sweat slicking my skin. At least every other contestant was in the same situation. The scent of rain hung in the heavy air and that made the carnival sugar and roasted meat smells more cloying. I picked at the front of my shirt, trying to get some relief from the heat, humidity and hopping thoughts. If I made it through this, I would never enter a contest again.

Dani leaned over toward my station. "This weather isn't good for baking."

"It's going to be a real test of all our skills, that's for sure."

She swallowed hard, her eyes taking up much of her face. She glanced at Luke, who was busy helping her set up her station. "I want to win this for him."

She was a good kid. "He'll be proud of you, no matter what."

Something I realized was absolutely true.

I was rechecking my station, making sure I had everything, when Natalie's phone rang. She frowned at her phone, then gave me sorry-I-have-to-take-this look, turned her back and spoke in rapid French. Natalie never got calls. I never saw her with anyone. So, I had to admit, I was curious. When she turned back, her face was ghost-pale.

"What's wrong?" I asked.

She slipped her phone into her apron pocket as if she were moving through a vat of honey. "My mother, she is in hospital. *Une crise de coeur.* A heart attack."

Her pinched face told me the direness of the situation. "Go," I said, waving her toward the baking tent's exit. "Go be with your family."

"But—" She looked around her as if lost. "I promise."

"It's fine. I'll be fine." I was used to baking alone. "Family comes first."

She nodded but stood unmoving. "Bread is not complicated like people."

Not sure where she was going with that. But if her family was anything like mine, complicated didn't begin to explain our relationships. And no matter how angry I was with any of them, if something happened, I'd go to them if possible. "Go, you have to."

She nodded again, gathered her bag with zombie moves, and lumbered away with unsteady steps. "Just be yourself, Maeve, and you will win."

Worried about her mother, she wouldn't have done me any good anyway. I reminded myself to check on her tonight.

I reached for my travel mug of coffee, took a steadying slug of java. Then another. My station was ready. It was okay. I'd be okay. I could do this. I could bake a simple cake.

Regina's voice penetrated the scramble of my thoughts. "Bakers, on your mark."

I looked up in time to see the red handkerchief fluttering down. "Bake away!"

When times were tight, another pair of hands to measure and prep was handy. I hadn't realized how much Natalie had done to organize me and smooth the baking process for me. If I won, she was getting a raise.

Having to do everything myself, I let the ticking clock get to me. Each tick sounded like a bomb. Each minute left me further behind. Reminding myself to breathe, to stay in the zone wasn't helping.

"Maeve?" Dani's strangled voice floated across her workstation. "My whipped cream is melting."

"Stabilize it." I pushed my container of stabilizer toward her end of my workstation.

She reached over for the can. "You're a life saver."

Five minutes to go. My whipped cream wasn't doing great in spite of the stabilizer because of the heat and humidity. I stuffed the whole thing in the fridge while I sliced extra strawberries for the topping.

I still had a few strawberries to place on the top when the time buzzer went off. I had to hope that was enough.

"Your time is up!" Regina said with glee. Today, she wore a red skirt, a white short-sleeved blouse, a red straw hat and a strawberry necklace and earrings. She picked up a basket of strawberries. "Today's berries were provided by Riverbend Farms. Make sure you stop by their booth and buy some of your own to take home. They are delicious!"

I looked around at the competition. All the cakes looked fancier than mine. I should've gone for spectacular instead of an old standby I knew tasted great.

Regina shifted toward the tasting table, inviting the other two judges, Sarah Mason and Peter Perl, up with her. "Now, it's time to test these cake creations."

The three judges tasted each one in turn.

"Oh, this isn't good," Regina said as she sliced into Jake Cunningham's PB&J Cake. "It's like a river of jam."

His strawberry jam hadn't set properly. His face turned as red as the sauce on the plate. Maybe I still had a chance.

"This cake is overbaked," Sarah said, picking away at Kenny's yellow cake with layers of strawberries and cream. It did indeed look too dry. The strawberry gel between his layers had managed to set, though.

"I agree," Regina said, moving on to the next.

Kimberly Kim's strawberry matcha cake looked spectacular with its pink and green stripes.

"I'm afraid the matcha overpowers the strawberries," Peter said, smacking his lips as if trying to dissipate a bad taste. "What a shame. It's such a beautiful presentation."

"This one brings me back to my childhood," Sarah said, reaching for a second forkful of Dani's cake. "Like a bite from a strawberry ice cream bar."

I smiled over at Dani, who took in a deep breath and held it, wringing her hands.

Next came Delia Horton's vegan rhubarb and strawberry

crumble cake. "It's interesting," Peter said, giving the cake a strange look, then going back for a second taste.

"This is a classic cake," Sarah said, slicing into my cake.

I held my breath, hoping the layers would stay together in this oppressive heat. I let my breath go when the slice came out whole and the whipped cream stayed firm.

"Oh, this cake may look simple, but it tastes divine," Regina said. She put her fork and napkin down. "As you know, only three bakers will move on to the third and final round to battle for the one-hundred-thousand dollar prize." She put on a pouty face. "That means that sadly, we'll have to say goodbye to three of you."

The judges knotted on the other side of the tasting table by the VIPs, who could overhear their discussions. While we waited for the judges' decision, my gaze roved the crowd. Aaron and Meredith were there, holding hands. I was glad for Aaron that he'd found someone but sad for myself that my own story wasn't going to have a happy ever after.

Zoe crowded in with Irene and the girls. Mom and Dad weren't there. I knew they were dealing with Snick's illness, that the dog needed them. Yet, I couldn't help wishing they were there for me. Mom and I really needed to talk.

And search as I might, I couldn't find Patrick in the crowd either. So much for wanting to make a life together.

I'd never be able to depend on him.

The realization hit me like a slap. I'd waited all these years for nothing. He wasn't going to change. He wasn't suddenly going to morph into the father Neve needed. Into the husband I wanted. My throat tightened and I reached for my coffee mug, which was, of course, empty.

I blinked away the tears that burned like lye. I wouldn't cry for him. He didn't deserve any more of my tears.

Regina picked up the mic and smiled her most benevolent

smile. "This was a tight race, and the judges weren't unanimous in their choices, but our final ranking is as follows: Maeve Carpenter, Danielle Saunders, and Delia Horton. Congratulations, ladies! We will see all three of you tomorrow at noon in the tent for the third and final phase of the competition: the sharing basket filled with individual pies, cupcakes and cookies."

Over at her station Dani squealed, jumping up and down and hugging Luke, so happy for her win. Luke looked so proud of his sister. Was Patrick ever there like that for me, for Neve? His absence wasn't making me feel loved and wanted. I'd been a fool to hang on to this dream of making a family with him for so long. Zoe was right. Love shouldn't be one-sided.

The crowd cheered. Aaron whistled. Merry clapped. Zoe and Neve yelled. These were the people I could count on to be there for me no matter what happened.

Dani took off her apron, revealing a pink "Donut Give Up" T-shirt.

I didn't want to give up on Patrick.

But I had to.

25

GRACE

I'd had a restless night, worrying about Snick. She was still refusing food and, most worrisome of all, water. Her nose was dry. Her gums were dry. Her skin sagged. Google promised kidney failure if dehydration went on for much longer.

I'd called Dr. Shaffer first thing this morning, but she'd had an emergency and couldn't see us until noon. Ansel had dropped us off, then gone to run some errands for me. I felt bad for missing Maeve's competition two days in a row. I'd make it up to her with a special celebration at Sunday dinner after the competition. I'd explain then. Hopefully, she'd understand.

I sat in the waiting room, with cartoon puppies romping around the chair rail of the celery-green walls. Snick laid on my lap like a blanket, unmoving. And that wasn't like her at all. If she was awake, she was sniffing or trolling or getting into trouble. She'd already added a new layer of liveliness to the house.

I stroked her coat that felt much too saggy beneath my hand, willing her to get well. "You can't do this to me," I told her. "You can't make me like you and then die."

She made a pitiful attempt at licking my hand, her tongue so dry it felt like sandpaper on my skin. "Save your spit, Snick."

Ava strode into the waiting room, zeroing in on Snick. "Hey, pretty girl, what's going on with you?"

The tip of Snick's tail went up and down.

"Poor baby. You look miserable." She glanced at me. "Let's get her up on a table and see what's going on."

In the exam room, Ava examined Snick, who laid sideways on the rubber mat on the stainless-steel table without moving. "She has a bit of a fever. Her tummy's bloated and tender. And you're right, she is dehydrated."

"What does all that mean? Will she be okay?"

"It could mean many things. I'll take some X-rays to see if there's an obstruction. Take some blood to check for an infection. And I'll give her some fluids under the skin for the dehydration." Ava reached for Snick. "Come on, pup, let's see what's up with you." She cradled Snick in her arms. "I'm going to take her to X-ray. She'll be back soon. We'll take good care of her, okay?"

I nodded, throat too dry to talk.

I sat on the plastic chair, wishing I'd brought a book to help make the time pass more quickly. I tried to play a word game on my phone but couldn't concentrate. All I could see was Snick's eyes, begging me to help her. Her lying unmoving on the cool tile floor. Her nose so dry. I couldn't help it, the tears flowed. I hadn't even wanted the stupid dog, and now she was making me worry about her.

"You better not die," I told the empty room.

An eternity later, Ava returned, Snick walking beside her. She already looked better and sported a hump on her back. "What's wrong with her?"

"I injected some water under her skin. This should take care of the dehydration."

Snick, tail wagging, insisted on jumping onto my lap. I held her close and stroked her ears. She leaned her head on my chest and I, once again, had to fight tears.

Ava brought her phone over, showing me the X-ray. "Her gut looks clean. It doesn't mean that there isn't something stuck in there. I'm just not seeing anything right now. See those bubbles there?"

She pointed to some spots on the X-ray. "Those are gas. That's probably what's hurting. Everything else— liver, spleen, kidneys, bladder —looks normal. I checked for a bladder infection. There are signs something's going on, so I'm going to send it out to be cultured."

She stroked Snick's head. "All signs point to gastroenteritis — an inflammation of the gut."

She put her phone back in the pocket of her lab coat. "I'm going to prescribe metronidazole for the inflammation and some low-fat dog food. It'll be easier for her to digest. She should be feeling better by tomorrow. If not, give me a call Monday morning and we'll run more tests. How does that sound?"

"Like a plan." I fiddled with the straps of my purse. "What could have brought on the gastroenteritis?"

Ava shrugged. "She probably ate something that didn't agree with her." She gave Snick a loving scratch under the chin. "No more of that, young lady."

As if she agreed, Snick gave a wag of her tail.

Win set us up with the medicine and the prescription dog food. Already, Snick had a little more pep in her step and her nose looked moist.

"For a free dog, you sure are expensive," I told her as I buckled her seatbelt. She curled up like a donut, ready for the ride.

As I drove home, a giant wave of relief flowed through me. Snick would be okay. I wouldn't lose her like I'd lost my sense of purpose and direction.

Later that evening, after Neve was in bed, Snick snored in her bed by the television where Ansel watched a baseball game. I couldn't tell who was playing, nor did I care. Instead, I trolled the internet on my laptop for product for my new venture— a self-serve pet care boutique I was thinking of calling Wash 'n Wags. I chuckled to myself at the tagline I'd come up with: "Come dirty, leave happy." I was making good headway.

Snick had turned up her nose at the prescription food, but she had accepted some of the chicken and rice I'd made the day before. She'd even lapped at her water, though not as much as I wanted.

As if she knew I was thinking about her, she got up, stretched and hopped onto the sofa next to me. She pawed at my arm until I moved the laptop, giving her access to my lap, where she curled up. Which, I had to admit, I didn't mind even though it felt as if I was wearing a fur coat on this hot night. I scratched behind her ear, and she licked my hand.

Something in my heart turned over.

The doorbell rang much later than usual. Snick lifted her head and made an attempt at a bark but didn't trot to the door to confront whoever dared to disturb us like she usually would. I slid her onto the sofa.

Of all the people that could have knocked on the door, the last person I expected to see there was Luke Saunders.

Tail wagging, Snick wriggled around me to get to the man, insisting on licking the skin right off the poor man's ankle. I grabbed her collar and pulled her back. "Enough, Snick!" I looked up at Luke. "Sorry, she can't hold her licker."

He crouched down to her height and scratched her under the chin. "It's fine. I love dogs. Always wanted one. But travel and pet care don't go well together."

"Is there anything I can do for you?"

He looked up at me, still petting Snick, and smiled. "I was looking for Maeve."

"She lives in the apartment around the back. But she's not home. She's at the bakery, getting ready for tomorrow's competition."

"Who's there?" Ansel asked from the living room.

"Luke Saunders."

"Have him come on back."

I opened the door wider. "Ansel is a huge fan of yours. Would you mind saying hello?"

"I'd be glad to."

In the living room, the men shook hands.

"Take a seat," Ansel said, pointing to his own recliner. "What's up with this pitch clock disaster?"

Luke chuckled. "It's supposed to make the game go faster and gain the sport more fans."

"It's making the game ridiculous." Ansel pointed at the TV. "How can the ump call a ball or a strike when there wasn't even a pitch?"

I tuned out at that point. Baseball was boring. I went back to my laptop but couldn't stop glancing back up at this man. I'd seen the way he looked at Maeve as if she was the moon to his sun. He had a solid look about him that had nothing to do with his movie-star face. Although, if you were going to spend a lifetime with someone, them having a nice face was a bonus.

He had an openness about him, as if talking baseball with Ansel was just what he wanted to do. Which was much nicer for family get-togethers than the uninterested, want-to-be-anywhere-but-here vibe that Patrick emitted. Not that he ever bothered to show up for Sunday dinner. Not even when he was in town.

I never thought he was good enough for Maeve. I never got what she saw in him, why she gave him so many chances to break her heart. She should have moved on as soon as he refused to act like a father to his own daughter.

Not to mention all the times he'd cheated on Maeve. It hurt to see her so invested in someone who could never return her love and loyalty. Patrick had toyed with her affection, making promises he never intended to follow through to keep her hooked. He'd even gone so far as to give her an engagement ring three years ago, just when we'd talked her into moving on.

She was a wonderful, loving woman. I wish I knew how to help her see that in herself. That she deserved to be loved and cherished. Treated like a princess. But anything that came out of my mouth seemed to automatically register as false.

Both she and Neve deserved someone who could love them with their whole heart, not with a bunch of exceptions.

Luke stood and shook Ansel's hand. "So good to meet you, Mr. Carpenter."

"Ansel."

Luke nodded. "Ansel."

"Luke," I said as I got up, hooked an arm around his elbow and walked him to the door, "why don't you and your sister come to Sunday dinner tomorrow night after the competition? We're having a little celebration to honor Maeve, win or lose. Although, I'm pretty sure she's going to win. Her bakes make you forget all about your good diet intentions. And, well, your sister deserves a little celebration, too. She worked hard and has done so well for someone so young. Say you'll come."

His smile made me wish I was a couple of decades younger. "When you put it like that, how could I refuse? What time would you like us here?"

"Around seven."

"What can we bring?"

"Yourselves. It's just going to be family, so you won't have to worry about autograph hounds."

He chuckled. "I appreciate that, and it sounds like a nice opportunity to get to know Maeve's family."

"Is that something you'd like to do?" I asked, putting all of my mother's nosiness into the question.

His gaze met mine, frank and true. "It is something I would absolutely love to do, if she'll let me."

"Good. Maeve deserves some happiness."

He took his leave and from the lightness of his step, I was almost 100 percent sure he wasn't heading to the B&B but to the bakery.

After the rotten way Patrick had treated her, I hoped Maeve could open herself up to the possibility of a good man.

26

MAEVE

After a day of too much noise and too many people, being here alone at the bakery, working on Mom's birthday cake, was a balm.

While my happy playlist wafted over the speakers and the cake layers cooled on a rack, I called to check on Natalie.

The usually unflappable Natalie answered her phone with an edge to her voice.

"How are you?" I asked, worried for her.

"I feel like I am being mixed with a dough hook."

I could imagine the roller coaster of emotions that came with dealing with a parent's illness. "How's your mom?"

"She had surgery. A bypass. She will be in hospital for another day or two."

"But she'll be okay?" If Natalie came back too soon, the regular bread customers were sure to taste the tears in her bread.

"Yes.... But I am afraid I will need to stay to help my mother when she get home."

"No worries, Natalie. Take care of your mom."

"You will not give my position away?"

I frowned. "Why would I do that? You're the best bread baker I've ever met."

"I could be away a month. Perhaps more."

I reached for my sketchbook. "Then it'll take a month or more. We'll all be glad to have you back when you're ready."

Silence filled the line. "Nat? Are you okay?"

"*Merci*, Maeve. You have no idea what this means to me."

I rifled through the junk drawer for a pencil. "Maybe one day you'll trust me enough to tell me."

We chatted for a few minutes more. She insisted I write down a list of steps for tomorrow's competition.

"Good luck, Maeve. I am sorry to leave you like this. But am I sure you will win, and I will get my new oven."

Natalie tried to laugh but it came out more like a strangled sob.

After I hung up, I sketched the decorations for the cake I'd promised Zoe would be spectacular. Lee Roessler's lyrics urged me to persevere, Roo Panes' to be myself and Andy Grammer's to keep my head up because everything was going to turn out.

I hoped he was right.

Instead of using the cake base I had in the freezer, I'd started from scratch. Snick, according to Neve, was doing better and Grandma wasn't sad anymore. That gave me the idea of making a snickerdoodle cake.

The vanilla cake had ribbons of cinnamon sugar running through it. I would make cinnamon-brown sugar buttercream and top it with cinnamon sugar.

Baking was love. The ingredients were like words in a sentence. I stirred them together to create a story. A story that would find its perfect ending with the *aah* of pleasure in the taster's mouth and linger long after the mouthful was gone.

As Neve's mother, I was in charge of her sugar consumption. But other people had to make their own decisions. All I could do was use the best ingredients I could.

Instead of rosettes along the top edge, I would attempt dog faces. At the foot of the cake, I would attempt paw prints. Mom had always had a soft spot for dogs. Nobody could have loved Oscar, the ugly mutt Lark had insisted belonged to Mom when we were little, as much as Mom had.

She cared, I had to remind myself. About Neve. About me. Maybe this cake would show her I did, too. This apology birthday cake would be my best one yet.

A knock on the back door startled me out of my scrambled thoughts. I needed to find a way to dim the lights so Colton would stop coming around for handouts when I was working late. How he could always tell when I was baking with cinnamon was a mystery.

"Colt—" I started, ready to tease Colton about his cinnamon addiction. But Luke stood there instead of the firefighter.

"If you're going to answer every knock in the middle of the night, you need to put in a peephole." Luke peeled his long body from the door frame. "I could've been anybody."

I exaggerated a huff, and opened the door wider to let him in. "This is Brighton."

"Where nothing bad ever happens?"

I shut the door behind him. "I wouldn't go that far. But nobody would knock on that door this late unless they knew me." I crossed my arms under my chest and narrowed my gaze at him. "Which brings me to: how did you know where to find me?"

That smile could melt icing as easily as a warm day. "A little bird told me."

"Neve?" I asked, patting my shorts pocket and realizing I'd forgotten my phone on the counter at home. I went back to the stand mixer and dumped in softened butter.

"Your mother."

"Ah." I started the mixer, creaming the butter, to let the

noise give my brain time to reset. What was he doing at my parents' house?

He leaned against the worktable, watching me as if I were something interesting. As if a mess could be interesting. "What are you doing here so late?"

"Mom's birthday is next Monday. We're celebrating tomorrow night after the competition. I promised my sister I'd bake a spectacular cake. With the competition..." I lifted a shoulder and let it drop.

"You forgot?"

"I just couldn't carve out the time. And now I've run out."

"Smells good."

I shot him a small smile. "Don't tell me you're as obsessed with cinnamon as Colton is."

"I can admire a good treat when I smell it."

"We're going to have to break you of that habit." I shook my head, remembering the pile of nutrition books on the end table in the apartment. "On second thought, you have the right idea with your no-sugar stance."

"Your mom invited Dani and me to dinner tomorrow night."

"She did?" Which wasn't surprising. Mom loved a full table on Sunday nights— the fuller, the better. She invited everyone, including strangers, to join us on a regular basis. Her cancelling last weekend? That was an anomaly. One I feared she'd done because of our argument. "Sunday dinners are a regular thing. She doesn't know we're planning a party for her."

"I won't tell," Luke said with a soft smile. "She's a nice woman."

I snorted. Most people would tell you she was a wonderful woman. Caring. Loving. She went out of her way to be helpful. Too helpful, in my case. And that created expectations of me that I couldn't live up to. But Luke didn't need to know all that.

"What?" He tipped his head, urging me to talk.

"My mother and I have a... difficult relationship."

"How?"

I rolled my eyes— I hadn't done that so much since I was a teenager. What was it about Luke that brought out the worst in me? I didn't really want to get into all the ways Mom and I managed to push each other's buttons. "Ever since I was a kid, whatever I did wasn't good enough. I wasn't good enough." Still wasn't. "I wish I could afford to move."

Now why had I said that? I tipped my chin toward the brown sugar container at the end of the table. "Hand me that container."

He pushed the brown sugar my way. I added brown sugar to the butter, hoping the sound of the mixer would invite him to drop the conversation.

"When you leave," he said over the mixer's hum, "you take your troubles with you."

He was right, of course. I'd put on my happy playlist because the thoughts in my head had taken a dark turn since the end of the cake competition. Which was also another reason I'd needed to bake tonight. To try to purge Patrick and his unreliability out of my mind. I had to make a decision about him. And I had to stick to it. For Neve's sake.

For mine.

The one thing I was starting to see was that winning the prize wasn't going to solve any of my problems. I'd still need help with Neve in the morning. I'd still have a bakery with narrow profit margins to run. I'd still have my mother and her stubbornness to deal with. Worst of all, I'd still be dependent on her for help.

A new oven or a trip to Paris wouldn't change any of that.

Even though Rob Thomas' "Someday" would have me believe that I could start all over again, moving would just complicate everything.

"You have great parents," Luke said.

I snorted. "You met them, what, two minutes ago?"

"They won't always be there."

I remembered him saying his parents had died a few years back in a car accident. "You're right."

His smile widened. "Your parents both bragged on you. I'm surprised your ears weren't burning."

With a fingertip, he touched the lobe of my ear, and the skin tingled as if he'd sprinkled hot pepper.

I turned away from the perplexing sensation, focusing on the cake, and tried to change the course of the conversation. "Tell me about your mom."

He bent his head forward, shaking it and smiling. "She told the worst jokes. Like: have you heard about the chocolate record player?"

I shook my head.

"It sounds pretty sweet."

I groaned. Yes, this was much better. Easy, fun, light.

"And if a child refuses to nap," he said, "are they guilty of resisting a rest? She used that one on Dani, a lot."

I laughed. "I could use that one for Neve."

"Wanna hear a joke about paper? Never mind, it's tearable." His smile wobbled and his eyes went hazy. "She'd laugh until she had tears springing out."

He looked lost in the memory.

"And her laugh was so embarrassing— more like a snort crossed with a bray —I'd beg her to stop." He tried to keep his smile up, but it fell. "Now, I'd give anything to hear it again."

I thought of Mom not being there. She was my rock— even if I sometimes resented the fact. I grabbed the powdered sugar bin. "I'm sorry. She sounds like a good mom."

"The best." He pulled the brown sugar container toward him and replaced the cover. "Even as wonderful as she was, she and Dani often butted heads. Moms, they want the best for their kids."

I ceded him the point with a jolt of my shoulder.

"You're a mother," he said. "Think about your fears for Neve. Your mother has fears for you, too."

I dumped powdered sugar into the mixer, but I had it on too fast and the sugar clouded the space between us. "She doesn't have any."

"Of course, she does. She's human."

I stopped the mixer and scraped the sides of the bowl with more force than necessary. "You don't understand. She's strong. The strongest person I know. She's the person you go to when your world falls apart. And she puts it back together." I didn't know what I would've done without all of Mom's help when Patrick left and my whole world crumbled.

"That's an awful lot to put on someone's shoulders." He tipped his head, studying me again with that unnerving gaze that felt as if it could see all the way down to my soul. "What fears do you have?"

He'd distracted me and I'd forgotten to add the cinnamon and vanilla. I snatched the cinnamon from the spice wall and added it to the butter mixture, poured a tablespoon of vanilla straight from the bottle. My fears trailed behind me like crumbs, enough of them to cover a dozen coffee cakes. "A whole industrial mixer's worth."

"Like what?" His attentive gaze said he was interested in the answer.

For some reason that had my insides feeling raw, exposed. "If I'm doing right by Neve, for one."

"You don't think that your mother had that fear when it came to you and your siblings?"

I stopped the mixer and tested the consistency of the buttercream, added a bit of cream, and turned the mixer back on. "She always had her stuff together. We had a great childhood. We felt secure and loved."

"You don't think Neve feels that way?"

"I hope so. I don't know." I stopped the mixer and scraped buttercream off the paddle. "Her father's not around often."

Neve was a sweet, wonderful girl, but she also carried a swirl of sadness that no child should have. Me, alone, I wasn't able to fix it. And that made me worry I wasn't a good enough mother. "She looks together when you meet her, but her ADHD... It's hard to deal with. And Mom doesn't think it's real. I'm trying to get Neve stabilized without drugs. I've explained this to my mother a thousand times, but she keeps going against my wishes."

He took the paddle from me and walked it to the sink. "How were you as a kid?"

I laughed. I got exactly where he was going. "They used to call me Monster Maeve."

"And your mother probably thought it was her fault somehow and worried about you and your future."

I doubted it. I was sure she blamed me for being so bad. "I'm still a monster."

My temper was still short. I still hurt people's feelings without meaning to by saying things without filtering them first. I still wasn't good enough for Patrick to stick around and be the family we— I'd —dreamed about.

"That's not what I see." The gentleness of his voice traveled down my spine like the softest of breezes.

I looked into his storm-gray eyes, clear like a summer sky and, suddenly, I wanted to see myself through those eyes. If he didn't see a monster, what did he see? Instead, I made a joke out of it. "I know who I am, Donut Guy. It's you who's confused."

"I know exactly who I am."

I snorted, reached for the cake turntable, and placed a cooled cake layer on top. "I've seen at least three Lukes since you've arrived." Having the conversation pointed in his direction instead of mine was much easier.

He glanced from side to side. "I see only one."

"Baseball Luke is different than Internet Luke. And he's different than Coach Luke." Mom liked a lot of icing, so I made sure to place a thick coat before sprinkling cinnamon crunchies and adding the next layer of cake.

He hiked an eyebrow. "Please, enlighten me."

"Baseball Luke is focused and driven." I worked on the crumb layer.

He gave a nod. "I can agree with that."

"Internet Luke is charming and approachable and could be your friend."

"Nothing wrong with that."

"It's not real Luke, though. It's a show. Real Luke is the one at camp, with the kids, teaching them how to play whack-a-mole with their gremlins."

That seemed to have stolen his easy words. He ambled around the kitchen, studying the labels on all my containers as if they were of utmost fascination. "People expect me to act a certain way."

I could understand that. People had impressions of who you were, expectations on how you should behave. Living up to someone else's views wasn't always easy. Especially in a small town. A lot of people in Brighton still saw me as the teenage troublemaker I once was. And being your true self was probably also difficult when the limelight was pointed your way.

He fidgeted with a measuring spoon on the table, rolling it so that it made a click-click sound. "As long as I kept winning games. As long as I showed up for clinics. As long as I signed autographs and took selfies with fans. Then I was worth something, you know?"

While the crumb layer set in the fridge, I took out a sheet pan and mixed the sugar-cinnamon topping. "Don't you think they'd like you if you were just yourself?"

He palmed the measuring spoon and lobbed it into the water-filled sink with a plop. "Fame is temporary."

"Way to sidestep, Luke." I smiled, joking.

But he stayed serious. "I can't live in the past. These past few weeks have shown me that. It's done. And I'm good with that. I have to look toward the future."

He'd let go of his baseball dream. Not just because his leg would prevent him from playing, not just because of Dani, but because the time was right. Some other player might grow resentful at the loss, scatter blame like sesame seeds. But Luke had taken stock of his reality and was moving on. He was playing a role now to help his sister. But he wasn't stuck in the past.

I thought of my dreams— Paris, traveling the world, a family with Patrick. It was as if I'd stopped time ten years ago when I found out I was pregnant. Even the little cottage by the lake was a nod to an ageing dream.

I was still stuck there.

"Hey," Luke said, close, too close, his voice a soft murmur. "Why so sad?"

Before I quite knew what I was doing, I leaned my head on his shoulder. His arms circled my waist and, instead of feeling like armor, they felt like comfort. Part of me wanted to stay there. *Safe*, I thought, *secure*.

As if he sensed the fragility of the moment, he said nothing and just held me. His scent, sunshine and rain, enveloped me. I thought about how I wanted him closer. I closed my eyes and tipped my head up.

"Maeve..." It was a question. It was a plea.

His lips met mine, warm, soft. The low, gruff sound at the back of his throat told me he wanted more. My stomach thrummed with the strangest sensation. His hands shifted, bringing his body closer to mine. His heart beat against me, slow and steady. I could feel myself fall into him. Skin hunger, I told myself. That was all. How long had it been since anyone had kissed me like this? And, oh, how I wanted him to go on.

"Maeve..." His breath caught.

Then a flood of fear came over me. Lips aching from the quick separation, I backed out of his hold, and got busy icing the cake. He gathered the dirty tools from the table, took them to the sink and washed them.

I couldn't go from Patrick to yet another man who didn't plan on staying still. I needed space to figure out who I was and what I wanted before I even thought of another relationship. I owed that to myself and to Neve.

When the icing had set, I turned the cake horizontally and rolled it in cinnamon-sugar topping. I hurried through adding some topping to the top of the cake and smoothing it. I'd pipe the decorations in the morning. Right now, I needed to get home.

After placing the cake in the fridge, I took off my apron. "I need to get some rest before tomorrow."

Because he insisted, I let Luke walk me home, but held my distance. The lingering heat of the day, the darkness of night while the town slept, the sparkle of stars in the sky seemed to throw a cozy shawl around us. One I couldn't allow myself to sink into. Once at the house, I raced up the steps before I could do something stupid like kiss him again. "Goodnight. See you tomorrow."

I closed the door behind me without waiting for his answer or looking back. I leaned on the door for a moment. *Do not go from one impossible dream to another. That would make you the world's biggest fool.* Something I was already in contention for.

I shook off thoughts of Luke and his kiss, and the way my heart wanted more, and checked on Neve. She lay sprawled like a starfish on her bed, a bunny tucked under one hand, a puppy under the other. I kissed her temple, love for her filling my heart. She was my number-one concern. Always would be.

As I did most nights, once I'd slipped into bed, I clicked on the Zillow tab for the cottage. I admired the cardinal-red door and Adirondack chairs. The flowers. The lake. Somehow, this gem was still available.

A heaviness anchored in my gut. A family with Patrick would never happen. I'd never be able to depend on him. He wasn't a good father. Neve needed someone who accepted her, someone who would be there when she needed him. I was a fool for having hung on so long to something that was more smoke than substance.

The pieces of my heart that belonged to Patrick cracked like a hot chocolate shell on cold ice cream, shattering, falling, leaving behind a sticky mess. All the might-have-beens leaked out, pooled, languished.

Sobs shook my shoulders. I stuffed a fist into my mouth to keep my cries from spilling out. I didn't want Neve to wake up. I didn't want to have to explain that all my hopes and dreams were seeping out along with the tears.

I curled into a ball on the pull-out bed, my heart hurting, hugging the hedgehog stuffie that was there as if its prickly fur could offer solace.

I wanted someone to tell me the hurt wouldn't last forever, that it would stop.

But there was no one.

I had to take charge of my own life.

I hugged the hedgehog closer so I wouldn't fall apart, while silent tears drenched my pillow.

Then, after one last look at the cottage on Hummingbird Lane, I deleted the tab.

I had to let that dream go.

I had to let Patrick go.

Easy to say; not so easy to do.

27

GRACE

Aaron arrived at 10 on Sunday morning to take me to see the house he and Meredith were planning on buying. I wanted to cancel. Snick was feeling better, but I hated to leave her behind, and I didn't think she was feeling well enough for a car ride and house viewing.

"Go, Grace," Ansel insisted, Sunday *Boston Globe* spread around him, mug of coffee in hand. "I'll watch the mutt."

"That would require you taking your nose out of the paper."

With a sigh, he placed the paper on the table and invited Snick onto his lap. She looked from me to him and back again.

"Go ahead," I said to her with a wave of my hand.

She hopped on Ansel's lap and settled in.

"Now go," Ansel said. "We'll be fine."

She'd had her medicine. She'd eaten her breakfast. She'd drunk a fair amount of water and done her business outside. She looked much better this morning. Still.... Aaron had asked for my opinion, and I didn't want to let him down. The sooner I went, the sooner I could get back. I grabbed my purse from the hall table. "I won't be long."

"We'll be fine," Ansel insisted.

"They'll be fine, Mom." Aaron urged me out the door. "We need to hurry if we want to be back in time to see Maeve in the baking contest finale."

Another thing I didn't want to do but would surely feel guilted into doing. I just wanted to be home with Snick. Although, I supposed that having missed both previous competition segments, I should attend the big finale. The guilt around children didn't disappear just because they were adults.

I settled into Aaron's truck with a sigh. "Where is this house?"

"It's just down the road from my workshop."

Which was a fair way out of town. So much for a quick trip. "Well, that's convenient."

He gave a nod and smiled, pleased. "That's what we thought."

He drove past his workshop, turned onto Lookout Road and bumped to the end where a small ranch house stood, nestled in woods on two sides. It looked rather plain with its off-white siding and gray shutters. Only the ox-blood door gave a pop of color. The landscaping left much to be desired with only a few scraggly, half-dead bushes hiding the foundation.

"There's only a one-car garage," I said, thinking of snowy winters and how far out of town the house was. "Your truck won't fit in there. I'm not sure Meredith's car will either." She'd sensibly gotten a four-wheel-drive, hybrid SUV.

"I can add on before winter."

The advantage of being a builder. He could fix the house any way he wanted. Which gave me an idea.

Aaron came around the truck and helped me down the high step. "It doesn't look like much from the outside but it's surprisingly big inside. And wait until you see the three-season porch."

I hoped that Ansel hadn't gone back to reading his newspaper and that he was still keeping an eye on Snick. As if he'd read my mind, Ansel sent a photo of Snick upside down on his lap, enjoying being petted. His caption? Proof of life.

I got the hint and put Snick out of my mind. For now. And focused on Aaron's excitement and on the house.

The first floor had some lovely hardwood floors throughout. The paint looked fresh. "Four bedrooms?"

Aaron's gaze studied the floor and he blushed. "We're thinking of applying for adoption."

"Adoption?" I hugged him. "Oh, Aaron, that's great! I always thought you'd make a fantastic father."

"You did?" He looked surprised.

"Of course. You'll be there for your kids. You'll spend time with them. You'll love them. Unlike some people we know." Of course, Patrick had set the bar low when it came to parenting responsibility. I hugged Aaron again and whispered, "Plus, I wouldn't say no to more grandchildren."

He laughed that big-hearted laugh I always associated with my first-born. He'd had a rough time for a few years after his fiancée dumped him like bad news as soon as she'd gotten what she wanted out of him. He'd tried to mold himself into what she wanted but I was glad he hadn't succeeded. He'd slowly found his way back to himself and his true calling.

Then Meredith had come into his life last Christmas. I hadn't seen him this happy in a long time. And all a mother wanted for her children was to see them thriving and happy.

I looked around the open-concept living room and kitchen. This house would make a great space for them to settle. The living room had a fireplace with a woodstove insert that would make winter nights cozy. "The kitchen's on the small side."

"It'll do for now."

I tutted, hoping he noticed the tease. "One of you will have to learn how to cook decent meals if you're going to have children."

"Yeah, we'll need to pinch pennies now that we'll have a

mortgage." He ushered me toward some stairs. "Wait till you see this basement."

Oh, it was wonderful. A finished space with what looked like a craft room that Meredith could use as an office. A laundry room. And a space that would make a terrific playroom, complete with a playful woodland mural on one wall. A full wall of windows opened onto a the three-season porch that offered views of Lookout Pond. Light flooded the whole basement.

"My only worry," I said. "Is that it's so far out of town, especially in winter."

"I've got the truck with a plow blade. There's a whole-house generator. We'll be snug in here."

I shouldn't spend any time worrying about Aaron; he knew how to take care of himself. And he would do anything to keep Meredith— and their future children —safe.

"You better snap this up before it goes," I said, imagining them enjoying summer evenings by the firepit and fall days sitting on the cozy porch, sipping hot chocolate. "It's not going to last long."

"We put in an offer," Aaron said sheepishly.

I frowned, irritated he'd made me come all the way out here when he'd already made up his mind. "Then why did you ask me to come see it?"

"You have good taste."

I knocked an elbow into his ribs. "You're trying to butter me up for some reason."

His voice went soft and vulnerable. "I wanted to tell you about our adoption plans. But we want to keep it quiet until we know if we'll be approved."

"Of course, they'll approve you." I patted his cheek. "You and Meredith will make wonderful parents." I traced a cross over my heart. "But, yes, I'll keep your secret and let you and Meredith make the announcement when you're ready."

As we drove back through town, I pointed toward North Brighton Road. "Would you mind taking a small detour?"

He raised his eyebrows, curious. "Of course not."

I had him stop in front of a redbrick, box of a building just off Main Street. Like his little ranch house, it didn't look like much from the outside.

"What's this?" he asked, peering at the empty building.

"A possibility." Suddenly, nerves overtook me. Would he think it was silly for someone old like me to start a new venture? I opened the truck door and stepped onto the sidewalk. "I want your opinion."

"You know I'm full of them."

I chuckled and unlocked the door and pushed it open. "I'm hoping to transform this into a self-serve dog care boutique."

"Okay," he said, looking at the space with his builder's eye. "What are you thinking?"

I pointed to the back wall. "I want to put two bathing stations there. Two tubs on legs." I opened a tab on my phone to show him what I planned to purchase. "Two grooming tables. Two dryers hooked to the wall."

"You'll need a plumber to install the sink and drains. And an electrician for the dryers."

"On my list." A list that kept getting longer and scarier. This idea was starting to give me as many nightmares as excitement. I turned to face the left wall. "Along here, I want to put a counter with bulk dispensers for shampoos, conditioners and cleansers. People would bring their own containers, or we could sell some."

I spun to face the right wall. "Along there, I'd have a checkout counter and maybe a rack with some doggie items like collars, leashes, neckerchiefs, coats and such, made by locals."

"That's a great idea, Mom."

I swiveled to face him, studying his demeanor. "Really?"

He nodded, looking around as if he shared my vision. "The area doesn't have anything like it. And there are tons of dogs around. Did you buy the building or are you renting?"

"Renting." I wasn't sure how long I wanted to keep this venture going, so it had seemed the prudent alternative.

"Make sure you get good insurance," Aaron said. "That flat roof could cause some damage if we get a heavy snow."

"Your father has that covered."

Aaron strolled around the empty space. "It wouldn't take too long to build it all up. We could have you in business in no time."

I swallowed hard. This project was starting to feel real, and my insides went all jittery. "I'd pay you, of course."

He sent me a crooked smile. "I'll hit you back in babysitting."

Joy filled my heart. "I'd love that."

As I locked the door behind me, I took one last look at the empty space, seeing it all decked out, happy dogs and owners milling about.

I did have something of value to offer.

28

MAEVE

S unday dawned like a toddler having a temper tantrum. Thunder rolled over the mountains. Lightning forked the sky. And rain poured as if competing for deluge status.

The outside weather matched the inside mood of our apartment with Neve crying, screaming and throwing things after Patrick failed to show up for their breakfast date. He'd promised to take her out for pancakes and that they'd spend the day together.

I wanted to throw a tantrum right along with Neve. Too bad one of us had to act like an adult.

By lunchtime, fingers of sun poked through the clouds. Neve had somewhat calmed down. But the fairgrounds were a muddy mess. Someone had spread hay over the tent floor to sop up most of the water. My sneakers still sank and wet my socks. This was going to be fun.

Because Patrick hadn't shown up as promised to watch Neve during the competition, she was here with me, getting underfoot as I tried to get ready. I was already hampered by the lack of an assistant, so this wasn't helping my sour mood.

"Neve?" Luke called over to her. "Can you come help me with something?"

She glanced at me, and I nodded, mouthing a "Thank you" over her head at Luke.

He popped her onto the stool he used to rest his leg during the competition. "Dani has to make some cookies, and I need help unwrapping these kisses." He opened a bag of white chocolate kisses and placed a bowl on the station and a garbage can next to her. "Kisses here." He pointed to the garbage. "And wrappers here." He pointed to the bowl.

She scrunched her forehead. "Um, don't you mean the other way around?"

He knocked the heel of his hand on his forehead. "Good thing you're on the ball, or we could have a mess on our hands."

Neve laughed, and hearing the sound after the temper tantrum she'd thrown as we were leaving was good.

She took her job seriously, counting each one to make sure Dani would have enough kisses for her three dozen cookies. She chatted with Luke, who somehow managed to make her laugh again. She was halfway through her task when Patrick sauntered along, looking as if he'd just stepped out of the shower. I glanced at my watch. Only three hours late.

"Hey, Neve," Patrick said, waiting as if he expected her to jump into his arms. "Ready to go play games?"

"I have a very important job to do." She kept her gaze on her fingers as she unwrapped another foil wrapper. "Dani needs thirty-six kisses plus some extras, just in case."

"Come on, kid." He waved at her to come. "Stop being such a baby. Let's go."

Her lower lip trembled, but she studiously kept unwrapping the kisses, rounding into herself. Not good. The next step: tears.

"Looks like she'd rather stay here," Luke said, his voice light as he kept setting up Dani's station.

Patrick glared at Luke. "You're not her father. Let's go, Neve."

Tears streamed down Neve's cheeks as she kept unwrapping kisses. "I need to finish."

I struggled to untangle myself from the mess of boxes at my station.

Patrick's dark eyes hardened. "Let's go!"

"She doesn't want to," Luke insisted, stepping between Neve and Patrick, ready to fight for this little girl he barely knew.

"It's none of your business."

"You're right." Luke pointed at Neve. "But it is hers, and she said no."

"Hey!" I said, but they both ignored me. "Enough!"

"I know my own daughter." Patrick's voice was tight, his words sharp bites. He turned to me. "Maeve, call back your guard dog."

No, he didn't know his daughter. Something he'd made abundantly clear since he'd come back to town. I headed toward the sure confrontation.

"Neve, come. Now!" Patrick looked ready to start a barroom brawl. Just what I didn't need happening with the whole town watching and WMUR setting up cameras in the background to film the finale.

"Enough!" I said, hands on hips. "Patrick, you're too late. Neve's busy right now, so leave her alone."

His face twisted into scorn. "Is this because of this washed-up has-been?"

"No, Patrick. It's because you promised your daughter you'd be there at 9 this morning to take her out for breakfast, and you're just now waltzing in."

"My alarm didn't go off," he said, his tone bordering on rude.

"That's no way to talk to your child's mother," Luke said. And it felt as if he would fight this dragon for me if I let him. "You were asked to leave."

So, this was what it was like to have someone stand up for you.

Not the right guy. Not the right time. But nice.

"Shove off." Patrick tightened his fists. "This is between me and Maeve."

I stepped in between them.

"Thanks, Luke. But this is my problem. I'll handle it."

He hesitated for a moment, gave a nod and moved back to his station. Dani, who'd gone to the porta-potties, came back. "What's going on?"

"The competition is about to start," I said, placing every inch of determination I had in my voice, "so I'd appreciate it if you left."

"What about Neve?"

"She wants to finish what she started. Then she'll go with people who actually care for her." I nodded toward Zoe ramming her way through the crowd and extending her hand toward Neve.

"I've got her." Zoe wrapped a protective arm around her niece's shoulders. "Come on, sweetie. I got us some good seats. Grandma and Grandpa are waiting."

"I gotta finish unwrapping the kisses."

"I'll help you."

Neve went back to the station with Zoe without a glance at her father. That was how I knew how deeply he'd hurt her.

"This isn't over," he said, his voice vibrating with threat. "She's *my* daughter."

Heart beating a hundred miles an hour, I turned my back on him. *Shake it off, Maeve. In five minutes, you have to bake for your bakery's life.*

∾

THE VIP TENT sported a series of small tables. The two dozen or so people seated there had paid for the privilege of sampling the picnic baskets' goodies after the judging.

Today, Regina wore a red dress dotted with white strawberry flowers. She tapped the mic, and nothing happened. "Is this thing on?"

She tried again, sending a feedback screech over the speakers that had the spectators blocking their ears and cringing. "Welcome to the last day of competition!" A la Vanna White, she presented a basket bulging with strawberries. "Today's berries were provided by Cloverleaf Farm."

She turned toward the baking tent. "Bakers, today you're tasked with creating a picnic basket containing three dozen individual pies, three dozen cupcakes and three dozen cookies. Remember that the star of each category must be the strawberries."

She lifted a red handkerchief. "On your mark!"

She let the handkerchief fall. "Bake away!"

Success today would depend on time management, which would be the most difficult part for me, especially without Natalie here to help me. I dug into my shorts pockets for the list Natalie had insisted I write down. Pie crust first to give it time to chill. Cupcake batter second. Cookie dough— why did a pick a dough that needed chilling? Pie filling. Frosting. Then assembly.

"Good luck!" Dani called from her station.

"You, too!"

Even with only three competitors, the baking tent buzzed with activity. The scent of strawberries hung in the thick air. The crowd came and went, throwing the occasional words of encouragement. Every half hour, Regina announced the passing time.

We were on the home stretch. The hand pies were done and cooling. Just before plating, I would dust them with my special sugar. The cupcakes were baked and cooling. All I had left to bake was the cookies. I sped to the fridge, grabbed the roll of cookies, sliced them and shoved them in the oven. While those baked, I iced a dozen of the Strawberry Champagne Cupcakes.

The cookie timer dinged and my nerves popped. I was so behind. I grabbed the cookie sheet from the oven. The sheet caught the edge of the counter. All my cookies went flying. They landed in the mud in a series of sickening plops. A horrified "Oh!" rose from the crowd. This, I was sure, would become a meme.

I stared at the cookies, sinking into the wet mess, and wanted to cry. *There's no crying in baseball or baking.*

I shook myself off. Okay, time to pivot. *I can do this.* I glanced at the clock. Not enough time to start the cookies over.

Luke appeared at my side. "What can I do to help?"

"Dani—"

"She's all set. Let me help you."

I launched some measurements at him while I dug through my containers, looking for the freeze-dried strawberries I'd packed on a whim.

I was halfway through mixing my compromise cookies when Dani shouted, "No, no, no!"

"What's wrong?" Luke asked, hobbling over to her station.

"My oven's not working."

"What temp do you need?" I asked, mixing dough as fast as I could.

"Three-fifty."

I moved aside while I continued mixing. "Use mine."

"But you need it."

"I'll kick you out in fifteen, so make it quick."

She hurried over and shoved her cookie sheet into my oven. Luke fiddled with her oven, trying to get it working again.

Ten minutes later, she pulled her cookies out, and I shoved in my two pans.

While that baked, I iced the rest of the cupcakes, added a decorative strawberry fan and started filling my picnic basket.

By the time my cookie timer rang, only a few minutes remained on the competition clock. These brookies— not quite brownies, not quite blondies —needed cooling, but there wasn't enough time. *Please, please, please stay together.*

I unmolded the pans onto a cutting board, grabbed a round cookie cutter and cut out circles as quickly as I could. Dani and Luke, even Delia, appeared at my side, placing them in the basket as fast as I could cut them.

"Bakers!" Regina announced. "Your time. Is. Up!"

The buzzer rang and I sagged. I'd done it. The presentation lacked the finesse it should have had, had I had time, but it was done. I had three dozen pies, cookies and cupcakes in the basket.

I did something I rarely did, I grabbed Delia, Dani and Luke into a hug. "Thanks!"

Regina perused all three baskets on the judging table. "These all look so wonderful!"

After the tasting, the judges conferred. Some sort of argument took place between Peter and Sarah, but eventually, all three judges faced the bakers.

"We've made our decision," Regina said. She cleared her throat. "It is with great regret that we must eliminate one of our bakers for not following the brief to the letter."

Well, shoot. There went my new oven.

"Maeve, as tasty as these cookie-shaped concoctions are," she pointed at the strawberry blondies sandwiching a chocolate brownie layer, "the judges feel they cannot be considered cookies. And because of that, you are eliminated."

"What?" Dani said, looking from the judges to me. "But that's not fair!"

"It's okay, Dani," I said. "Technically, they aren't cookies."

"But—"

"Ladies," Regina said, calling over Dani and Delia. She picked up a giant crystal strawberry from the table. "Although both remaining baskets raised the bar on strawberry baked goods, the judges felt that one had a slight edge over the other." Regina paused, trying to squeeze drama out of the moment.

I rolled my eyes at her habit, and that's when I caught sight of Patrick scowling at the edge of the crowd. He'd come back.

And I felt nothing.

Not happiness. Not sadness.

Just nothing.

"And the winner of the First Annual Strawberry Festival Sweet Spot Baking Contest is..." She pressed the giant crystal strawberry forward. "Delia Horton!"

The crowd applauded. "Ladies," Regina said, opening one arm toward the VIP tent, "please join your adoring fans."

Three helpers grabbed the baskets and circulated through the VIP tent, offering goodies for their tasting enjoyment. I grabbed one of Dani's strawberry cookies with kisses as her basket went by.

"These are delicious." Graham crumbs dusted the strawberry cookie's outside, and a white chocolate kiss added an unexpected creamy richness.

"I call them strawberry kisses," she said, blushing at the compliment. "Your s'more cookies gave me the idea."

"Let's talk later. I may want to add them to the bakery's offering."

"Really?" Her smile rivaled Luke's. I would miss her when she left.

I hooked an arm through her elbow. "Let's go mingle."

I'd thought I'd feel crushed if I didn't win. Except that my baking skill hadn't cost me the win; it was pure bad luck in dropping those cookies. And that came down to rushing— something I didn't have to do when I baked for myself.

I was sad about the bills that wouldn't get paid, about the

oven I'd promised Natalie and the updates I'd planned for the bakery. But not about not winning. Which didn't make sense because I loved to win. It was one of the reasons Coach Mac had insisted I come back and play for him senior year— that need to win.

I glanced at Luke, charming the VIPs with his stories and his smiles, and Dani, blushing at their compliments. They'd gone out of their way to help me, jeopardizing their own win.

The worst part of this loss was disappointing Natalie. I'd let her down. She'd generously offered to pay the contest's entry fee, and I hadn't won her a new oven.

I'd find a way to pay her back the entry fee.

I'd find a way to get her a new oven.

In the meantime, I'd take in the compliments the VIPs offered about my bakes, do my WMUR interview, and find a way to use my treats to grow the bakery's reputation as a destination.

29

MAEVE

I circulated through the VIP tent, answering questions about my basket's bakes. Patrick, standing by the red velvet rope, waved at me to come closer.

"We need to talk," he said when I drew close, the red rope separating us.

I crossed my arms under my chest. "So, talk."

"Not here."

I glanced around at the milling crowds. "Why not?"

"Okay, have it your way." He shoved both his hands into his pants pockets. "You should've won."

I shrugged. "That's life."

He ran a hand through his short hair. "No, Maeve, you don't get it. If you hadn't helped that girl, you would've won."

"The cookies fell in the mud, Patrick. There's nothing I could do to save them. And that happened before I let Dani use my oven."

His dark eyes had none of the warmth I usually associated with them. They were hard, unyielding. "I was counting on you winning. For our future."

I frowned. "What do you mean?"

"The prize money," he said as if I was stupid. "I was going to invest it in our future."

Laughter and contended murmurs filled the VIP tent like a backdrop to a bad sit-com. "Where did you get that idea?"

"We talked about it," he said between gritted teeth. "When you took me to the cottage."

That wasn't the conversation I remembered. "We most certainly did not."

Patrick stared down at his expensive sneakers, streaked with mud. "I want to be part of Neve's life."

It sounded like a rehearsed speech, like something he could use to get me to change my mind. The worst part was that this tactic had worked in the past.

No more.

"Since when?" I thought of all the chances I'd given him, of all the times he'd failed Neve, left her disappointed and me having to dry her tears and find a sensible explanation for Patrick's failure.

He startled as if I'd spoken gibberish. "I'm her father."

"Not according to her birth certificate."

He stared at me as if I was some specimen he didn't recognize. "What do you mean?"

"The day she was born, you didn't even bother coming to the hospital. You said, and I quote, 'I don't want a baby. Ever.' So, I left the spot for father blank." I'd been so hurt, so angry that, when the nurse presented me the paperwork, I'd filled in N/A in the spot where Patrick's name should have gone. I'd given Neve my last name— a name she could always count on. And Patrick had proved me right, hadn't he? Every single day since. He'd been a big N/A in Neve's life.

His jaw flinched. "I'm still her father."

"According to your actions, you never have been." Luke, in the few weeks since he'd arrived in Brighton, had gotten to know Neve better than Patrick had in the past nine years.

I lifted my shoulders and let them drop. "I always thought you were the one person who saw me as I truly was, who got me and still loved me. Now I get that you don't see me at all, that you can't see past your own nose."

His gaze narrowed, glaring over my shoulder. I followed his gaze to Luke, who regaled his fans with some sort of story. "I'll sue you for custody."

This was a sweep of the legs I should have seen coming. My heart thundered. My anxiety rocketed.

Patrick didn't want me. He'd never wanted me. He hadn't wanted Neve. I'd had to beg and bribe him to spend time with his own daughter. And now that I'd done all the hard work, he wanted her in his life? Was willing to use her as a pawn against me? For money?

Neve was worth more than a $100,000 bakery contest win.

So was I.

I fisted my hands. I had to breathe. I had to calm down.

All the time I'd wasted waiting for him to come back to us. All the time I'd wasted waiting for him to step up for Neve. All the time I'd wasted waiting for us to become a family. How could I have been so stupid?

Because he'd made a promise, and I'd taken his promise as true.

I stabbed at finger in the middle of his chest, the last of my hope crumbling like overbaked cake. "Go ahead and try. It's going to look really good in court when I show that you've paid exactly zero dollars in child support. That you see your daughter for only a few hours every year. That you don't know the first thing about her."

"I do—"

"What's her favorite color?"

"Pink."

I made a losing buzzer sound. "Purple. What's her favorite food?"

"Anything with sugar."

I buzzed him again. "Pancakes. She'd eat them three times a day if I let her. What's her favorite book?"

He didn't even try to answer that one. Instead, he jerked his chin in Luke's direction. Luke, who kept glancing in at me all the while chatting with his fans, who was close enough to come to my rescue, but far enough to do as I'd asked, let me handle the situation on my own. "This is all because of that guy."

"No, Patrick. This is all because of *you*." I sighed the mother of all sighs. I'd had a long week, and I was ready for a long nap. I didn't need or want this fight. "I'm just tired. I have a lot on my plate right now. I have a ton of bills to pay for Neve's care— bills you haven't offered to help with even though she's your daughter. I have to find a way to get a new oven for the bakery. I have a bread baker to replace." For a little while anyway until Natalie came back. "The last thing I need is you stirring the pot when you have absolutely no intentions of ever acting like a father to Neve."

I felt nothing for Patrick now, except pity. He didn't understand what he had, what he was letting go. He wanted adventure. He wanted a posh lifestyle. One he wouldn't find here in Brighton. "What's it going to take?"

He stared at me. "For what?"

"For you to leave us alone? To stop jerking your daughter around like she has no feelings."

He hesitated, then named a sum.

My heart sank. My mind spun.

The price of his love.

When I looked at him, it was like watching a bad cake collapse through the oven window, distant and detached.

Paying him off would clean out what was left of my savings and my emergency fund. It would make paying the bills for Neve's therapy much more difficult. It would pause every plan I had for the bakery.

But to give Neve stability, I'd pay any price.

If I'd learned anything from this whole baking contest adventure, it was that I had people I could count on in my life. All I had to do was ask for help. I'd be stuck in the apartment at my parents' house for the foreseeable future, but I had a home. The bakery may look dated, but it had a good reputation. It would take longer to get the new oven I'd promised Natalie, but I would get it eventually.

For all my faults, I'd built a viable business. And if I just kept putting out product with unexpected flavors, if I kept being the baker I was born to be, it would eventually be a success.

All my feelings knotted in a tight ball. "Done."

"What'll you tell Neve?" he asked, looking at his daughter, circled by my family— Mom, Dad, Aaron, Meredith and Zoe. The people who truly loved her and accepted her the way she was.

He was more upset about my losing the contest than losing his own daughter. That saddened me beyond measure.

I'd made the right decision.

For both of us.

"Here's the sad reality, Patrick. I won't need to tell her anything at all. She's used to you letting her down."

Patrick's chin dropped to his chest. "I'm sorry, Maeve. I'm sorry I can't be what you want, what you need."

I sighed. "I'm sorry, too."

I slid the engagement ring off my finger and plopped it into his hand.

As I turned my back on him, a new lightness filled my body, as if I'd gotten rid of an anchor.

30

GRACE

"Ansel, where in the world are you going?" I asked as he drove away from the fairgrounds in the wrong direction. I needed to get home to check on Snick. She'd been alone too long. What if she'd had a relapse and nobody was there? I also needed to finish getting Sunday dinner ready. Everyone would start showing up in half an hour.

"I have to make a quick stop at the office."

I frowned at him. "On a Sunday?"

"It's just a quick check I need to make for a client." He kept staring at the road ahead. "Won't take but a minute."

"Snick—" I started.

"Is fine. She's probably glad for the break and you not hovering over her every second."

"Hey!"

He glanced at me and raised his brows. "You've been hovering."

I toyed with the strap of my purse. "I'm worried about her."

"She's doing much better."

She'd had more pep this morning. Her nose had been moist. And she'd eaten most of her breakfast. Although by the look on her face, she wasn't exactly pleased with the taste of the prescription food.

I hated counting on others, though. Even Ansel. I hated being late for my own hosting duties. "I still have a lot to do for Sunday dinner."

"I've got all the grilling ready." He glanced at me with a tease in his eyes. "That's the important part, right?"

I laughed. "You have no idea what goes into getting ready for these Sunday dinners."

"Which, I will remind you, is something you instituted yourself."

I tipped my head to one side. "I like a full table."

He reached for one of my hands and squeezed it. "I know you do."

"Maeve's favorite potato salad won't have time to chill at this rate." Still hanging on to Ansel's hand, I stared out the window at the scenery going by.

"Maeve won't notice if it's not there."

I turned back to him. "You're missing the point. I *want* her favorite potato salad to be there. It's a celebration of her accomplishment at the baking contest."

"She might be sad she lost and not want a celebration."

He was right, of course. Maeve's moods were mercurial. She might see the celebration as a failure on her part to— I didn't know what. Could be anything. That I was making light of her loss. That I hadn't expected her to win in the first place. I sighed. "I'll see what her mood is. If she's sad, I'll just make it an ordinary Sunday dinner."

Ansel smiled, that smile I fell in love with all those years ago, the smile that still made me feel warm inside. "See, all fixed."

I shook my head. "You know, I wish everything was as easy as you make it out to be."

"I'm not sure why you have to complicate things."

"Relationships aren't easy. Especially mine with Maeve."

"You love her. She loves you." He shrugged.

Love wasn't enough, though. "Think of it as a balance sheet that doesn't quite add up and you're looking and looking for the place where you made a mistake so you can fix it. And the paper you're using is thin, so it might rip easily."

"As much as I love to play with numbers, I do understand that people aren't black and white. And I don't think there's as much to fix as you think." He sent me a pointed look. "You two just need to sit down and talk. This ignoring each other isn't helping your cause."

We did need to talk, but I still wanted to set the scene properly, have Maeve see that I did love her and care about her. "The point is, I don't see why your stop at the office can't wait until Monday. You're an accountant, for heaven's sake, not a doctor."

"Getting that answer today feels like a broken bone to this client. It's a few minutes to make a client happy."

And when you worked for yourself, keeping your clients happy and spreading the good word of mouth was how you kept the business open. "Fine. Just make it quick. I'll wait in the car."

Ansel's couple of minutes turned into nearly twenty. The car's air conditioning sounded like a growl that mirrored my frustration. I kept watching the time turn over on my phone, getting more frustrated by the minute. Just as I was about to go drag Ansel back, he came back out, talking on his phone.

I rolled down the window. "Can you hurry?!"

He shook his head, said something into the phone, then placed the phone in his pants pocket.

When we finally got home, I recognized Aaron's truck, Zoe's Prius and Maeve's van parked on the street, as well Kate's silver SUV. I groaned. "Looks like the gang's already all here."

Ansel hooked his arm through my elbow. "Let's go say hello."

I grumbled. "Fine."

This wasn't the way I liked to do things. I liked for the scene to be set properly before the guests arrived— table, food, atmosphere. I wanted people to walk in and feel at home, to relax and have a good time.

He led me around to the backyard. Snick, who was playing tug with Neve, dropped the toy and galloped toward me, tail wringing, tongue flapping, insisting I pet her. I crouched down and scratched her chin. She licked my face as if I'd been away a week.

Everyone— Aaron, Meredith, Maeve, Zoe, Paul, Kate, Lark and Neve —stood, lifting a glass of lemonade my way. "Surprise! Happy birthday!"

My mouth dropped open. They'd remembered. And then, for some silly reason, tears flowed down my cheeks. Snick licked the tear from my face, and I hugged her close, even though she tried to wriggle away.

"Sit, Mom," Maeve said, coming over to lead me to a chair on the patio. Snick followed and jumped into my lap. "Merry's got this whole party under control."

And she did. The backyard looked inviting, everything organized as if planned by a professional, which I supposed Meredith was.

"But the potato salad—" I started.

"Taken care of," Maeve said with a smile.

I frowned. "Really? How did you know?"

"What's a Carpenter cookout without your famous potato salad and macaroni salad. We found your recipes."

I wasn't sure if that made me obsolete or pleased. I looked around the yard at the picnic table set with a red-checked tablecloth, featuring a red-and-silver glitter balloon bouquet centerpiece (probably picked out by Neve), pitchers of lemonade and iced tea. The outdoor tableware was all set, including a fancily folded napkin on each plate.

String lights hung from the fence. Neve's giant Jenga and ring toss games, Aaron's cornhole game, and Zoe's old croquet game were set up on the lawn. Soft love songs wafted from the speakers Ansel had installed a few years ago. Aaron had started the grill while we were driving back, which made me wonder if Ansel had had an emergency, or if he'd just stalled for time. Even the colorful clay pots filled with peppermint, basil and lavender that Irene had helped me put together seemed to have caught the jubilant mood, swaying in the soft breeze. Someone had lit the citronella torches around the picnic table to keep the bugs at bay.

Every detail taken care of for a successful dinner.

I didn't know what to say, so I just said, "Thank you."

Dinner unfolded with laughter and stories. I didn't mind the ribbing because it was done with love. These were all my favorite people, and I loved having them around me. I kept looking toward the front of the house, hoping to see Luke and his sister come around, for Maeve's sake.

Every time I tried to get up to get something. Zoe or Maeve or Meredith stood and said, "Sit. Enjoy your party. I'll get it."

Then Maeve disappeared inside the kitchen. When everyone oohed, I twisted around in my seat at the table. She carried a Snick-colored cake with red candles that shot sparkles.

Everyone burst out in song. "Happy birthday to you...."

Maeve carefully set the cake in front of me on the picnic table. Cinnamon sugar covered the frosting. The top was decorated with rosettes that looked like Snick's face and wandering pawprints decorated the side of the cake. "Is this a snickerdoodle cake?"

Maeve hugged me. "It is."

"It's the most beautiful cake I've ever seen." My heart felt all kinds of wobbly, so I placed a hand on my chest to keep it steady.

They'd remembered my birthday. All their stories reminded me that they loved me. I blew out the candles, my eyes going moist. Here was exactly where I wanted to be.

I stood up and clanged a fork against my glass. "I don't know if you've noticed but I've had a hard time for the past few months, anticipating this birthday."

My family had the nerve to raise eyebrows and murmur, "Yeah, we noticed all right."

I ignored their comment and continued. "It feels as if none of you needed me anymore."

"Oh, Mom," Zoe said, reaching over to hug my waist. "Of course, we'll always need you."

"That I was old and useless."

"Mom—" the kids started, shaking their heads, but I shushed them.

"But something's happened in the past couple of weeks." I skewered Lark with a narrow glare. "Someone brought me a dog I didn't want."

The whole family laughed as if me having a dog was a given.

"I've discovered that I'm a strong woman, who's turning a young sixty." I reached for my glass of iced tea for courage. "I still have plenty of life left in me. Age doesn't limit me. It empowers me."

"Hear! Hear!" my brother Paul said, lifting his pint glass my way.

"I've discovered the next phase of my life."

Kate shot me a knowing smile. "You've found your joy."

"I did." Kate was right. I'd been acting like a martyr in need of sainting. "I will be opening a new self-serve dog care store, where people will be able to bring their dogs and bathe them with professional equipment, buy shampoos, conditioners and cleansers in bulk, cutting down on dog care costs. They'll be able to stay closer to home."

"Go, Mom!" Aaron said, lifting his half-eaten burger my way.

"I've gathered a truckload of wisdom caring for all of you and intend to use it in this new venture." Figuring that out had taken a while. Cleaning may be my only skill, but it was a skill people with pets needed me to share.

I looked at Lark. "If you can give me a stack of brochures for your training center, I'll have them at the counter."

"Of course." Her joy-bubble laughter sparkled through the air.

"I also plan to support local canine crafters." I placed my glass back on the table. "Anyway, that's it. That's all I wanted to say." I sat back down. "You all may not need me, but the area dogs do."

I was suddenly mobbed with hugs and kisses from all my children. Snick insisted on joining the fray.

And there it was, the feeling I'd sought these past few months— belonging, community.

Love.

Nothing could stop me from the joy, happiness and abundance I wanted, except my own thoughts.

"One more thing," I said, pulling away from all the hugs. "From now on, if you want help, you're going to have to ask for it."

31

MAEVE

"Has anyone seen Neve?" I asked as I took the last of the dishes from the picnic table outside to the kitchen.

"She's out front," Zoe said, putting away the leftover potato salad and macaroni salad in the fridge while Merry and Aaron did the dishes. Zoe gave me a concerned look. "Waiting for Patrick."

My heart sank, and I bit back a swear that would have Mom threatening to wash my mouth out with soap. The man was gone and still creating chaos. "Thanks."

I grabbed my travel coffee mug and took a slug for courage. I headed out the front door and found Neve scrunched into a chair on the porch, purple polka-dot shorts riding up her thighs, her sneaker heels kicking at the rattan loveseat leg, creating a disjointed tattoo.

"Hey, what are you doing out here?" I sat on the cushion next to her. "The party's out back. Grandpa's starting the fire pit."

"Waiting for Dad." Her fingers worked the ball inside the heart-shaped fidget. "He promised to come."

Before or after our talk? Another broken promise that left me picking up the pieces. "I know you were looking forward to seeing Daddy." I took in a long breath and reached for one of her hands. "But I don't think he's going to make it tonight."

"Cuz I wanted to help Dani instead of playing games?"

"Oh, no, honey bunches, of course not. This has nothing to do with you." How could I possibly explain that I'd exchanged her freedom from his yo-yo visits and constant disappointments for a few thousand dollars? That wouldn't bolster her self-esteem. "You are the brightest, most wonderful part of our lives. Daddy just needs some time to figure things out. His leaving is absolutely not your fault."

Her fingers worked her fidget in her lap so hard, I thought the ball inside the flannel fabric would pop out.

"Why does Daddy not love us?" she asked, focused on her fingers.

Oh, wow. That was a loaded question. One that stopped me in my tracks. For all his faults, Patrick was still her father. And if she wanted a relationship with him as she grew older, that was her right. I wouldn't taint her ideas of him, like his mother had done of his father, for a bit of sympathy.

I had to choose my words carefully.

I turned in my seat so I could look straight into her eyes. I thought I'd have more time to figure out this conversation. That it wouldn't show up until after another long stretch of absence on Patrick's part.

"He does love you," I said, taking both her hands in mine. "But you see, Daddy wasn't lucky like we are. We have Grandma and Grandpa that love us and care for us. His parents were sick and didn't know how to love him. So, he doesn't know how to love people back the right way. It doesn't mean he doesn't love you in his own way. He's just decided that it's best for him to stay away for a while."

Her head dipped lower, her hair curtaining her face. "How long?"

"I don't know, honey bunches. But no matter where Daddy is, you'll always have me right here with you."

She pulled her hands out of mine and reached for the fidget in her lap. Round and round went the ball under the flannel. I couldn't tell how my words were landing. Was I making a mess of this? "Does it make you sad?"

Her forehead pleated. "I don't like his way."

I kissed the top of her head. "It's okay to be sad and angry and to love him and miss him all at once."

She slammed her fists into her thighs, her whole body vibrating. "I'm mad at him, and I want to yell at him to go away and never come back."

I wanted to take all that hurt away from her and didn't know how. "I'm sorry, honey bunches. I know it hurts when Daddy makes a promise and breaks it."

"He—" She made the huh-huh sound she did when her feelings were all jumbled, so I gathered her onto my lap, willing my body to absorb her pain. "He's never here."

And that was the crux of it all. He'd never been there when we needed him. "He's looking for a way to stop the hurt inside him."

"But he has us." Her little body stiffened in my arms. A meltdown was just around the corner. We should be enough, but we weren't.

"And we are the best," I said, trying to lighten the mood. I covered her in kisses. "You've got me, kiddo, and I love you more than the whole galaxy."

She giggled, then went back to serious mode. "Will he ever come back?"

He probably would if he thought he could get another handout from me. I had to make sure that payoff was a one-time thing. That he couldn't use Neve to bleed me dry. Add that to the list of things I needed to save for: a family lawyer.

"I don't know, honey bunches. One day, I think he'll be sad he missed out on how wonderful you are. Right now, he needs to figure things out. Just like we're doing with the therapy."

She leaned her head against my chest. "Charlie's dad is breaking her family. She goes to therapy, too. Her nana takes her."

Another thing they could bond over. I didn't want Charlie to leave in August. For Neve to deal with another loss. "It's good to have a friend who knows what you're feeling. Let's invite her for a sleepover next weekend."

Neve perked up. "Princess movie?"

"Is there any other kind?"

I felt her smile against my heart. "Cupcakes?"

"Don't push your luck, young lady."

She settled in my arms, and I felt sorry for Patrick, sorry he was missing out on such a wonderful girl. "Mommy?"

"What?"

"Do you love me more than coffee?"

"What kind of question is that? Of course! I love you more than anything in the whole wide world."

Gaze meeting mine, she reached up and twirled a hank of my hair, the way she used to do as a baby while nursing. "I like sugar the way you like coffee."

"That is true."

"Grandma says all that coffee isn't good for you."

Grandma should mind her own business. "It helps me focus."

"Let's make a deal."

"Uh-oh. I'm not sure I like where this is going."

She glanced at the ever-present travel coffee mug I'd set aside on the end table when I'd come out to find her. "If you stop drinking coffee, I'll stop eating sugar."

"Oh, wow. I'll have to think about that." Could I give up coffee to help Neve deal with her sugar restriction? She was dealing with so much lately. I could make the sacrifice.

"We'll do a hard thing together," she said.

When she put it that way, my heart melted. "Deal! You'll have to give me a few days to get the caffeine out of my system."

She gave the hank of my hair a gentle tug. "Um, I think that means I can have a cupcake with a princess movie. To get the sugar out of my system."

I laughed and tickled her until she giggled. "You are devious."

Her giggles died and she went back to working the fidget in her lap.

"I'm sad Mr. Luke is leaving, too." She focused on pinging the ball back and forth between her thumbs. "I wanted to play baseball better so Mr. Luke would stay."

"Oh, Neve." Another loss she had to deal with. One I hadn't seen coming. "You played so well. I was so proud of you. And Mr. Luke is so proud of how you learned to whack your gremlins like a pro. And he likes you whether you play baseball or not. He thinks you're great."

I realized that these weren't just words to appease Neve, but a fact. He'd been so good with all the kids at camp. That was where his true self had shone, where all his best qualities had come out. Too bad he couldn't see that.

"Not great enough," she said, tears zigzagging down her cheeks.

I brushed away the tears with my thumb. So many losses for a little girl and the summer was just getting started. I wanted to shield her from more pain even though the task was impossible. "He and Dani came here just for the baking contest. We talked about that."

"But I want them to stay." Her lip drooped into a pout.

"I know. I'd like that, too." As soon as I said the words, I knew they were true.

Neve looked at me with those deep brown eyes, filled with hope. "Can we ask them?"

Luke had said that he would stay wherever Dani landed. I wasn't ready for another relationship. Not yet. But if Luke stayed around Brighton, in the future, we could see if anything might develop.

What if I could convince Dani to apprentice at the bakery?

"We can try."

Had I just set Neve— us —up for another disappointment?

32

GRACE

Maeve sat in an Adirondack chair, away from the rest of the family busy building s'mores by the firepit. Now was my chance to talk with my eldest daughter one-on-one. I took the sunflower-yellow chair next to the cardinal-red one she'd chosen.

"What are you drinking?" I'd expected to see her usual travel mug of coffee, but the liquid in the glass was clear.

Maeve glanced into the glass and made a face. "Water."

"Water?" I settled back into the chair, watching Paul, Kate, Lark, Ansel, Aaron, Meredith and Zoe talk and laugh around the firepit. Snick went from person to person for pats and possible treats. They'd all been warned not to feed her under penalty of my wrath, but those eyes were hard to resist. I turned back to Maeve. "Who are you and what have you done with my daughter?"

She drank in a long breath and held it for a moment. "Neve and I made a deal."

"This I have to hear."

She slugged down half the water in the glass. "I have one

week to get the caffeine out of my system. After that, Neve said she'd stay off sugar as long as I stay off coffee."

I chuckled. "Smart cookie."

A small smile danced on Maeve's lips. "Maybe a little too smart. This is going to hurt."

So would the next words that I had to say. "I owe you an apology."

Her gaze found mine. "What for?"

"I saw you with Neve earlier. You're a good mother. I don't tell you that often enough. But I'm proud of everything you've accomplished since you had to forgo your dream of culinary school. It couldn't have been easy to work in a sandwich shop when you'd wanted to travel and bake. Starting your own business wasn't easy either."

Maeve turned back to examining her glass and snorted. "Yeah, because every almost-thirty daughter should still be dependent on her parents." She reached for my hand and squeezed it. "Don't get me wrong, Mom. I'm grateful for everything you and Dad do for me. I just long for a little independence."

"I understand." That was what I wanted too— a way to be myself. "I'll do better. I promise to respect your boundaries."

Maeve took her hand back and twirled the glass in her lap. "Thanks, Mom."

I knitted my fingers into a tight knot, trying to choose my next words carefully. "I also owe you an apology for the way I harped on you when you were younger. I honestly didn't know you had ADHD."

"I just found out myself. I can see how I might have looked stubborn and uncaring. But I really did try to live up to what you wanted me to be."

And that made me so sad. This beautiful little girl had suffered because I'd misread her needs. "I read up on how getting organized can be difficult. I tried one of the methods they mentioned to help Neve clean up her room."

"I wondered if you'd done it."

"No, we made it into a game. Gamifying, they called it. One category at a time. We made a chart. She's probably going to need help for a while but, eventually, she'll be able to organize her room herself." I tsked. "I wish I'd known about that when you were struggling. Maybe then you'd have more confidence."

Maeve stared at her glass, rolling it back and forth between her hands.

"Patrick left," she said, her voice so neutral that I felt the depth of her hurt. She'd loved him so much, given him so many chances. And he'd let her down every single time. She lifted her left hand and waggled her fingers. The engagement ring was gone. "For good this time. Cost me all my savings but he won't be disrupting Neve's life anymore."

He'd left my girls for money? Something nasty roiled through my gut. I wanted to hunt him down and make him feel how badly he'd hurt two beautiful human beings. He'd never been good enough for Maeve. Good riddance. "I'm so sorry."

"It's for the best." She tipped her head from side to side. "I just wish it hadn't taken me so long to figure things out."

"One of your best qualities is your loyalty."

Silent tears ran down her cheeks. "I wanted what you and Dad have. To walk into a room and have my partner light up. I wanted a family for Neve like you and Dad gave us. Two parents. Safety. Security. Love. I thought when he gave me the ring after I opened the bakery that it would finally happen."

"You can still have that family, security and love." I reached over and thumbed the tears away.

She shook her head, sending her curls cascading around her shoulders. "Not with the hours I work."

"You never know. Love could be closer than you think," I

said, thinking of Luke and the way he looked at Maeve as if she was precious.

"Luke didn't come, after he said he would." She shrugged as if it was no big deal, but having another man break a promise had to hurt.

Why hadn't he come? Because of the confrontation with Patrick at the baking contest? I wouldn't have thought he'd let a little thing like that get in his way. I needed to have a word with him. No. That was exactly what Maeve would call meddling. I had to let her work things out on her own.

"Plus, he's leaving," Maeve said. "Tomorrow morning. Moving on to the next baking contest." She sighed long and low. "Besides, I need time to figure out what I want, not jump right into another relationship."

"Very wise."

"Enough about me." Maeve shook her head, drained the glass of the remaining water and smiled at me. "So, you're going to become a business owner."

She thought it was a stupid idea. "You think you're the only one with shattered dreams, Maeve? I was young once, too. I didn't spring up fully grown as a mother."

"Mom, I was just asking. I'm curious. That's all."

"Sorry, it still all feels tender." I stared at the night sky, glittering with stars. "When I was a teen, I wanted to be a champion dressage rider."

"As in horses?"

I nodded. "As in horses. Dressage, it felt like dancing, and I loved the close relationship you had to develop with the horse to have it trust you enough to make the maneuvers look effortless."

"I never knew you rode."

"It was a long time ago. Before kids. I haven't sat a horse in about forty years." Other dreams had filled my mind once I'd met Ansel. "Not in the budget once you have three young kids running around."

A choice we'd made, knowing full well it would entail sacrifices.

"I'm actually impressed," Maeve said.

I smiled. "I used to be quite the athlete, too. Field hockey in the fall. Gymnastics in the winter."

"Gymnastics? Really?"

"Really." I wasn't ever going to make the top ranks, but I'd enjoyed each and every sport. Mostly, I'd enjoyed the way practices and games kept me away from home. Sad really. "Track in the spring."

"Wow, Mom, you're full of surprises today."

Home hadn't been a warm and loving space. "You don't remember my mother because you were too little when she died." I'd taken care of my mother during her dark episodes the way I'd wanted to be taken care of. "She was depressive, and she seemed to have energy only to point out everything I did wrong. Cleaning was what got her attention and the few compliments she handed out. It wasn't something I particularly liked."

If I was honest, it made me feel like a servant growing up instead of a cherished daughter. I'd tried to be a better mother to my daughters, but apparently, I'd failed in a different way. With both of them.

And yet, the cleaning had also made me feel useful, needed. Part of keeping the peace between my parents' difficult relationship was keeping the house clean, something my mother couldn't do. Maybe she had ADHD, too. I'd read that it was hereditary.

"Horses, riding were an escape." I gave a rocky chuckle. "Come to think of it, the way I earned riding lessons was to shovel manure." That and braiding other people's horses for shows.

"I get that," Maeve said. "That's what baking was for me in high school."

As much as Dot Carpenter had made my life difficult, she had provided a bright spot in Maeve's. "I'm so glad you found baking and had your grandmother to give you what I couldn't."

I drained the rest of the iced tea from my glass. "And that's what I wanted to be for Neve. A grandmother she could always turn to." I shook my head. "In my mind, that meant spoiling her now and then like I'd wanted to be spoiled growing up."

"Baking is love." Maeve looked at me. "That's why I baked a special dessert every Sunday for your dinners."

To show me she loved me, and the gesture had gone completely over my head. I glanced at the half-eaten cake on the picnic table. She'd made it to show me her love.

"When I needed a job to help out with the bills while you kids were in high school..." I shrugged. "Cleaning was something that gave me the flexibility to be around for you and your brother and sister."

"And that helped give us that loving foundation. It's why I came back to Brighton after I found out I was pregnant. I wanted that for Neve. I wanted her to have grandparents and aunts and uncles. To be surrounded by love."

"Oh, darling girl. We adore Neve, and we're so glad you came back home and allowed us to share her with you."

I leaned over and hugged my eldest daughter, letting her feel my love for her in every cell.

"I'm sorry I was so hard on you," Maeve said, tears in her voice. "I thought you disapproved of everything I did, and it hurt."

"Oh, Maeve. And here I thought you disapproved of everything I did."

Maeve moved out of my hug and wiped at tears. "Do you want me to bake some dog treats for your store?"

"Would you?" I hadn't expected the offer, but now that she'd made it, I could see bins of treats displayed at the checkout counter, little bags with the bakery logo for customers to take them home. I got that the offer was her way of forgiving me.

"All you have to do is ask."

"I would like it very much if you baked some treats. Could you make them different sizes? I find most treats are too big for a small dog like Snick, especially one that tends to look at food and gain weight." I laughed, pinching my waistline. "Like her owner."

"Let me do some research."

Maeve looked out to the firepit where Snick trolled, looking for a handout. "So, you're keeping her?"

As if Snick knew we were talking about her, she trotted up and jumped into my lap. I kissed the top of her head, and she licked my chin. "Looks that way."

"Neve will be happy." Maeve reached over and scratched Snick under the chin. "You always did like dogs."

"They love unconditionally." I reached over for Maeve's hand. "Unlike humans. I'm sorry that you felt as if you didn't measure up when you were growing up, that I didn't love you. I never meant for you to feel that way. I will always love you, Maeve, even when I'm not showing you the right way."

She leaned her head against my shoulder. "I'll always want you in my life, Mom. Even if I move away."

33

MAEVE

W hat I loved best about Mondays was sleeping in. To anyone else 7 a.m. would sound early but, for me, it was an utter luxury. I took my time making a breakfast for me and Neve. And half-caff coffee, which I had to say, wasn't quite as satisfying as full-caff. I shuddered at the thought of no coffee at all by the end of the week.

But Neve was right; we would help each other through a hard thing and both be the better for it.

After I dropped Neve off at art camp, I made my way back to the bakery.

I still couldn't get over Mom riding horses when she was a teenager. Playing all those sports? I shook my head. I'd never thought of her as wanting to be anything but a mom. I never thought of her as having a desire for adventure.

Maybe that was where I got mine. Dad certainly had no yen to travel. I'd always thought of Mom as a homebody but really that title belonged to Dad. And apparently my athletic ability also came from Mom. I smiled. Who would've thought?

Maybe Mom and I weren't so different after all. That was something to ponder— later. I had too many other things crowding my mind this morning. For now, Mom and I had come to a truce. One I would work harder to keep.

Instead of going into the bakery and dealing with the mound of paperwork, I tucked my key fob into the waistband of my shorts and headed toward the B&B. I had a two-part plan. I was pretty sure how part one would go.

Part two had my stomach rumbling like a volcano.

I hadn't walked one block when C.C. Bass with her drab brown skirt, smushed-pea-colored blouse and sensible sandals stopped me. "Maeve! When are you opening?"

I did not want to deal with the town gossip today. "It's Monday. We're closed on Mondays."

She blinked behind her owlish glasses. "Since when?"

"Since always. Sundays and Mondays. Closed."

With the rolling of her lower lip and her tightening fists, she looked as if she was about to throw a tantrum. "But I need scones for book club!"

"Not today."

"Are you sure? I'll take some day-old ones."

"One hundred percent sure. There's nothing in the bakery cases."

She narrowed her gaze at me. Then her eyes took on a sparkle of mischief. She placed a hand beside her mouth and whispered, "I hear Patrick's moved on."

"Did you now?" There it was. She just couldn't help herself. What was going on in her life that the way to make herself feel good was by spreading other people's pain like everything topping on a bagel? I made a noncommittal noise, shifted my purse to my other shoulder and went by her. I didn't have the time or the energy for this.

"With Amy Tucker." Her voice was filled with smugness.

I lifted a hand, waved and kept moving forward. "She's welcome to him."

"Hey! What do you mean she's welcome to him?" C.C.

trotted after me, grabbed my arm and stopped me. "You guys broke up?"

"Took me long enough."

A gleeful smile filled her face at the first-to-know gossip she'd get to strew all over town. "Well, well, well, isn't that interesting." C.C. all but skipped beside me. "Does that mean that you've moved on to Luke Saunders?"

I rolled my eyes. The last person I would choose to discuss any relationship was C.C. "Haven't you heard? He's leaving this morning."

"Really?" Her lower lip curled again. "That's too bad. You guys looked good together."

"As if looks make any difference to a relationship." I picked up my pace, hoping C.C. would get the hint. She stared after me. "Bye, C.C. See you later."

"Where are you going?"

"Falls into the need-to-know category. You don't."

"Well, the nerve!"

I didn't bother looking behind. She was no doubt plotting how to best scatter her malicious tidbits. I chuckled. If she only knew what I was about to do.

At the Lilac Inn, I chatted with Lilah Copeland, the B&B's owner. Lilah, with her dandelion puff of white hair and her everpresent lilac shirtdress, looked like the gracious hostess she was. Then I went up the stairs and knocked on Dani's door—the Lavender Room —pulse kicking up.

Dani opened the door and furrowed her brow. "Maeve?"

I pointed inside. "Can I come in?"

Using the door as a shield, she ushered me into a room Lilah had lovingly appointed. By the window sat an upholstered chair with cushions bearing the image of lavender sprigs. By its side was a small table with a stack of books and a lamp. A white desk held a drink station on one side. The antique white dresser had a lace runner and several antique vases filled with lavender. The whole room gave off a cozy vibe that invited the guest to stay and relax. Lilah had done a great job with her renovation. I carefully placed my purse on the dresser before turning back to Dani.

Giving me a confused look, Dani plucked a stack of T-shirts from the open dresser drawer and dumped it in the open suitcase on the bed. "Luke's not here, if that's who you're looking for."

It wasn't but now I wondered where he could be. "I came to see you."

"Me?" She swiveled to face me, and the stack of donut T-shirts toppled onto the area rug.

I chuckled. "Where did you get all those donut shirts?"

"A catalog." She glanced down at the mess at her feet. "They're all too big because I ordered them for Luke. When I was trying to convince him going from baking contest to baking contest was a good thing." She crouched down and retrieved the T-shirts, holding them tight in her arms. "Really, it was just an excuse to visit a ton of bakeries." She pointed her chin in the direction of the tote on the desk that held her notebook. "And taste."

Her expression darkened as she rose and let the T-shirts fall back into the suitcase. "That was before I knew about our father."

"What do you mean?"

She nibbled at her thumbnail. "I feel I kinda have to explain about Luke."

"There's no need." I waved her comment away. I didn't want to think about Luke. Not right now. One step at a time, or I'd lose my focus.

"Actually, there is." She plopped down on the edge of the bed and worried the hem of her tie-dye "Donut Stop Believing" T-shirt. "It's been a rough couple of years for Luke."

I leaned my rear against the dresser. "It's hard to lose your parents and your career at the same time."

"It's more than that, though. My dad... he was a big man." She gave a sad smile. "Big smile. Big belly laugh. Big personality. Everybody loved him."

Tears slid down her face, but she made no attempt to wipe them. I let her unroll her story at her own pace.

"When I was a kid, he was my hero. But it turns out he was a zero. When he died... he left behind a lot of debt. He'd used Luke's name to scam people." She shook her head. "Not quite sure I get how he did it, but he got a lot of money and, instead of investing it like he promised, he wasted it all."

She took one of the T-shirts from the messy pile in her suitcase and carefully refolded it.

"It's like he was a person I didn't know. And it messed me up for a while. If it wasn't for Luke, I don't know where I'd be right now." She started a pile of folded T-shirts beside the suitcase. "Paying back the people Dad scammed just about wiped out everything Luke had." She shrugged one shoulder. "Me? After I got back from rehab, I baked away my feelings."

That explained a lot— why Luke couldn't pay for her tuition to culinary school, why Dani had needed to win the contest, why Luke was so determined to get me to help her, why he worried about Dani.

If I'd known, things might have gone differently.

"The truck?" Dani continued, reaching for the next T-shirt. "That was the last of his savings. I was supposed to earn tuition to culinary school with the baking contest wins. He did clinics and autograph sessions to pay for our expenses on the road. That was our deal. And I wanted to win for him, so bad."

She rolled her lips inward and pinched them with her teeth. Her gaze met mine. It shimmered with fresh tears. "Then I found out what happened, and I wanted to pay him back for all he'd done for me. I wanted him to stop worrying about me and start worrying about himself. If I did like he wanted and went to school, then he could go on with his own life."

I certainly understood what it was like to owe an emotional, if not a financial, debt to someone.

She knife-edged the next T-shirt with the side of her hand. "I don't want to disappoint him, you know, because he's done so much for me." She sighed so loudly that her whole body deflated, crumpling the freshly folded T-shirt in her lap. "But I really don't want to go to school right now. Maybe later. Just not now. Right now, I want to focus on the baking to see if that's what I really want. Because, the donuts, they're mixing me up."

"Because of your dad?" She'd mentioned he took her out for donuts before going to see Luke's ballgames.

She nodded. "There're good and bad memories, and they're all jumbled. One minute I miss him horribly, because we had some good times, you know. Like our donut dates. And I know he loved me." She stared out the window, chin wobbling. "And the next I hate him so much for what he's done to ruin our grandparents' orchard, to us, especially to Luke."

"Yeah, that's a lot. Relationships are complicated." I both loved my mother and resented her at times. Sometimes at the same time. Dani's father's betrayal also explained why Luke had the argument with Patrick, protecting Neve. He'd seen what I wasn't ready to admit— that Patrick was self-centered and would always put himself first. Like Luke's father had done with his investors' money...and confidence.

"These past two week here?" Dani went on, her gaze pleading. "They've been the best I can remember in a long time. I really liked baking with you, Maeve."

"And I quite enjoyed having you in my kitchen." I'd loved the company, loved showing off, loved seeing her learn. Loved the fun we'd had.

She blinked. "Really?"

"That's what I want to talk to you about." Arms folded

under my chest, I cleared my throat. "How's your bread baking?"

She sucked in a breath, holding herself statue-still—as if any movement would make me change my mind. "It's good. And I learn fast."

"I have a proposition for you, then."

Her eyes widened.

"And I think it would solve both your desire to bake, and Luke's desire for you to get an education."

She sucked in her lips and nodded madly.

"Natalie, my bread baker, has to deal with a family emergency and most likely won't be back until fall. I could use your help at the bakery."

She pumped her heels up and down and clasped her hands over her heart. "Really?"

"Then in the fall, you could go to Hopewell College. It's not a fancy culinary school but they did add a decent culinary program a few years ago. I suggest adding some business management classes if you plan on ever owning your own bakery." I tried to keep a straight face, but her excitement was catching. "And you could apprentice at the bakery when you're not in school."

Her smile took over her face, making the rings at the corners of her brows shake. "Really?"

"Yes, really. Warning: I won't be able to pay you much."

"I'd work for free!"

"Okay, lesson one." I shook a finger at her. "Never undervalue yourself. You don't work for free. You are worth a salary for your time and talent. You'd be doing me a favor. And I'm going to work you hard. I'll pay you."

She nodded like a bobblehead doll, then launched herself at me and hugged me so tight I thought my ribs would crack.

"Luke, he's one of the good guys," she said, still hanging on to me. "Everything he's done for the past few years has been for other people. Being here, with you, it's the most relaxed I've seen him since we hit the road."

"Okay," I said, moving out of her death-grip hug, not quite ready to deal with Luke yet. "Tuesday morning, 4 a.m. Come to the back door."

"I'll be there!"

I grabbed my purse from the dresser top, making to leave. "If you want, we could add your donuts to the menu."

Preemptive strike so Luke wouldn't park his truck in front of my bakery again. Plus, if people liked them so much, it would bring them *into* the store and buying other baked goods.

"Really?" She plucked her notebook from her tote and flipped the pages, showing me a complex diagram. "I've been thinking about mail order. I mailed some to myself last week." She reached to the desk for a mailer box and pushed it toward me. "What do you think? Did they stay fresh enough?"

This youthful enthusiasm was what the bakery and I needed right now. I took a donut and tasted it. They really were good. No wonder a long line had queued for a taste. "The idea has potential."

She dropped the mailer box back on the desk and scurried around the room like a mouse in a maze. "I have to find Luke. I have to tell him I'm staying. OMG, I have to find a place to stay. And a car."

"Whoa, Dani. Slow down."

She stopped in place, nodding. "Yeah, one step at a time."

"First, ask Lilah if she can hold the room for you until you can find a place to stay. I can give you the name of a realtor." I toyed with the strap of my purse. "Would you let me talk to Luke first?"

She stared at me for a moment, then a slow smile crept over her face, making her eyes glitter. "Yes, of course!"

"Do you know where I can find him?" This wasn't going to

be an easy talk, and I already felt the butterflies bashing around in my stomach.

"At the fairgrounds, collecting the truck."

"How long ago did he leave?"

A smile filled Dani's voice. "If you hurry, you can still catch him."

34

MAEVE

When I got to the fairgrounds, I couldn't see the donut truck. The place was deserted. The gate was locked. All the vendor and game tents were put away. All the porta-potties were gone. All the food trucks had moved on to the next event. The only thing that remained was the carousel, and even that had a fence around it to keep kids with nothing better to do from vandalizing it.

I called Dani. "Did Luke come back?"

"Hang on a sec, I'll find out where he is." She put me on hold and came back a moment later. "He's at the sports field. I didn't tell him you were the one looking for him."

I wasn't sure if that was good or bad. The delay in finding Luke wasn't doing the butterflies in my belly a favor. I could really use some coffee about now. But I'd promised Neve I'd quit, and someone had to keep their promises to her.

I found the donut truck parked by the equipment building. For a moment, I sat in the parking lot, hands unwilling to let go of the steering wheel. What was I doing? What if I'd imagined his interest? And really, how stupid was it to tell someone you liked them, then tell them to keep their distance?

But I needed to tell him how I felt, that I had put the past behind. That I could look toward a different future than the one that had kept me stuck for so long. Maybe this wasn't my original dream but whatever came next could be just as wonderful. And I wanted him to be part of that future.

"Right," I said, pushing open the van door. "Here goes nothing." I wasn't sure how he'd react to my confession, but I was strong enough to let him go if he didn't want me in his life.

I'd be fine.

And Neve and I would have a great life.

Sucking in a breath, I headed toward the equipment building and almost ran right into Luke rushing out, carrying a clipboard.

"Maeve?" His smile made the side of his eyes crinkle as if he was happy to see me and lit warmth low in my belly.

"Hey," I said, suddenly tongue-tied. I stuck my hands in my shorts pockets.

"You were my next stop." He tucked the clipboard under his arm, closed and locked the equipment building door.

Okay, already this wasn't turning out anything like I'd planned. Things rarely did, I reminded myself. I almost laughed. "I was?"

He pointed toward the donut truck. "Want to go for a ride with me?"

"Not particularly." That donut truck had stirred up enough trouble to last a lifetime.

"There's something I want to show you."

I couldn't imagine what, but I needed time to figure out how to say what I wanted to say without sounding insane. "Fine."

He opened the passenger door for me. It creaked so loudly, I was sure it would fall right off its hinges. "Is this thing safe?"

"It's on its last leg, but it'll have to do for now."

As he drove, I tried not to focus on his hands, not to remember how they felt holding mine. I really tried to keep myself from looking at his lips and remembering how they'd felt on my lips. I had to pull myself together, or I'd make a mess of things. And I wasn't going to let emotions take charge, the way I had with Patrick. I pulled my gaze to the passing landscape, seeing none of it go by.

"Mom missed you at Sunday dinner," I said. Although Mom hadn't mentioned Luke not being there at all.

"Mom?"

"Neve, too." I couldn't quite keep the accusation out of my voice. "You made a promise."

He frowned. "Ah, Maeve."

"Ah? That's all you have?"

"I'm sorry. I wasn't thinking." He hitched a shoulder. "I didn't want to intrude on a family event." He tipped his head. "And after what happened at the contest, I wasn't sure you wanted me there."

I had told him to stay away. I'd just meant then, not forever.

"Fair enough." I looked outside again. Trust was such a fragile thing. One Patrick had shattered piece by piece. But not trusting, not hoping wasn't what I wanted for the rest of my life. "I did, by the way. Want you there."

"Then I truly am sorry I missed it."

He reached for my hand and wove his fingers with mine. I couldn't stop staring at our entwined hands, or the sigh of contentment.

"Where are you going next?" I asked, trying to fill the loaded silence between us. What I really wanted to say was, *Please stay here with me and Neve.*

When he said nothing, I turned back to him, and all he did was smile that press-conference smile. What was he up to?

"Wow! Luke Saunders without a story? What is wrong with you?"

"Oh, there's a story all right. It just needs the right setting." He took his gaze off the road and glanced at me. "Because this person, she's really stubborn and needs physical proof. Words aren't enough for her."

My heart skipped then rolled like water at full boil. Where on earth was he taking me? What was he trying to prove?

At the stop at intersection of Pine and Lakeshore, he took back his hand, leaving me not knowing what to do with mine. I missed its solid feel, its warmth.

"Close your eyes," he said.

I narrowed my gaze at him, unsure where this was going. *You are crazy, Maeve. You're planning on telling him you like him, that you want him to stick around.* "Why?"

He sent me a pointed look. "Can you just do it and not ask so many questions?"

"I'm not sure."

He tilted his head, pleading. "Do it. Please?"

"Fine." I closed my eyes, leaving a slit.

"All the way."

I growled but did as he asked.

A few minutes later, he turned onto a dirt road that needed grading. The roll of the truck from side to side as he navigated the road had me hanging on to the door for dear life.

He stopped. "Ah, ah, keep your eyes closed."

He opened his door and came around to open mine. He held my hand and, as if it had found home, it willingly let his fingers wrap around my palm, warm and firm. With his other hand on my elbow, he helped me down the truck's step. Then he stood behind me. My whole back tingled. Part of me wanted to pull away. The other wanted to lean back against him.

But I had to take it slow this time. I had to make sure. For both Neve's and my sake. So, I stayed exactly where I was.

He leaned his head over my shoulder and whispered in my ear, sending a quiver of pleasure down my spine. "Okay, open your eyes."

There before me stood the cottage on Hummingbird Lane that I'd coveted.

I spun to face him, ice filling me with dread. "Is this a joke?"

He frowned. "Never been more serious in my life."

I'd never told anyone about the cottage. How could he know? "You bought *this* cottage?"

"Made a rent-to-own deal with the owner." He shrugged. "When I saw it, I thought of you."

"Of me?"

He suddenly looked shy, a creep of pink coloring his neck. "I could see you puttering with those flowers. Neve running around the backyard." He shrugged again as if the vision was foolish.

"For months I had the Zillow tab featuring this cottage open. I looked at it and dreamed about buying it every night..." I swallowed hard. "Until Patrick came back and made it clear that he had no intentions of ever being a family."

"Oh, wow!" He put a hand over his heart. "I swear I had no idea."

Luke couldn't buy the cottage because of the financial mess his father had left him, but he'd found a way to get it anyway. Because he could imagine me there. The thought all but melted my resolve. "Dani told me what your father did. I'm really sorry."

"She wasn't supposed to."

"Why not? There's nothing to be ashamed of."

He stuck his hands in his jeans pocket and turned toward the water, staring far away. "Dad was always after the big score, the thing that was going to make him rich. What he had was an aversion to actual work. He'd look for the quick way out. Got into investment schemes that tended to go south." He glanced over his shoulder at me. "When I went away to college, he even lost the family orchard his grandparents and parents spent a lifetime building into a thriving business."

"That's awful." I wanted to hug the hurt away but kept my distance.

He turned back to the water. "Our family was never on a stable financial footing— either feast or famine. But growing up, Dani and I never knew. Our house was filled with love."

Like my family's house still was. Why had I concentrated on everything I'd missed out on instead of everything I already had?

"Dad loved us and supported us as best he could. He made it to almost all my games from Little League to majors."

"That's something special." I'd always had someone— either Mom or Dad or both or the whole family —at my games, too. Someone cheering for me. Someone in my corner. I hadn't realized how special that was. How I'd needed that support.

"He left a mountain of debts when he died," Luke said, running a hand through his hair. "Going through his office, I saw all the people he hurt."

"And you paid them all back," I reminded him. Someone else probably wouldn't have.

"He'd used my name to float his latest scheme." His jaw flinched. "I wanted to strangle him. I'd worked hard to build a solid reputation. I couldn't do anything about him, but I could clear my name."

"You have. I saw how all your fans still adore you." I knocked my shoulder into his. "You're a good man, Luke."

He nodded, turned to the house, looking at the sad paint. "Part of the rental deal is fixing up the cottage."

"I can give you the name of a great carpenter," I teased, trying to lighten the atmosphere.

He lifted his brows. "Aren't you wondering why?"

I came to stand beside him, mimicking his hands-in-pockets stance. "Why you need a carpenter?"

"Why I'm renting a house."

Like him, I kept staring forward. "Because you want to be

able to make a quick exit?"

"Ah, Maeve." He shook his head. "I would've bought it if I could."

Was he saying he planned on staying? My heart beat too fast, filling with hope that I didn't want to feel. Not right now, anyway.

We both kept staring at the cottage, at the bushes that needed trimming, at the weeds that needed pulling, at the paint that needed scraping.

"I offered Dani an apprenticeship on the condition she takes courses at Hopewell College in the fall," I said.

He crooked a smile. "What a coincidence!"

"What do you mean?"

"Coach Mac is retiring, and I was offered the Athletic Director position at Hopewell College this morning."

The blasted hope sprung up again like a soufflé right out of the oven, golden, puffy, beautiful. "You accepted?"

"I jumped on the chance to stick around for a while. Dani'll be able to get free tuition." He laughed. "I was wondering how I'd sell her on going. She doesn't think I get that she doesn't want to go to school. But I saw how she came to life in your bakery. I was going to beg you to take her on, even if I had to pay her salary myself."

For his sister's sake, he was willing to stay in middle-of-nowhere Brighton, pay me money he didn't have. "You're staying, then?"

"Looks that way." He turned toward me yet left enough room so I didn't feel caged. He reached for one of my curls and rolled it around a finger. I swear I could feel the heat of his touch all the way down to my toes. "There's this beautiful, prickly woman I'd love to get to know better."

My heart went all soft and wobbly. "Neve and I would like you to stay."

I wanted to wrap my arms around him and kiss him, but I

had to make sure he understood my boundaries. I wouldn't make the same mistake twice. "But I can't jump from one bad relationship to another."

"Bad? Me?" he teased.

"To be determined."

He laughed. "I get that." That stormy gray gaze didn't waver, letting me see the truth of his intention. "You need time to figure out what you want." Then his smile went wicked. "Doesn't mean I can't stick around to show you what you're missing."

I laughed. A real laugh that came from way down in my belly. "OMG, the ego on you!"

He reached for both my hands. "I fell for you that first day."

"You mean the day you almost caused my bakery to fail."

"Yeah, well, I'm sorry about that. But people usually tend to want to give me what I want. And you didn't. And I really wanted to give Dani a leg up at the competition. You stuck by your guns. I admire that."

He took a step closer, and my traitorous body felt his pull. "I like the way you challenge me."

"I like the way you keep your promises. I like the way you are around Neve. She's part of the reason I can't just jump into another relationship."

"I like Neve. A lot." He wrapped his hands around my rib cage. "I like you, Maeve. A lot."

"I like you, Luke. A lot." My hands crept to his shoulders. "But it's not enough. I refuse to be another notch on Internet Luke's belt."

"Internet Luke's reputation is highly overinflated." He glanced toward the cottage. "I'm planning on buying this place, and I'm really hoping that, one day, you and Neve will feel comfortable enough to share it with me."

"You're saying all the right things." My hands were shaking. My whole body was. Tears pooled hot at the back of my eyes, afraid to hope, yet desperately wanting to. Because I really did like Luke. A lot.

"I plan on doing more than talking," he said. "I'll show you every single day that I mean every single word. You and Neve."

I grinned. "Won't take much to win her over. She already likes you and wanted me to ask you to stay."

"So, you looking for me is just because Neve likes me?" he teased.

"I spent so many years hoping." I shook my head. "All for nothing."

"I get that. After everything that happened with my dad and my injury, I'd given up hope. No career. No savings. I saw nothing in my future. Until I met you. Then everything changed. Then suddenly, the future didn't look so bleak." Luke shook his head. "He was the wrong guy."

"And you're the right one?"

"I'll prove it to you— even if it takes a lifetime."

I sucked in a breath. A lifetime! I couldn't let Patrick and his inability to commit to his family rob me of possible happiness. I had to be willing to take a chance.

"He's gone, by the way." I snorted, filling it with all the scorn I could muster. "He traded his relationship with Neve for the contents of my savings account."

Luke swore. "He doesn't deserve her. Or you."

"I know that now." I leaned forward and kissed him. A slow, soft kiss filled with promise.

He looked up from the kiss, a smile lifting the corners of his mouth. "I won't let you down, Maeve."

I placed a finger on his lips. "No promises."

"But—"

I kissed him again. I wanted to stay in the present. To let this relationship grow slowly. To take my time.

This— Luke, the way he looked at me as if I were something special even with all my prickliness, the way he cared for

Neve, his wanting to make a family —was everything I'd ever wanted. It wasn't the way I'd imagined it... and yet, I could see it growing into something as solid as what my parents shared.

Instead of a bank of dark clouds, the future seemed bright. Luke wasn't just saying the words I wanted to hear; he was showing me with his actions that he meant them. He was going to stay. He was going to let me set the pace. He was going to be there.

Throat tight, I glanced at the white donut truck with its neon donuts plastered on the side. "You parking that thing in front of my bakery was the best thing that happened to me."

"Yeah?"

"Yeah." Life was messy. Relationships were messy. Love, especially, was messy. But living in the moment beat living in the past, waiting for a future that would never come. I was stronger, wiser this time around. "We'll take it one day at a time and see what happens."

"I'd like that very much." He sealed his promise with a kiss that had every single thought flying right out of my mind except, *Yes.*

Authors depend on word of mouth. So, if you have time, I'd be grateful if you would post a short review wherever you can.

All the best,
Sylvie

Want to keep up with what's going on in Brighton Village? Join my VIP Readers List today. The newsletter comes out once a month and contains book updates, behind the scenes tidbits, recipes, specials and extras that only my VIP readers receive. Go to https://sylviekurtz.com/newsletter and sign up now!

DANI'S STRAWBERRY KISSES
COOKIES

Ingredients

- 1 ¼ cups all-purpose flour
- ½ teaspoon baking powder
- ¼ teaspoon baking soda
- ¼ teaspoon salt
- 8 tablespoons unsalted butter, softened
- ½ cup sugar
- ½ cup graham cracker crumbs
- ½ cup powdered freeze-dried strawberries
- 1 large egg, room temperature
- 1 teaspoon strawberry extract
- 2 tablespoons strawberry jam
- 10-12 large marshmallows, halved
- 20-24 white chocolate candies

Directions

Preheat oven to 350 F. Line two baking sheets with parchment paper. Whisk the flour, baking powder, baking soda and salt in a bowl.

In the bowl of a stand mixer fitted with a paddle, beat butter, sugar, ¼ cup of the graham crumbs and ¼ cup of the freeze-dried strawberry powder on medium speed for about 3 minutes, until pale and fluffy. Add the egg and strawberry extract and beat until incorporated. Reduce the speed to low and slowly add the flour mixture. Mix until just combined.

Place the remaining ¼ cup of crumbs and ¼ of strawberry powder in a shallow bowl. Working with 1 tablespoon of dough at a time, roll into balls, coat with the crumb mixture. Space the dough balls evenly on the prepared baking sheets. Bake 1 sheet at a time, for about 10-12 minutes, until just set and beginning to crack on the sides.

Switch the element to broiler to heat. While the cookies are still hot, press a finger in the middle of each cookie to create an indent. Place ¼ to ½ teaspoon of strawberry jam in the indent. Top the jam with 1 marshmallow half, cut side down. Broil the cookies until the marshmallows are golden, about 30 seconds, rotating halfway through to keep the browning even. Transfer the sheet to a wire rack and immediately place a white chocolate candy in the middle of the marshmallow, pressing down gently.

Repeat with the other baking sheet. Let the cookies cool completely before serving.

Notes:

My plan had been to use white chocolate kisses, but apparently, they don't exist. Hershey's Cookies and Cream kisses work well, as do Crème Brulée hearts from Ghirardelli. In a pinch, a sprinkling of white chocolate chips works.

To make strawberry powder, blitz freeze-dried strawberries in a small food processor.

ACKNOWLEDGMENTS

First, I'd like to thank Tanya Crosby-Straley and Oliver Heber Books for welcoming me into their family. It is really nice to have a team in one's corner.

Thank you to Sally O'Keef for knowing where commas and hyphens go and catching all my missing words.

Thank you to Ann Roth, Karen Coulters and Lorrie Thomson for seeing me through a really tough year and encouraging me to keep writing.

Thank you to Chelle and Joanne, my two biggest fans. I appreciate all the support more than I can say.

Thank you to my family for putting up with my writing craziness, my questions and my culinary experiments.

A special thank you to Callie, the inspiration for Snick. Writing with a dog in one's lap isn't easy but it does offer comfort.

As always, thank you to you, dear reader, for choosing to spend time in the fictional world of Brighton Village.

ALSO BY SYLVIE KURTZ

Love in Brighton Village Series

Christmas by Candlelight

Christmas in Brighton

Summer's Sweet Spot

Brighton Village Cozy Mystery

Of Books and Bones (novella)

Midnight Whispers Series

One Texas Night

Blackmailed Bride

Hidden Legacy

Alyssa Again

Under Lock and Key

A Rose at Midnight

Pull of the Moon

Remembering Red Thunder

Red Thunder Reckoning

Personal Enemy

Detour

The Seekers Series

Heart of a Hunter

Mask of a Hunter

Eye of a Hunter

Pride of a Hunter

Spirit of a Hunter

Honor of a Hunter

Action-Adventure Romance

Ms. Longshot

Paranormal Romance

Broken Wings

Silver Shadows

Holiday Romance

A Little Christmas Magic

ABOUT THE AUTHOR

Sylvie writes stories that celebrate family, friends and food. She believes organic dark chocolate is an essential nutrient, likes to knit with soft wool, and justifies watching movies that require a box of tissues by knitting baby blankets. She has written 25 novels in various genres.

Her first Harlequin Intrigue, *One Texas Night*, was a 1999 Romantic Times nominee for Best First Category Romance and a finalist for a Booksellers Best Award. Her Silhouette Special Edition, *A Little Christmas Magic* was a 2001 Readers' Choice Award Finalist and a Waldenbooks bestseller. *Remembering Red Thunder* was a 2002 Romantic Times Nominee for Best Intrigue. She was a 2005, 2007 and 2008 Romantic Times nominee for Lifetime Achievement for Series Romantic Adventure. Twin Star Entertainment optioned *Ms. Longshot* as a possible TV movie.

For more details, visit https://sylviekurtz.com.

facebook.com/sylviekurtzauthor

instagram.com/sylviekurtzauthor

Milton Keynes UK
Ingram Content Group UK Ltd.
UKHW011224280324
440101UK00005B/572